A Pirate's Possession

MICHELLE BEATTIE

BERKLEY SENSATION, NEW YORK

THE BERKLEY PUBLISHING GROUP
Published by the Penguin Group
Penguin Group (USA) Inc.
375 Hudson Street, New York, New York 10014, USA
Penguin Group (Canada), 90 Eglinton Avenue East, Suite 700, Toronto, Ontario M4P 2Y3, Canada
(a division of Pearson Penguin Canada Inc.)
Penguin Books Ltd., 80 Strand, London WC2R 0RL, England
Penguin Group Ireland, 25 St. Stephen's Green, Dublin 2, Ireland (a division of Penguin Books Ltd.)
Penguin Group (Australia), 250 Camberwell Road, Camberwell, Victoria 3124, Australia
(a division of Pearson Australia Group Pty. Ltd.)
Penguin Books India Pvt. Ltd., 11 Community Centre, Panchsheel Park, New Delhi—110 017, India
Penguin Group (NZ), 67 Apollo Drive, Rosedale, North Shore 0632, New Zealand
(a division of Pearson New Zealand Ltd.)
Penguin Books (South Africa) (Pty.) Ltd., 24 Sturdee Avenue, Rosebank, Johannesburg 2196,
South Africa

Penguin Books Ltd., Registered Offices: 80 Strand, London WC2R 0RL, England

This is a work of fiction. Names, characters, places, and incidents either are the product of the author's imagination or are used fictitiously, and any resemblance to actual persons, living or dead, business establishments, events, or locales is entirely coincidental. The publisher does not have any control over and does not assume any responsibility for author or third-party websites or their content.

A PIRATE'S POSSESSION

A Berkley Sensation Book / published by arrangement with the author

PRINTING HISTORY
Berkley Sensation mass-market edition / December 2010

Copyright © 2010 by Michelle Beattie.
Cover art by Judy York.
Cover design by George Long.
Cover hand lettering by Ron Zinn.
Interior text design by Kristin del Rosario.

ISBN: 978-0-425-23820-2

BERKLEY® SENSATION
Berkley Sensation Books are published by The Berkley Publishing Group,
a division of Penguin Group (USA) Inc.,
375 Hudson Street, New York, New York 10014.
BERKLEY® SENSATION and the "B" design are trademarks of Penguin Group (USA) Inc.

PRINTED IN THE UNITED STATES OF AMERICA

10 9 8 7 6 5 4 3 2 1

To my daughters, Natalia and Taryn. I love you! You are, by far, the best treasures in the world!

One

Claire Gentry pushed open the heavy door and made her way across the crowded tavern, through teetering drunks—though it was barely sunset—and down to the table that held her destiny. Without more than a nod to the three other men that sat around the table, Claire took her seat.

"You sure you're in the right place, boy? This here's a bettin' table and the stakes are high. Bigger men than you have wanted in and were tossed out."

Keeping her gaze cool, Claire dug into her jacket pocket and dropped two fistfuls of coins onto the scratched surface.

"I'm in," she answered, keeping her voice low. Not many people looked past her dirty clothes and face, and she'd learned over the years that people mostly saw what they expected. And since they didn't expect a young woman to be bold enough to walk into such an establishment dressed as a downtrodden sailor, they didn't see one. It was what had kept her alive for the last few years.

She'd run from her duplicitous marriage, and the lying bastard who had tricked her into it, determined never to count on anybody again. Her future, her life, was her own, and by God, nobody was going to let her down ever again. However, looking at the shiny coins and knowing how hard they had been to come by, how long it had taken her to save them, she could only hope that she wasn't about to let *herself* down.

She'd been looking long and hard for the missing half of the map, and when word had gotten round that it would be here today, she'd taken everything she had. It all sat before her now.

The man to her right whistled between his teeth. "Looks like he's in the right place," he said.

"Where's the map?" she asked, keeping her coins close. She wasn't pushing them into the middle until she saw what she'd come for.

"You think you're man enough to find this treasure, boy?"

"It's not muscle that's needed to find the treasure, it's brains. And I have more than enough of those."

The men who'd circled the table, curious to see who'd bet on part of a treasure map, guffawed at Claire's taunt. Though the man across from her chuckled and his grin ate up a portion of his large square face, there was little humor in his gray eyes. When his gaze, as sharp as the knife she had tucked away in her boot, locked on to hers, she felt a snap of cold against her cheeks.

"Spoken as though you already know what's on that map." He leaned forward and his sticky breath floated over the table's surface and slid up Claire's nose. "How would that be, given that the map is at least five times older than you are?"

Claire knew she had to be careful. He was right. She

had half the map memorized in her head, thanks to her father, but it would be more than foolish of her to let anybody know that. It would likely cost her her life.

She shrugged. "Hearsay, is all."

His eyes narrowed, but he leaned back in his chair. Claire slowly released her breath.

"Hearsay will get you killed," came a rumble from her left.

She looked past the last chair, the one that had yet to be occupied, to the man who'd spoken. She watched as he pulled out a wrinkled piece of paper, spread it out before him. Claire's stomach turned inside out.

"But the map is real, and if you want to play for it, you have to pay for it," he said with a gravelly voice that sounded as though it hadn't been used in a long time.

Claire eyed him curiously. His hair and beard were black, his eyes a deep blue. It was a striking combination, one made all the stronger by the emptiness she saw in his eyes.

"Why haven't you found it?" one of the onlookers countered.

The man raised his gaze. "I lost more looking for that treasure than I ever would have gained by finding it. It means nothing to me now."

The pain in his voice drew Claire, and though her heart went out to him, she didn't move. Nothing would give away her gender faster than such a womanly gesture. But then again, maybe not. She looked over at the women in low-cut dresses, their breasts straining against their corsets, and mentally sighed. There was a reason she could get away with posing as a boy and it had nothing to do with hiding her curves. There simply wasn't enough there to worry about concealing.

"He's got no problem taking your money for it, though," someone called.

The man with the map silenced everyone with a cut of his icy glare.

"Well, I'll take my chances," Claire said and pushed her coins to the middle.

"As will I."

Though the room was filled with loud conversations and bad singing, Claire's ears heard only that one sentence. She hadn't seen Nate Carter in eight years, not since he went back on his word, but she recognized the voice even before her eyes rolled up his tall body and latched on to the face she'd dreamed about more often than the lying bastard deserved.

Her stomach dove to her toes. Nate was here. He was here and so was the map she'd told him about when she'd still been foolish enough to believe that a man's word meant something. Betrayal burned a hole to her belly. He'd come for the treasure, the treasure they'd talked about together. The treasure he'd promised her they'd find together. Only he'd never come back for her. It was only one of the lies he'd led her to believe.

From under the brim of her hat, a hat she tugged a little lower, Claire willed herself to remain still, a difficult task with her heart racing and her hands wanting nothing more than to slap Nate's lying face, despite how handsome it was. She wasn't concerned about being recognized, not with her hair cut short and the auburn color hidden under the wide hat. Not when he'd likely forgotten about her once he'd stepped out of the orphanage doors. Stepped out and never looked back.

And damn him for looking better now than he had then. Nate's shoulders, which had already been substantial at sixteen, were even broader now. His dark brown hair was much the same and still had a few loose strands that fell over his forehead. Skin bronzed by the sun and further darkened by a shadow of beard covered his chiseled jaw.

Nate reached inside his jacket, put a black leather pouch bulging with jingling coins onto the table before taking the empty seat.

The man to her left picked up all the coins, dropped them into a small sack. He slid the map into the middle of the table.

"Best hand wins," he said. The cards snapped as he shuffled.

"My name's Sid," said the man to her right. "Just thought I'd tell you now who it'll be winning the map."

The man across from her shook his head. "That'll be me, James."

"What's the matter, boy, don't have a name?" Sid asked.

"Clarence," Claire said, using her father's name, as she usually did if anyone bothered to ask. She held her breath, but Nate wasn't paying her any more mind than he was the other players, less in fact since he didn't bother to do more than nod that he'd heard. His eyes barely touched on her, certainly not long enough to see past the shadow of her hat and the dirt on her face. Did he not think her capable of coming on her own? Did he believe she'd given up on ever finding it, or had he long since forgotten she even existed? Her eyes narrowed. None of those possibilities sat well with Claire.

Although she really should be relieved that he wasn't looking too closely.

"And you?" Sid asked.

"Nate."

There was a long pause as everyone turned to the man who was shuffling.

"Cale," he answered grudgingly, dealing each of them five cards.

With the cards now in play, more spectators circled the table. Unfortunately with them came the combined smells of men who stank of rum and stale tobacco, and who'd gone far too long between visits to the bathhouse.

Claire looked at her cards one by one. A ten, an ace. Her heart pumped, another ten. The last two cards were useless, a six and a five. Still she had a pair and she had to hope it was good enough.

"You're first," Cale said to Sid.

"Why me?" the grown man said. Though he had to be at least fifty, if the field of gray hair on his head was any indication, it didn't stop him from whining.

"Because you were here first."

Sid sighed, turned over his cards.

"Ace high."

Claire exhaled slowly then looked at James.

"Pair of eights, king high," the man said, his eyes sliding from Claire to Nate as he tried to gauge their reactions.

Claire swallowed hard. She was one step away. Hunger for the map gnawed along her nerves. She needed this. Her life was consumed with finding this treasure and she was tired, so very tired, of coming up short. If she lost . . .

She took a deep breath. She wouldn't; life wouldn't be that cruel.

"Pair of tens," she said, flipping over her cards. "Ace high."

James inhaled sharply.

All eyes turned to Nate. Claire's palms were damp and her feet tapped under the table. Please, please, let him have less than her pair.

For the first time since Nate had arrived at the table, he

smiled. And as his teeth flashed against his golden skin, Claire felt her world begin to shatter.

"Three threes," Nate said. He laid them out one at a time but all Claire saw was a blur of suits.

She'd lost. Just like that. Feeling sick, she rose unsteadily.

"You all right, boy?" Nate asked.

Claire couldn't look at him, not at him or anyone else. She had nothing. Nothing! The paper on the table was so close and her body shook with a need to take it. Take it and run. Her hands curled at her sides, but she didn't move them. She'd never get out of the tavern with it; Nate would catch her before she made it to the door.

Nate. The bastard didn't deserve it! She bit her lip when tears stung her eyes. With a last look at the paper that would have made every difference in the world to her, she pushed her way through the crowd.

"Hey, boy," Sid called. Claire could hear him work his way toward her.

She increased her pace. She needed to get out now. The last thing she wanted when her world was falling apart, when her plans and dreams were turning to dust, was to talk. Despite her hurry, however, he managed to grab her arm before she made it to the door.

"Hey, what's your hurry?"

"What do you want?" Claire asked, pulling her arm free.

"Easy," he said, raising his hands. "You just look so down I thought maybe a wench would help you forget your worries."

"I don't have any money," she mumbled, keeping to her ruse.

"Well, there's one just outside that's so besotted she won't know if you stick it in 'er." He smiled. "At least she didn't when I was back there."

Claire's stomach roiled.

"When I want a tumble, I'll find a partner that's willing. I won't need to prey on anybody that's so drunk they don't know any better. *I'm* not that despicable."

Sid went red, and just as Claire figured out his intention, it was too late. His fist connected with her cheek. Fiery pain rippled across her face and sent her careening backward. She crashed into a table. Her hands scrambled for purchase. Warm liquid sloshed over her fingers and trickled down her face. She lost her balance and tipped sideways, taking the table down with her. It knocked her on the head and sent her hat rolling.

"Get the hell away from him," Nate roared through the ringing in her ears. She looked up, saw Nate give Sid a hard shove. "Step back or you'll know what it is to be hit by a man who more than doubles your size."

Sid muttered a curse then wove back into the crowd, shoving past James, who'd also come to see what was happening.

Nate turned his attention back to her.

Oh hell, she thought. Clambering to her hands and knees, sliding on the wet floor, Claire reached for her hat.

She was too late.

Nate's strong hand reached it first. She'd be lucky to get out now without being recognized and she didn't want him to know who she was. She'd envisioned seeing him again, after she was wealthy and had found the treasure. After she was dressed in the prettiest fashions and could show him what he'd turned his back on. She hadn't ever imagined it would be like this, when she had nothing. Feeling as though the walls were closing in on her, heart pounding in her veins, Claire sprang to her feet. With her eye on her escape, she yanked her hat from Nate's grasp and ran for the door.

"Wait!" he called, but this time she didn't let anything slow her down. Shoving and pushing her way through, ignoring the curses aimed her way, Claire hit the door before Nate could stop her and, once outside, ran for the jungle and the cover it provided.

Two

It couldn't be. It was a trick of his eyes, the light, or something. Yes, the boy was small, had hair the same color as Claire's, but hers was long and curly, not chopped ragged like the lad's was. Besides, she would never step foot into such an establishment, and she certainly wouldn't need to gamble for a piece of a treasure map, even one she'd spoken about in great length. Not when he knew for a fact that she already possessed more money than she could ever spend.

But then, he thought angrily, maybe she would come here for the damn map. How the hell would he know? It wasn't as though he was an expert on the woman and it certainly wouldn't be the first time she'd proven him wrong. Given all this time, who knew what she was capable of now?

"Get out of my way!"

Nate turned. Cale was making his way over.

"Is the kid all right?" he asked.

"Yeah, but he'll have a hell of a bruise come morning."

It was lucky that *hadn't* been Claire, or Sid would be lying in the street about now wishing he were dead. Despite Nate's feelings toward her, he wouldn't stand by and let harm come to a woman. It was a rule he'd lived by since he'd been a young lad and had seen firsthand the abuse a man was capable of inflicting on a woman.

"Stupid idiot," Cale muttered, jamming his thumb in the direction Sid took. "Anybody could see the only thing that kid was interested in was the map."

"Yeah," Nate agreed, his eyes drawn to the door despite his reasoning. It wasn't her. She was likely in San Salvador, where he'd last seen her, surrounded by a passel of children. The thought did strange things to his guts.

"Well, he may not think so right now, but he's better off without that treasure."

"How long did you look for it?" Nate asked, pulling his gaze from the door.

Cale's blue eyes hardened. "Too damn long." And without another word, he strode outside.

Nate was contemplating Cale's words when a full-bosomed wench rubbed up against him. She was much shorter than Nate, and with her low-cut bodice, Nate could nearly see down her gown.

"Can I interest you in anything?" she asked, trailing her fingers up his chest. She licked her painted lips, pressed herself up against him.

Looking at her, long hair loose and curly around her shoulders, all he could think of was that it wasn't red. And that just made him angry.

"Not tonight." He smiled to take the sting off the rejection. Not that he really believed she was interested in him. He'd seen her lingering about the table and no doubt figured if he could put up the stake for the game, he had more where that came from.

"Are you sure?" she asked, taking a deep breath that pushed her already impressive breasts upward.

"Yeah, I'm sure."

Nate watched her stroll away, generous hips swinging beneath her full skirt. If only he wasn't partial to more slender women. He gnashed his teeth, shook his head. He felt as much as saw the other man come to his side.

"I'm not sure even the promise of a treasure would distract me from that," James said as he stepped beside Nate. Because of the crowd, they stood shoulder to shoulder.

Nate shrugged. He'd never met this man before and knew the only reason James wanted to talk was the map Nate had folded and put in his coat pocket. Since Nate had no intention of discussing the map or the treasure, he saw no point in encouraging the conversation.

"A man of many words, I see."

"I can be. When they're important."

James chuckled. "Why don't you let me buy you a drink? You don't have to say a word, just listen to my proposition."

"I don't want or need a partner."

It was impossible to miss the tightening of the man's jaw. But it eased as quickly as it had come. Then he swung an arm around Nate's shoulders, a task not just anyone could do considering Nate's height.

"Well, then, you have nothing to lose and you'll get a free drink from listening to my rambling," James cajoled.

James grabbed a nearby table as soon as it emptied. Once Nate sat down, James nodded and went to fetch their drinks. With the game now over, those people that had come only for that were making their way outside. Nate felt himself breathe a little easier.

He'd always hated crowds and he wasn't particularly trusting of strangers, a trait that served him well in his work. Therefore, he accepted the drink and was content to enjoy his rum while he waited for James to begin what would no doubt be a proposition to go looking for the treasure together.

If he'd bet on it, he would have won again. Barely swallowing his first sip, James began to talk.

"A joint venture would be profitable," James said.

"The only one who stands to gain from a joint venture is you."

James shrugged that off with a wave of his hand. "But since you only have half the map, surely another pair of eyes trying to decipher it would be better? You'd waste less time."

Nate chuckled. "Actually, the more people who look at it, the more trouble I've got." He eyed James over his crockery mug.

"You have a ship, then?"

Nate set his drink down, studied the man across from him. Cool gray eyes regarded him out of a rather square-looking face. From what Nate had sensed of James thus far, he wasn't a man easily fooled. And though some would think James foolhardy for even discussing such a venture, Nate had a different thought altogether. It wasn't foolhardy if the man knew going in he wasn't going to convince Nate that a partnership was a sound decision.

James didn't expect Nate to agree to something so ridiculous, because, as Nate had already explained, he had the map. Why share the treasure when he didn't have to? Nate leaned forward, his gaze locking on to James's. He knew the real reason they were talking. James was digging for information.

Nate didn't plan on giving him any. Other than his crew and a handful of people he considered family, nobody knew anything about him. That was best, considering the fewer people who knew he sailed under the name "Sam Steele," the better. And the longer his life expectancy became. Not that he was incapable of defending himself; hell, he'd managed just fine these last three years. However, he was a man who preferred to keep things close to the vest. It was simply less messy that way.

"I have my ways of getting around," he answered vaguely.

"I'm sure you do. But I have a ship. You're welcome to sail with me."

Nate's lips pulled into a smile. "As I said, I have my own ways."

"It's been said that the map hasn't been seen in its entirety for near a hundred years. Are you confident you'll be able to find the treasure simply based on what you won today?"

"As confident as you were when you put your coins into the pot."

James took a swig of his drink, wiped his mouth with the back of his hand. His nostrils flared as he contemplated Nate.

"Men all over the Caribbean have told one version of it or another. I've heard it's more of a riddle than an actual map."

"Is that so?"

"A map leading to a treasure of that size isn't a secret. You won't be the first to go looking for it."

"Nor the last, I imagine."

"Not unless you already know what the other half says. Seems to me a person would have to have some idea of what's written on the other half or searching would be a complete waste of time."

"You know someone then?" Nate asked, despite the fact that he knew full well what James was doing.

James nodded. "I do," he said.

There was no trace of a lie in the man's eye that Nate could see and it gave him pause. Could it be that James also knew what was on the other half of the map, the half that Claire's father had possessed?

Nate finished his drink. "Then I hope they remember this half as well," he said as he patted his pocket. "Thanks for the drink."

He unfolded himself from the chair and was heading to the doorway when his first mate and good friend, Vincent, strode into the tavern. The dwarf came directly at Nate, who was easy enough to spot because of his height.

"Well?" he asked, hands braced on his hips. "Did you get what you came for?"

Nate frowned. He hadn't told Vincent or his crew about the treasure. Part of that was because until he had the last piece of the map, there was no point. The other part was, though he had no intention of mentioning Claire, he'd no doubt be thinking of her in the telling of the tale regarding the map and the treasure. Since he never gained any joy from thinking of her, and since she was already too much in his thoughts for his peace of mind, Nate delayed it yet again.

"I didn't come here for anything."

"Then why were you in such a bloody hurry to make port?"

"Maybe I just needed to get away from your endless badgering for a few bloody minutes. What are you complaining about anyhow? I thought you had an errand to run."

"Errand? Oh, right. All done." He took a breath; the smile he gave Nate was forced. "What did you mean, you needed to get away from me? Having me as your fist mate is the best thing that's ever happened to you."

"Sure it is. Right after scurvy."

For a moment it looked as though Vincent believed the words, but then he rolled his eyes. "You're not going to tell me, are you?"

"It's not hard to see you were raised with a bunch of women," Nate commented, referring to his friend's need to know everything.

"Fine. I'll tell you what." This time Vincent's smile was real. "You keep telling me there's nothing, and I'll promise to stop trying to get it out of you."

"I'll believe that when I see it."

Vincent sobered. "If there's nothing, then why do you look as though you've just lost something that mattered?"

Because that was exactly as Nate felt. He'd been thinking of or searching for that treasure for years and he'd come to Nevis for the missing piece to the map. The map that would lead to the biggest treasure in the Spanish Main. He had it now; he should be pleased. The ironic part was that by having it, he was also reminded of what he didn't have.

Nate found a table, one as far from James's as possible. Making himself as comfortable as the wooden chair allowed, he caught a passing barmaid and ordered two tankards of rum. Then, thinking that was a good start, he ordered one for Vincent as well.

Claire thrashed her way through the jungle and over the haphazard path she'd created a few days ago to the small camp that, as of Thursday, had been her home. The moon was nearly hidden by clouds and offered little relief to the cloaking darkness but Claire knew her way. She hadn't kept herself alive this long by making a habit of getting lost.

She arrived at the small encampment and saw, if only in her memory, a cold pile of rocks surrounding black coals and a small cleared-out area that was no bigger than the blanket she used to keep warm. Claire dropped to her knees. She'd put her hopes and efforts into locating the map. She'd worked until her bones ached, and more times than not, she'd fallen asleep at night too exhausted to undress. She'd trudged ahead despite fear and pain, loneliness and heartache, believing it would be rewarded in the end. Believing justice would prevail. Never, never, had failure entered her mind. If it had, she'd have given up long ago.

Great heaving sobs shook her, and soon warm tears were meandering down her cheeks. After everything, she had failed. Her money, her hope, it was all gone.

As was her father. And despite having only just seen him, as was Nate. She pulled her knees to her chest, held them tightly. After so many years, why wasn't she used to this feeling of being alone?

When her father had left her at the orphanage to seek the treasure, she'd believed it was temporary, that he'd come back rich and take her away. As the weeks turned to months, that belief had become hard to cling to.

The one good thing had been Nate, who'd also lived in the orphanage. He'd been first her friend, someone she could talk to, then her confidant, when she'd told him about the map her father had, and then finally he'd become the boy she'd loved.

Together they had spent hours talking about the treasure. Where would it be found? Would it be mostly gems or coins? How would her father carry it out? They'd envisioned crowns made of rubies, swords fashioned with emeralds and diamonds.

But when the months turned into years and Claire could no longer pretend her father would ever come back for her, it was Nate who'd held her, who'd comforted her. It was Nate who'd discussed trying to locate it themselves. It was Nate who'd kissed her, who'd made her feel beautiful. And Nate, like her father, had left and never come back.

She couldn't very well damn her father because she had no way of knowing if he was alive and still looking for the treasure to this day or if he'd perished along the way. It was a thought that plagued her. Was he hurt? Had it been discovered that he had a piece of this most famous map and was killed for it? Until she knew, she had no reprieve from those troublesome thoughts. And as he was her father, she loved him, and if he were to come back, she'd forgive him for leaving her. If only she could see him again.

She'd once thought the same of Nate. But seeing him today, knowing *he* was alive and hadn't bothered to come back for her the way he'd promised yet could continue to search for a treasure for eight years, stoked her anger until it raged within her.

Him, she could damn.

Wiping her tears, wincing as her fingers brushed where Sid had hit her, Claire got up and made a fire. It wasn't for warmth as the night was mild, but rather for company. Feeding the flames gave her something to do with her hands, and the crackling wood filled the silence. But watching the fire dance and flicker couldn't distract her from her thoughts or the truth that pressed upon her as much as the humidity.

Nate had the missing piece. Combined with what she'd shared with him as a young girl, he had enough to go looking for the treasure she'd always considered to be hers, or at least her family's. There'd be no stopping him now.

Claire inhaled sharply as bitterness overtook her. Over her dead body.

Coming to her feet, she kicked dirt over her fire, packed her few belongings into her worn bag, and headed for the tavern. As far as Claire was concerned, Nate was stealing the treasure from her.

It was only fair she return the favor.

I oughta just leave you out here to sleep it off," Vincent complained as he tried, with very little success, to pull Nate along the meandering street. It wasn't easy to steer him in any direction. Not when he careened more than a ship caught in a hurricane.

Vincent cursed when Nate once again stumbled. Lowering his voice, he grumbled, "I know you said to play along with whatever ruse it is you're up to, but could you help me a little, you big lubber?"

"You're doing fine," Nate whispered. "Jus' take me home, mate," he roared drunkenly. "My house is that-a-way." He gestured vaguely to the back edge of town.

As they left behind the taverns and harbor, the glow of the streetlamps faded and the cacophony of noise drifted away until it was nothing more than a dull murmur. Night sounds were now able to be heard, and the repetitive songs of crickets and frogs were a relief after the din of the tavern.

Vincent dug in his heels when Nate veered left and nearly took them both down. "Keep your damn eyes open!"

"They are," Nate answered.

"Then use them," Vincent ground as he yanked hard on Nate's arm.

He didn't have to feign frustration. It was gnawing on him like rats to a rope. What the devil was going on? Nate had said he'd wanted to get drunk, but he'd soon switched his drink to water. Still he kept it delivered in the same crockery mug in order to keep up the pretense of drinking. All he'd offered as way of explanation was that he was being watched. Vincent could only assume they were also being followed. Otherwise it made no sense to go this way, not when the bloody ship was bobbing in port behind them.

"Don't be such a woman," Nate teased.

"Say that again and I'll kill you," Vincent threatened, though it was an empty one. The big lubber could be annoying and downright stubborn, but he was a good friend and Vincent treasured friendship above all else.

Though it looked as though Vincent was guiding Nate, it was Nate, in fact, who was leading the way. He led them now past one of the last houses on the street. Its lights were out, and other than a horse lifting his head from where it had been dozing in a small paddock nearby, all was quiet.

Nate and Vincent rounded the corner. All pretenses of being drunk vanished. Nate pulled his pistol from the waist of his trousers, pressed his back against the wood planks of the house, and waited.

He knew James was following. The man had been watching them far too closely in the tavern, and Nate had seen James shift when he and Vincent made their way to the door. More than once as Nate feigned a stagger, he'd seen a shadow cut behind a house or tree.

He heard boots crunching on rocks and slid his finger against the trigger. His heartbeat was calm. His focus was complete.

When he heard the man's breathing near his ear, Nate made his move. He crouched then lunged when the man rounded the corner. Nate caught him at the waist and, with his speed and weight, took them both down.

"Ooof," the man groaned when Nate landed hard on top of him.

Years of sailing at night had honed Nate's eyesight and he saw, as he straddled the man and grabbed him by the throat, that it was, in fact, James.

"Your luck wasn't good at the table. What made you think you'd fare better trying to follow me?"

"I—" James tried to swallow but Nate's hand didn't let up. "I wasn't going to hurt you."

Nate smiled. "Not by yourself, you couldn't." He lowered his hand from James's throat and grabbed a handful of his shirt. "Are you alone?"

The man's head bobbed.

Nate shook his head. "Then that's the second dumbest thing you did tonight. The first was following me," he said as he brought his pistol down on the side of James's head.

"You're going to leave him there?" Vincent asked when Nate lowered James's head to the ground and stood up.

"Yes, and let's hope he wasn't lying about being alone or it'll make getting back to the ship and slipping out of port quietly a little tricky."

Three

She arrived back at the tavern in time to see the dwarf and Nate step outside. Jumping back into the shadows of the trees, Claire remained still as the dwarf and an obviously drunk Nate meandered away from both the tavern and the harbor and headed to where the bulk of the houses were nestled quietly for the night. Though she had every intention of going after Nate and the map, she certainly didn't want to get caught following. Therefore, while the streetlamps kept the men well lit, she remained where she was. For now.

When they were far enough up the road, when she was contemplating moving from her hiding spot, another man came out of the tavern. James from the poker game. He looked around, saw Nate and the dwarf, and then he, too, stepped into the darkness. Claire waited to be sure, but it soon became apparent, as the man crept from building to tree, that he was also following Nate.

Claire narrowed her eyes and set her jaw. If James was

following Nate, it could be for only one reason. Her map. Well, he wasn't going to get it any more than she planned on letting Nate keep it.

Still, as she followed them past taverns, closed businesses, and a graveyard marked with a tall white cross that shone despite the limited moonlight, she couldn't help wondering just where the devil Nate was going. And when they arrived at their destination, just how she was going to get the map back. Though she had a fair arsenal in her bag—pistol, dirk, and blunderbuss—not to mention the knife in her boot, Claire had never anticipated having to use them on someone she knew.

Even if the lying weasel deserved it.

However, before she could contemplate it further, Nate and the dwarf disappeared behind a darkened house. Not long after that, James followed. Claire took a step forward, saw Nate ram the man to the ground. She jumped, then slapped a hand over her mouth to keep her gasp contained. She watched, shocked, as words were exchanged before Nate's pistol came down on the side of James's head. The sound overrode that of crickets and frogs, and the dull whack as metal met skull made the hair on the back of Claire's neck stand on end.

She watched Nate relieve James of his weapon before leaving him behind like refuse, and she knew two things. Nate wasn't drunk and he wasn't to be underestimated.

Taking her pistol from her effects, Claire readjusted her bag over her shoulder and once again followed Nate. Nate wasn't the only one to be underestimated.

Now are you going to tell me what's going on?"

"Nothing's going on."

"You just knocked a man unconscious, Nate."

"He was following me."

"Well, let me assure you I don't think it was because of your good looks."

Nate's lips twitched. "You're sure about that?"

"What are they after? Did that man figure out who you are?"

"No."

"You're sure?"

"Yes, I'm sure. Let's just get back to the ship."

"Where you'll tell me what we're running from?"

Nate said nothing, simply increased his pace and lengthened his stride. Vincent had to run to keep up.

"You come ashore for some secret meeting, or whatever it was you were doing while I . . ."

Nate glanced at him. "You told me you were getting sugar. Didn't you find any?"

Vincent bobbed his head quickly. "Right. Sugar. It's, um, in the longboat, under some canvas."

Nate had been more than happy when Vincent claimed he needed to run an errand, since it had allowed him to attend the game without distractions and explanations. But his behavior since arriving at the tavern had been off balance. Unlike Vincent, however, Nate wasn't one to pry.

They were approaching the commercial part of town, and lights once again glowed at the far end of the street.

"You know," Vincent gasped as he ran alongside, "for someone who claims not to be running from anything, you're sure in a mighty hurry."

Nate sighed, and shook his head. "You never give up."

"Neither do I," Claire said as she stepped out of the shadows and planted herself directly in Nate's path.

Nate lurched to a stop; the dwarf followed suit. Claire

pushed the hat up onto her forehead, then aimed her pistol at Nate's chest. "And I'll be taking that map now."

Though they weren't directly under the lamps, there was enough light to see clearly, especially up close as they were now, and she saw the instant recognition dawned on Nate's face.

"Claire."

Hearing her name come out of his mouth for the first time in eight years, even if it wasn't said warmly, gave her an unexpected jolt. And it made her angry. He shouldn't still have that effect on her.

"I'm surprised you remember me. Should I be honored?"

She felt the heat of his glare. "It *was* you, at the game?"

"What game? You two know each other?"

Both she and Nate ignored the dwarf. "It was. The map, Nate. Hand it over."

He jutted his chin at her pistol. "Or you'll shoot me?"

She set her jaw. "It's the least you deserve. Don't think I'd feel guilty about it."

"Holy hell, Nate. What did you do?"

"Go back where you came from, Claire."

He slid his pistol from the waist of his trousers into his hand. Though it stayed down at his side, it was a threat nonetheless. Clearly she wasn't the only one ready to shoot if necessary. She sneered.

"Are you going to knock me out the way you did to James or will you shoot me outright?"

His lips flattened. "Which do you prefer?"

"Hell, Nate. She's a woman!" Vincent reminded him needlessly.

"And she's in our way. Good-bye, Claire," Nate said as he moved to step around her.

She wouldn't have any of it. She stepped to the side and pressed the barrel of her pistol into his chest. Cocked it. "The map."

She braced her legs and steadied her hand. Though he was taller, she'd been forced to battle more than a few men in the last years and she'd learned to fight. Strength didn't always dictate the winner. Sometimes it was cunning.

With blood tingling in her veins, Claire waited for Nate's move. Seconds passed with only the sound of their breathing filling her ears. She studied his face, his shoulders, for any sign of movement. Whatever way he moved, she'd be ready. When his lips curved, when warmth softened his eyes, Claire's heart jumped. She balanced on her feet, ready for anything.

"Meet me at the longboat, Vincent. I won't be long."

"But—"

"Go, I'll meet you there."

The dwarf hesitated, but then out of the corner of her eye, Claire saw him stride toward the harbor. She didn't move. She didn't trust Nate, and she wasn't going to so much as blink until she had what she wanted. Which she had every intention of getting. Only instead of raising his pistol, or his other hand, or even a leg as she expected he'd do, all he did was smile at her. The way he had before he'd left her all those years ago.

Visions of the past raced through her mind. The first time he'd held her hand. The first time he'd pulled her into his embrace. The first time he'd kissed her. Her cheeks warmed.

"You remember, don't you, the times we had?"

She clenched her jaw, forcing the memories back. "No," she lied. "I don't." And she'd die before she ever admitted it to him.

A flash of teeth. "You do. I do." His voice lowered at the same time his head dipped. "Do you taste the same, I wonder?" he whispered as his lips hovered closer to hers.

Her heart hammered now. It beat frantically against her chest. Her mouth went drier than a desert storm, but her brain was working fine. She pushed the pistol harder against his chest. His chuckle reverberated through the weapon to her palm and from there it sizzled through her veins like lightning. Her hand twitched.

"Tell me you haven't thought of this." His breath skimmed her mouth. He was but inches away.

"I haven't."

"Liar."

His lips were nearly upon hers. Claire took a sharp breath.

They moved at the same time. She reached for his pistol as he effectively grabbed hers from her hand. They jumped apart, each holding the other's weapon.

"Well, that was interesting," he said, his eyes once again cool and calculating.

"I'm no longer young and naive. I've learned some hard lessons." His pistol was heavier than hers but she had no problem pointing it at him. "And I still want the map."

"I can disarm you easily enough."

"Not if you're wounded. Or dead."

"Is that what you want? Me dead?"

"No. I'd rather you suffer."

His mouth flattened. "I hate to disappoint you but that's not going to—"

He spun at the crunching noise that came from behind him. James had come to and he was staggering their way, blood winding down his cheek, yelling for his men who, Claire feared, weren't so very far away. She needed to get the map!

"Sorry to cut this short, but I have to go."

Claire grabbed his jacket, held on with all her strength. "Not with the map, you're not."

Three men came running down the street from the direction of the tavern.

"Get him!" James yelled. "Don't let him get away." He pointed wildly in Nate's direction.

Shots fired at them. They whirred past her ears, coming close enough to steal her breath. Both she and Nate stooped low, swerved, and kept moving forward. Nate fired as he ran directly for their attackers.

"What are you doing?" she yelled at his back.

"Trying to stay alive. Are you going to shoot or not?"

Nate had been accurate with his first shot and there were only two men coming for them now. Claire stopped, knelt, aimed. Fired. One more of their chasers fell. There were two left. James from the back and one from the front. She knew James had no weapon.

Nate pulled another pistol—it must have been James's—from the small of his back and drew back the hammer. The shot was as true as his first.

After the ringing from the shot faded from her ears, Claire heard James's cussing getting closer.

Nate spun round. "Run!" he ordered.

Claire didn't believe he'd meant for her to go alongside him, but she had nowhere else to run to. If she ran to her camp, it would only be a matter of time before James caught up with her. Though she saw no other men coming to James's aid, she didn't doubt for a moment he had more. Somewhere. Besides, she still didn't have what she'd come for. She followed Nate.

"Where the devil do you think you're going?" he asked

when he'd reached his longboat and the dwarf, who'd already pushed it out into the water.

"With you."

"Not a bloody chance," he growled.

He held the edge of the boat in his large hand. His mouth was hard. Water lapped around his thighs. It was mere seconds before shots pinged into the water far too close for Claire's comfort.

"It's either that or we all get shot here bobbing like ducks. What'll it be?"

He opened his mouth just as a shot ripped through the longboat, missing his fingers by a breath.

"Get in!" he ordered.

James Blackthorn wiped the never-ending stream of blood off his brow and tried to focus on the horizon. Darkness wasn't his only enemy. He kept seeing two of everything. He blinked, shook his head. Nothing seemed to fuse the two images together. There were two longboats rowing out to sea, three people in each. There were two ships on the horizon, flickering lanterns along the gunwale waving cheekily.

Frustrated, he covered one eye with his hand. Though he now saw clearer, and only one boat rowed out to sea, it didn't help his predicament. He'd only brought three men ashore with him. He'd stumbled past their dead bodies, more than happy to leave them there. Dammit, they weren't supposed to let the map off the island. He'd only asked them for one thing and they'd failed miserably. That they paid with their lives seemed only fitting to James. But now the map was leaving, a herd of horses galloped against his forehead, and blood trickled between his fingers.

His stomach roiled, but he swallowed the nausea. He couldn't afford the time it would take to be sick. If he wanted the map—and he sure as hell did—then he had to get to his ship quickly. How in blazes was he supposed to accomplish that? he wondered, when the minute he opened his eye, he once again saw two of everything. Add to that the pounding in his head, his churning stomach, and the unusual weakness that had cloaked him since he'd come to.

Hell, he couldn't even walk a straight line let alone row one.

"Troubles?"

James blinked, tried to focus through the dimness. He couldn't see too clearly but he recognized the voice. He never forgot a voice.

"Sid?"

The man stepped closer and James felt his anxiety ease when he was able to see the man clearly.

"You're not looking so good." Sid smiled.

"Get out of my way," James muttered. He had enough to worry about without wasting time on a man like Sid. What kind of man wasted his time punching a kid, anyhow? Didn't he have anything better to do?

"How about a little appreciation? I shot at them for you."

James had wondered where those last few had come from. "You missed," he said, weaving his way toward his own longboat. When they split into two, he gnashed his teeth, closed one eye.

"That your ship?" he asked, keeping up easily.

James didn't bother answering.

"You needin' help?"

James looked to his left, where the yellow lights of a ship glowed, then to the longboat, which had almost reached it. With the way he was feeling, and the way his body was betraying him, James knew he needed to get to his own vessel as fast as possible. If Nate was any kind of a sailor, he'd douse the lamps to make following his ship as difficult as possible. It was what James himself would do, what he'd planned to do when he'd figured it would be *him* leaving Nevis with the legendary piece of the map.

Well, that hadn't happened, and though he was without the map, he didn't intend to be far behind. He wiped more blood, felt it smear across his eyebrow.

"How fast can you row?" he asked Sid.

Hell, Nate thought as he pulled the oars through the water, propelling the boat closer to his ship. What in blazes had he just done?

Granted, he hadn't been given much choice as he couldn't very well leave her there while she was being shot at. But having Claire on board his ship was a huge mistake for many reasons. The biggest of which was why he angled the longboat in such a way that she couldn't read the name written on the ship. Not that there weren't many *Revenge*s peppered throughout the Caribbean, but if she even suspected it was Sam Steele's ship . . .

He shook his head, dipped the oars back into the water. If she knew, she wouldn't hesitate to bring the law down onto him. A woman who was willing to shoot a man over a map wouldn't pause to call in the Navy if she knew he sailed under Sam Steele. And if she ever realized he *was* Steele . . . He craned his neck as though he could already feel the pressure of the noose. No. He couldn't let that happen.

Vincent was first to climb out of the longboat and up the side of the sloop.

Nate grabbed Claire's pistol, tucked it into his trousers. He wasn't worried about her shooting him as she hadn't had a chance to reload, but he didn't want to leave her the chance to bash his skull in either.

"After you." Nate gestured to the ladder that had been swung over the side of the *Revenge*.

Claire shifted the bag she wore across her chest, pulled her hat low on her brow, and put her foot on a rung. In the tavern Nate hadn't looked at her too closely because he'd thought her a boy. In the street, he'd been busy keeping himself from getting shot. But now, following her up the ladder, he couldn't help noticing the way her trousers pulled across the curve of her buttocks.

And he swore silently because at one time he'd considered Claire to be his. Knowing she'd given herself to another rather than wait for him still had the power to cut him if he let it. He shifted his eyes to his hands.

The crew was on deck, awaiting Nate's orders. There was a moment of surprise when they looked from each other to Nate. Since it was the first time he'd brought a stranger on board, he'd expected their surprise. Luckily he knew he could depend on their loyalty. And with Claire's hat covering her features and the men's clothes she wore, his crew didn't suspect she was a woman. For now, he had one less worry, though he didn't doubt her gender would be discovered easily with the morning's light. Hopefully by then he'd have figured out what in blazes he was going to do about her.

"Hoist the anchor, drop the canvas. And douse the lights," he said of the lamps that flickered along the gunwale. "I suspect we're going to be followed, let's not give them a target."

His men nodded, then dispersed to their duties. Though

he could see Claire gaping at him in surprise, he ignored her and turned to Vincent. "Take the helm, I won't be long."

"What are you going to do?" He nodded toward Claire.

Nate sighed. "Hell if I know."

Vincent grinned, and before Nate could do more than shake his head at him, he'd moved to the quarter deck, where he pushed a crate up to the wheel before standing on it.

Nate turned to Claire. With some of the lights not yet extinguished, the fury on her face was unmistakable. Her eyes were narrowed and cold, her mouth was pursed. Her hands were tight fists at her sides.

"This is your ship?" she gasped.

"Come with me," he said and moved past her.

She grabbed his arm. "Wait a minute! Is this yours?" She gestured with her other arm; her gaze never left his.

"If you want me to answer, you'll have to follow me."

He pulled her hand off his arm and walked around the boom to the base of the quarter deck, where he opened the hatch. Claire glared at him but soon followed his instructions.

"Close the hatch," he instructed as he made his way through the small darkened cabin to the table, where he lit a cluster of fat candles.

As the flames flickered to life, the silver plate beneath them shone. Though the light illuminated the cabin, there wasn't much to see. A large bed dominated a corner, shelves for his maps had been built into the back wall behind the table. Behind the ladder were a few trunks for his belongings. Five chairs were tucked around the table but he ignored them for now, as he did with the mess on it. He shoved aside his breakfast dishes, his ink and quill and the papers he kept anchored down with a metal trinket given by his best friend's wife. He faced Claire. In the small of the cabin her anger pulsed like a beating heart.

"This is yours? Your ship, your cabin? Seems you've done well for yourself. You'll forgive me if I don't congratulate you on your success," she sneered.

He couldn't help looking her over from head to toe. A wide hat covered in layers of grime, a face that was thinner than he remembered, dirty, mended clothes that hung on her slender body and leather boots that were worn white where her toes pressed against the sides. Though he couldn't help wondering what had happened to her, and feeling some concern for her, he wasn't ashamed of what he had either. It would take more than her scathing glare to change that.

"Give me your bag, Claire."

Her eyes went round as moons. "Why?"

"I want to see what's in it. I'm not foolish enough to let you onto my ship armed. Not after you've already threatened my life."

"What makes you think I'm armed?"

"Let's just say I've done enough gambling for one day. Give me your bag, Claire."

"You really want to see my underclothes?"

Hell, he was a man, wasn't he?

"Just hand me the bag," he sighed.

"If you want to see what's in this bag, you'll have to show me the map."

She'd threatened to shoot him, was an unwelcome presence on board his ship, and still she had the audacity to try to bargain with him? She'd played him for a fool once, did she really think she could get away with it a second time?

"I didn't bring you here to negotiate," he growled.

She pulled out a chair and sat in it. "Then you've wasted your time."

"Claire." He leaned over her, forcing her head back. He saw himself reflected in the depths of her blue-green eyes. "Do you really think I can't get it from you if I try?"

She glared at him, then snarled. Looping the bag's strap over her head, she shoved it at him. He grasped it, surprised at the weight of it. He opened it and dumped its contents onto his table.

Along with a blunderbuss and a dirk, there was a small bag of ammunition, an undershirt, an extra change of clothes—as dirty as the ones she had on—soap and a hairbrush. He took her weapons and ammunition and stuffed the rest back in her bag. He dropped it onto the table. She grabbed it, placed it onto her lap, and settled her hands protectively over it.

"Happy now?"

"No." How could he be, he wondered, when seeing her turned him inside out? He hadn't ever expected to see her again and here she was, in his cabin, within arm's reach, and a part of him couldn't help thinking that if she hadn't betrayed him, she'd have been his wife by now.

"This is your own doing," he said instead. "You wouldn't be here if you hadn't followed me and tried to steal the map."

"Don't think I don't regret that," she spewed before stomping her way up the ladder and disappearing on deck.

Nate dropped into a chair, spread his long legs out before him, and sighed deeply. He had questions, lots of them. They bombarded his brain and pulsed at his temples. What had happened to her? Where was her husband? Why hadn't she waited for him the way she'd promised?

After all this time he finally had the map. And through some ironic twist of fate, Claire was with him.

"God," Nate thought as he threw his head back and closed his eyes, "what in hell am I supposed to do now?"

Dammit. The lights on the other ship vanished one by one. James looked up, cursed the clouds that obliterated all but a sliver of moonlight. Three men gone, the map was on another ship that knew it was being followed, and there wasn't enough moonlight to keep it within sight for much longer. The best James could do was douse his own lamps and follow their current direction, hoping it would be good enough. A part of him knew it wouldn't be.

The smartest thing Nate could do was alter his direction. Hell, James expected him to, that wasn't the problem. It was the direction he'd choose that James had no reckoning of. Any way James picked could be the wrong one. And the wrong one would put him behind. Too far behind.

Damn his men for failing.

Sid, who'd followed James onto the deck and had been a shadow ever since, stood next to him at the bow.

"Did you know that Nate fella was workin' with that kid?"

James turned from the horizon. "What kid? What the blazes are you jabbering about?"

Sid smiled, rubbed his right hand. "The kid from the game. The one that looked about ready to cry when he lost."

Knowing who Sid meant, James shook his head. "The kid ran out of the tavern long before Nate, and I don't see how he'd be any help to a man Nate's size." James fingered the throbbing cut at this temple. "Besides, I hardly think the man needs any help."

"Well, he's with him sure enough. Maybe you couldn't see because you was seeing poorly, but there was three of them climbed into that longboat, Nate, a dwarf, and the kid from the game."

James looked from Sid's self-satisfied smile and once again focused on the darkness beyond his ship. He remembered seeing three people in the longboat, but he also knew he'd only chased two, and the dwarf wasn't one of them. He supposed it could have been the kid, since he really hadn't been paying close attention. He'd followed, sure enough, but he'd been in the back and his vision, as Sid pointed out, hadn't been very good at the time.

But why would the kid be with Nate? To what bloody purpose? James shook his head. A kid and a dwarf. What the hell kind of disparate crew was Nate sailing with?

"Whooee, this is some pickle," Sid laughed. "They got the map, and you don't know which way they's going, not with those lights out."

James looked at Sid, knew right then what he had to do.

"You're right," he acknowledged. "I am in a predicament. And before I get in a worse one . . ."

James pulled his pistol, smiled at the terror that claimed Sid's face, and fired.

"Take care of that, will you?" he asked a passing crewman. James tucked his pistol back into his trousers and made his way to the helm.

Four

The cool moist air did nothing to douse her temper. The gall of that man, she fumed as she marched to the bow. With the lights out and the moon mostly hidden behind the clouds, she had to pick her way carefully. A small sloop such as this one didn't have a great deal of open deck space with the men about, tying lines and adjusting sails. Claire maneuvered around them. Because of her clothes and hat, not to mention the darkness, they didn't give her more than a fleeting glance.

Claire braced her forearms on the gunwale and hung her head between them. Nate. How the devil could fate be so cruel as to send Nate back into her life? And to make it worse, he not only had her map but she was confined to his ship. Her head snapped up. When in blazes had he acquired a ship? She'd spent enough time on ships to know by the condition of the deck and the gunwale, not to mention the hull as she'd climbed it, that it wasn't an old ship.

If he could own such a ship, and pay a crew as well—was he a merchant sailor, she wondered?—why did he need her bloody map? The injustice of it raged within Claire until she wanted to hit something. Or rather, someone. Someone very tall.

"I thought you could use this," came a voice from her side.

Claire turned, saw the dwarf and the cup he extended to her in his little hand.

"It's coffee, but I added a healthy dollop of rum." He shrugged. "Thought after dealing with Nate, you might need something stronger."

The dwarf smiled. A shadow of beard darkened his cheeks. His voice was deep as any man's should be, yet with his round cheeks and short stature—his chin was level with her elbow—he looked as adorable as a child. It wasn't something she planned on telling him.

"Thank you. The man's insufferable."

He laughed. "That's the best you can do? I'd have gone with stubborn, frustrating as hell, or at the very least a pain in the arse."

Claire couldn't help it, she smiled. "You do know him, don't you?"

He nodded. "I've sailed with him for six years, three spent on this ship and three on our best friend Blake's vessel. I'm Vincent, by the way."

"Claire," she said. There was no point hiding her gender to him since she'd made no secret of it back on the street.

"How is it you know Nate?"

She took a tentative sip of her coffee. It was hot but not enough to scald her mouth and it was indeed heavily doused with rum. She took a bigger sip, looked out to sea. There wasn't much to watch. Nevis was behind them and everything else was just a large blanket of onyx. Water lapped the hull and the smell of seawater rode the waves.

She contemplated Vincent's question. She'd never made a habit of discussing her past because, in order to keep to her ruse, she needed to keep to herself. However, he already knew she was a woman and that she shared a past with Nate.

"We were in the same orphanage."

Vincent's head jerked back. "He was where?"

"You didn't know? I thought you were friends."

"We are."

Claire arched a brow. "Yet you didn't know about the orphanage?"

"Nate doesn't talk about himself, and believe me, it's not because I haven't tried to get him to."

Apparently some things hadn't changed, because she'd tried as well. As they'd become friends, she'd often asked him about his past, where his parents were, did he have any brothers or sisters. He'd always evaded her questions by talking of something else. When their friendship had turned to love, or what she'd believed was love at the time, she'd asked again.

He'd become very serious, told her it was a past he was ashamed of and was trying to forget. She'd loved him enough not to press, but she'd often reflected on the sorrow that had come to his eyes when he'd said that.

"Some things don't change," she murmured.

"Why, did you try to shoot him when you were younger as well?"

Claire scoffed. "No. But looking back on it, perhaps I should have."

She lifted her cup, the heat from the liquid warming her chin. The potent smell of rum mixed with that of the coffee beans.

"How long were you at the orphanage together?"

"Three years."

"And how long has it been since then?"

She looked at Vincent's eager expression. "Do you always ask this many questions?"

He shrugged. "I'm curious. As you've said, Nate doesn't talk much."

"I don't even know you. What makes you think you'll fare better with me?"

His grin was innocent and very endearing. "Because I'm likable?"

She smiled, and passed him her empty cup. "Good night." Turning, she almost bumped into Nate.

"Where are you going?" he asked.

How did a big man move so quietly? Claire wondered. She hadn't heard so much as a step, and suddenly there he was.

"To sleep. I assume you'll allow me to do that. Or do you need to recheck my bag first in case I might have slipped another weapon into it?"

He crossed his arms. "Where had you planned on sleeping?"

"With the crew," she said.

"No."

"Why in blazes not?" she asked. "It's where I've slept on every other vessel I've sailed on."

His inhale was sharp as any sword she'd ever seen. "I don't pretend to know where you've been or why, and while it's possible you could have sailed around most of the bloody Caribbean sleeping with any number of men, you won't be doing it on my ship."

Claire gasped. "You think I whored for them? They didn't even know I was a woman!"

"Keep your voice down," he warned while casting a worried glance around, "or this crew will know it sure enough."

Claire stepped toe to toe with him. "Then don't question my virtue."

Nate's gaze battled hers. "I wasn't aware you had any left."

"Holy hell, Nate," Vincent gasped.

Shame flooded Claire. Dammit she knew she wasn't virtuous, but it wasn't by choice, and she'd certainly never whored herself. Is that what he thought of her now when he looked at her? How could a man she'd once loved, who had once treated her with nothing but respect and kindness, think so little of her? He'd had the right to search her bag—even if she'd been angry about it—because she had given him cause not to trust her. But to think her capable of whoring?

Nate scoured his face with his hands, then dropped them woodenly to his sides.

"I'm sorry."

"Because you didn't mean it?"

Nate's silence bruised her already battered heart.

"I see," she said. She left before either man could see her tears.

Needing a place that would offer some level of privacy and shelter, Claire slipped beneath the lifeboat, which rocked gently above her. Rolling onto her side, Claire tucked both her bag and her shame close to her chest as warm and silent tears fell over her cheeks.

Vincent poured Nate a cup of rum and slid it across the table. It was a tradition they'd started on Blake's ship and they'd carried it from the *Blue Rose* to the *Revenge*. Every night before retiring they shared a cup of rum in the galley. Tonight was the first night since that tradition had begun that Nate didn't want to partake in it.

He simply wanted to be alone with his thoughts. But then, maybe that wouldn't be wise as he already knew the only thing he'd be able to think about was Claire.

"You know what this reminds me of?" Vincent asked. He had his cup in his hands and was swirling the liquid around within it.

"I'm afraid to ask," Nate replied.

Vincent grinned. "It's like the time Blake found Alicia stowed away on his ship."

"It's nothing like that." Nate scowled, took a long drink.

"Sure it is. Remember how he was all tied up in knots, having Alicia on board? How he pretended to hate her when what he really wanted to do was—"

"I'd stop right there if I were you."

Vincent leaned back in his chair. The seat wasn't high but his feet nevertheless dangled above the floor. "I'm not scared of you, you big lubber. Besides, you know I'm right."

"No, you're not. Blake did hate Alicia at first. It wasn't until he got to know her that he changed his mind."

"But you already know Claire."

Nate took another long swallow. "She's married." Since the words tasted bitter on his tongue, he finished the rest of his rum.

Vincent angled his head. "Then where's her husband?"

Nate sighed. Where *was* her husband? Surely he wouldn't leave her to sail around the Caribbean by herself, a fact that scared the hell out of Nate if he gave it too much thought. Besides, why did she look destitute when he knew for a fact that her husband was very wealthy?

"I don't know."

Vincent leaned forward. "Don't you want to?"

"No." And hell, didn't he know where this was leading? "Neither do you. Stay out of it, Vincent."

Nate didn't like the look his first mate was giving him, the one that said he'd do it anyway. He'd done that with Alicia and Blake as well, gotten into the middle of it to push them together. In that case, it had worked, and Nate hadn't minded so much, as long as Vincent had kept him out of it.

But now that it was his life being meddled in, he didn't like it. Not one bit.

"I can't help if she talks to me. She seems to like me," he grinned.

His friend's stature made him look innocent, but Nate knew that look in Vincent's eyes. It didn't bode well for him.

"Then I'll have to ensure you don't get any more time alone."

"Even the captain has to sleep," Vincent said before raising his cup to his lips.

He didn't do it in time. Nate saw Vincent's smirk before he hid it behind his mug.

Nate closed his eyes and sighed.

How long could a man stay awake, he wondered?

Clouds had melted as night wore on. Moonlight now beamed down on the deck, reflected off the polished wood. Claire had managed a few bits of sleep but she was used to sleeping lightly—a handy trait when she mostly camped by herself or was surrounded by men—and she'd been waiting for Nate to go to his cabin. He had. Hours ago.

She'd overheard him tell Vincent he'd be up later, and

from their discussion she'd reasoned that he'd be trying to get some sleep before coming back to relieve Vincent of his duties. Claire had dozed in that time, coming awake to see how the clouds had shifted, where the moon hung in the sky.

The deck had been quiet then, and it was even more so now. Peeking out from under the lifeboat, she couldn't see anyone about at all. Not even Vincent. She slid out from the boat, hesitating. No movement came from the quarter deck. Leaving her bag where it lay, Claire looked around. Vincent wasn't at the bow. She crept toward the stern, unable to see any shadows or movements there either.

Her heart lurched when she heard whistling, and she froze. Logically she knew she was being ridiculous. She wasn't doing anything wrong. Yet.

It took her a moment to realize the whistling wasn't coming from the deck, but rather from the galley below. She breathed a sigh of relief, slowly unclenching her hands. Luck had never been her ally, and she hoped that the fact that Vincent was below and Nate was asleep was a sign that her fortune was changing. Not about to waste the chance if that was indeed happening, Claire stole over to the captain's hatch.

Her heart beat quickly with her intent, and her palms were suddenly damp. She wiped them on her trousers and grabbed the handle. Biting her lower lip, Claire eased open the hatch. Thankfully Nate kept a well-tended ship and the hatch swung open soundlessly.

No light came from below, and as she strained to listen, the only sound was that of Vincent's soft whistling and the whisper of wind sliding between the sails. Claire swallowed hard, closed her eyes, and said a brief prayer. Opening them again, she stepped onto the ladder.

With each step down, she paused to listen. It was only once she'd made it far enough to be able to close the hatch above her that she heard Nate's even and deep breathing. Her shoulders sagged. He was asleep. The hatch closed as silently as it had opened.

Since it had been dim above deck as well, her eyes didn't need time to accustom to the darkness. Recalling where she'd seen everything earlier, Claire crept toward the berth. She'd hoped she'd step on some clothing as it would mean she could simply search through his clothes for the map, but her feet hit nothing but smooth wood.

She dared breathe only in short, shallow breaths. Soon she was at the bedside, her heartbeat thumping loudly in her ears. It seemed as though he'd fallen asleep without meaning to, spread out over the blankets. He hadn't even taken off his jacket.

Claire wiped her quaking hands onto her pants, reminded herself to remain steady. She could do this. She *had* to do this.

He was sleeping on his back and his large hands were at his sides. His head was turned slightly away from her. The part of her that remembered what they'd meant to each other, or rather what she'd believed they'd meant to each other, wanted to linger. It wanted to trace the arch of his brows and feel the roughness of his beard. It wanted to once again be taken in his arms and to be cherished.

For God's sake, stop it, she scolded herself. *The map, remember the map. Remember the lies, the hurt.*

To that end, she deliberately kept her gaze off his face. Reaching forward, she slid her hand into the pocket of his jacket. Her fingers brushed against the paper and Claire's heart leapt to her throat. She had it!

She slowly pulled her hand away. When Nate didn't move, Claire exhaled a trembling breath.

She looked at him once more, had a moment when she wished things could have been different. But knowing they weren't, could never be, she backed away from.the berth, tucked the folded map into her undershirt, and turned for the ladder.

She got as far as the base of it before she was grabbed from behind.

The scream ripped from her throat.

"Goddammit, Claire," he swore as she thrashed to break free.

Her arms flailed wildly, desperate to connect with some part of him that would make him release her. Her elbow struck his chest. Her foot came down hard on his. Growling, he spun her around. Her right knee came racing up.

"No, you don't," he said as he deftly wrapped a large hand around the back of her knee and held it there, a mere breath away from where she'd intended to strike him. His other hand grabbed her left wrist and held it shackled down at her hip.

Luckily Claire was right-handed. Smiling sweetly, she aimed for his jaw.

Five

Nate dropped her leg and caught her fist. He angled his hips when her knee tried again.

"Dammit, Claire!"

With his right hand holding her left, he quickly grabbed her leg again, but this time he raised her clear off the ground. She had no choice but to grab on to him for balance. Moving to the berth, he tossed her onto it. Before she could scramble away, he'd covered her with his body. She was trapped. But it didn't stop her from trying.

"Get off me!" she raged, pushing and bucking. She nearly managed to crack her head against his, but he pulled back in time.

"That's enough!" his voice rumbled from deep in his chest, frustration coating every word.

He clasped each one of her wrists and shoved her arms over her head, effectively trapping it within the frame of her limbs. His lower body pressed hers into the mattress. His eyes latched on to hers.

Claire's breath heaved, her heart raced within her chest. Sweat dampened her back. Nate's breathing was rapid and the heat of it moistened the exposed skin at her throat, sending a wave of fire skimming over her skin. Suddenly she became aware of just how intimately they were touching. Her breasts grazed his chest, and with each breath she took, the sensations doubled. Despite herself, her nipples went rigid and her blood began to pound between her legs. She shifted uncomfortably, a mistake she realized too late when it placed his hardness directly at the place she throbbed.

Her eyes flew to his. Reality slapped her in the face. He wanted her, at least her body. And dammit, her own was betraying her. How dare it! After everything she'd had to endure the last eight years, her body was foolish enough to desire him? And how dare he want her after all this time! He'd had his chance.

Claire set her teeth, arched her back, and began thrashing. "Get off of me!" she yelled. He didn't seem to require any effort to hold her down, which only infuriated her more. She turned her head as best she could, opened her mouth, and nearly succeeded in biting him.

"Would you settle down!"

"You'll never get what you want from me, Nate. Never."

He angled his head. "And what would that be?"

She felt the burn in her cheeks and wisely kept her mouth shut. She wouldn't bring lust further into this and neither would she remind him she had the map. Not that he'd forgotten, she was certain, but as it was, if he wanted to get it . . .

She swallowed hard. The thought of his hands on her made her belly flutter. Damn him.

"If I let you go, will you sit calmly or will you come after me again?"

She glared at him. She'd love nothing better than to get in at least one solid shot. As though he read her mind, his eyes hardened.

"I'll tie you up if I have to," he threatened.

Claire had learned to fight since the orphanage but she'd also learned to choose her battles. Swallowing her pride hurt, but she did it.

"I won't fight you," she agreed.

He angled his head again as he studied her. He must have realized she meant it because he released her arms. When she made no move to hit him, he slowly eased away. He moved to the table, lit the candles. Soft light bathed the room. Claire scrambled off the bed but kept her distance, as much as the cabin allowed. Nate leaned against a beam near the base of the ladder. If she hadn't already figured she was trapped, she would have known then.

Though she could feel her knife against her leg, she didn't consider using it. Where would she go? They were too far away from land for her to swim to shore and she couldn't possibly overpower his whole crew. Still, it didn't mean she planned on making it easier for Nate. She crossed her arms, waited.

Nate looked her over, couldn't see the map anywhere. Where had she managed to hide it in such a short amount of time?

"You're not leaving this cabin with the map."

"You can't have it."

"Where is it?"

Claire's eyes shone like the polished blade of a sword.

Her knowing grin warned Nate he wouldn't like her response and her words confirmed it.

"It's in my undershirt."

"Hand it over."

"No."

Nate ran a tired hand through his hair. "How are you
going to go after the treasure, Claire?" He took in her dirty
clothes and face, the chopped hair. While it was apparent
she'd fallen on hard times, Nate wouldn't let himself be
moved by that. She'd had choices, goddammit. It wasn't
his fault she'd made the wrong ones.

"I'll find a way. I've managed without you this long,
haven't I?"

Nate set his jaw. "The clue doesn't leave this cabin."

"You'd hold me prisoner?" Claire gasped.

"Not if you give me the clue. Then you can dance yourself right off the ship as soon as we make port."

"You want it?" Claire asked, glowering. "You'll have to
take it. It's the only way you'll ever see it."

Nate strode to the berth, where he loomed over her.
"I've got no problem fishing it out of your undershirt."

"You wouldn't dare," she seethed.

He arched a brow. "Are you certain?" He moved toward
her. Claire took a step back—all she could do with the berth
at her back—and her eyes widened. He smelled the wind in
her hair, the lingering aroma of campfire on her clothing.
Her breath whispered against his neck. He stepped closer
still, until their clothes brushed and his legs bracketed hers.

That her eyes never left his only heightened the aware-
ness between them. The hardness that hadn't fully abated
from when she'd thrashed beneath him on the bed came
surging back to life.

The gray shirt she wore beneath her vest had only one

button open at the neck, but it was enough to allow his fingers to slip behind it. Her skin was hot and it seared the backs of his hands. He flipped open another button. At the base of her throat he saw her pulse increase. She inhaled sharply. Another button opened, revealing the white edge of her undershirt.

He freed yet another and her shirt gaped open. He exhaled a troubled breath. Her skin was white as porcelain. He skimmed his fingers over the exposed flesh and felt both her shiver and her heat. He'd kissed her many times in the orphanage, but he'd never touched her inappropriately. He'd never seen this much of her before.

And he'd never ached to see more than he was aching to in that moment.

He wanted to tear off the shirt, rip open the undershirt, and feast, both with his eyes and his hands. Then, if there was a God, his tongue. She swayed slightly, drawing Nate's attention back up to her face.

Her eyes were dark, her lips parted. Desire hammered his lower body. He slid his hand into her undershirt and felt the slight swell of her breast.

Her hand clutched his, locking it into place.

"That's enough," she said, sounding out of breath.

"I don't have what I'm after yet," he said and he couldn't have said which it was he wanted more, her flesh in his hand or the map he'd been after for years.

They both reared when the hatch suddenly opened.

"Oh good, you're awake," Vincent said as he came down the ladder. He stopped dead when he looked at Claire, her shirt still unbuttoned, then to Nate, whose arousal was painfully obvious. Despite his own embarrassment, Nate stepped in front of Claire to allow her some privacy while she fastened her shirt.

Vincent's cheeks flamed but he didn't move. He wiggled his eyebrows and his grin reminded Nate of a very satisfied cat who'd just discovered a bowl of cream.

"I'm sorry, had I known . . ."

Nate hadn't thought Vincent's grin could get any wider. He was wrong. It spread across his friend's face until his eyes almost disappeared.

"I came to wake you but I can see that's not necessary," he chuckled.

"I was just leaving," Claire said. She stepped around Nate but he grabbed her hand.

"Not with the map."

"That's twice you mention a map. What map?" Vincent asked.

Nate scowled. He knew by saying it now, only after he'd had it taken from him, that it would seem as though he'd deliberately tried to keep Vincent from one of the most notorious treasures in the Caribbean, which he hadn't been. He'd never do that to his friend. But he knew, under the circumstances, that it would appear that way.

His gaze raked over Claire before he faced his friend.

"You were right. In Nevis, I was after something. It was part of a treasure map."

"So why didn't you say so when I asked?"

"Because Nate wanted it all for himself," Claire said.

"You don't know what you're talking about," Nate growled.

"Don't I? Vincent already told me you've known each other six years. Why didn't you tell him about it before now? It's not as though you haven't been looking for it for the past eight years."

Vincent looked struck. His eyes were huge in his face, but it wasn't Nate he turned to, it was Claire. The slight wasn't lost on Nate.

"What treasure are you talking about?"

"From the *Santa Francesca*," Claire said.

"The *Santa Francesca*? She suffered a storm and ran aground nearly a hundred years ago!"

"Yes, but only *after* leaving Nombre de Dios with a treasure room full of silver, gold, and gems of every color."

"And she was empty when she run aground. The treasure had already been moved to another ship," Nate added, earning him another dagger from Claire's direction.

"That's legend talking," Vincent said.

Claire shook her head, and the light caught the bruise that Sid's punch had left on her cheek.

"It's real."

"But—"

"It's too late to get into all this tonight," Nate interrupted.

"I'm not tired," Vincent argued.

Nate sighed. No, Vincent didn't look tired. His brown eyes all but twinkled.

"Well, someone has to man the helm. Get some sleep, Vincent. In the morning, once the crew's about, we'll continue this conversation. In the meantime"—he turned to Claire—"I'll be having that map back and don't think I won't try to get it again just because Vincent's here."

Her spine went straight as a mast. "I hope you rot in Hell." Vincent's eyes almost popped from his head. "Jesus, what happened between you?"

"Nothing important," Nate said, anxiousness skittering in his gut. He'd worked damn hard to keep his past where it belonged and he'd succeeded, dammit. He wasn't about to have it dissected now.

Claire's venomous gaze raked over Nate. Her eyes

narrowed and her quick breaths told him just how angry she was. He remembered that, the fiery temper that went with her hair.

Vincent took a chair, plopped into it, his feet hovering above the floor. "Then you won't mind discussing it," he said.

"Vincent, I'm needed on deck."

"Go," Vincent said with a wave of his hand, "but I'm not leaving. I've known something was going on, and only this afternoon you denied it. Now suddenly there's a treasure, a map, and a woman stealing into your cabin. Clearly the only way I'm ever going to get to the truth is to hear it from her."

Claire suddenly smiled, though her eyes didn't warm at all. Hell, Nate thought a moment before she turned that smile on Vincent.

"I'll tell you anything you want to know."

She glanced at Nate and raised her brows in challenge. She was relishing his uneasiness. And damned if he was going to let her see just how much he hated to have his past discussed. Instead, he crossed his arms over his chest, forcing his tight shoulders to shrug.

"You can talk all you want, *after* you give me back the map."

Her eyes jumped from his to Vincent's, as though weighing her choices.

"You can have the map," she countered, "*after* I talk to Vincent."

Nate ran a tired hand through his hair. Vincent jumped off his chair, took hold of Nate's arm, and guided him to a corner. "Let me talk to her."

"I don't trust her with that map."

"Where can she go with it? Besides, you're not having much luck on your own."

"I was," he snarled, "before we were interrupted."

Nate realized too late how that sounded and, to his horror, felt heat rise into his face.

"Well," Vincent smiled, "I can be the one to leave if you think you'll fare better . . ."

"I'll go. I'll rouse someone to take the helm for me while we get this sorted out." He sighed. "Whatever she tells you," Nate said quietly, feeling a little sick now that some of his past, a past he'd fiercely guarded, would be revealed, "stays in this cabin."

For once Vincent didn't tease or badger. He nodded seriously. "It always would have."

Nate nodded. What could he say? It was a little late for apologies. Besides, he reminded himself, Vincent couldn't divulge all of Nate's past because he didn't know it. Nobody did. The knot in his stomach eased. Nobody ever would.

"I won't be long."

But once Nate was on deck, with the air cooling both his face and his temper, he didn't immediately go fetch a crew member. Instead he checked the horizon. It was too dark to see anything, Nate couldn't see if James was following but he changed his heading anyway when he took the helm. It was a habit he'd used over the years never to leave any port in the direction he really intended to go. It was always more prudent to head one way and then alter his course after he was away from watchful eyes.

Although that matter was easily taken care of, he knew sorting through his thoughts wouldn't be quite so simple. He was mad at her. Hell, the way she'd betrayed him those years ago, he had a right to be angry. And he knew, after following her onto his ship and clapping eyes on her backside, that there was lust there as well. What he hadn't realized, what he would have believed impossible, was that, after touching her again, after seeing the desire in her eyes, he still cared for her.

And hell if he knew what he should do about that.

Six

Vincent had every intention of honoring Nate's wishes. Whatever he learned tonight wouldn't go past his ears. Or more importantly, it wouldn't go past his ears and out his mouth. But he'd been with Nate for six years. He'd treasured every moment, every battle, every storm, and every long day bobbing on the still water. But in that time, he'd learned little of Nate.

Of course Nate was honorable and trustworthy. He was a damn fine sailor and an even better captain. He worked hard and talked little. It was the latter that drove Vincent crazy. He was used to chatter. He had five older sisters, and with his brother out of the house by the time Vincent was seven, Vincent had grown up with constant gossip and chatter.

And he'd loved it. There was always motion and energy around his sisters. He likened it to watching bees flit from flower to flower, never seeming to tire. But besides gossip, he'd learned respect, patience, and understanding from his sisters. They were skills that had served him well. Especially patience.

With Nate, he needed a lot of it. The man kept everything to himself. If it didn't have to do with the ship, the weather, or where they were headed to next, it was damn near impossible to hold a conversation with him. Where Nate was from, his family, and his birthday were all mysteries to Vincent.

There was one mystery about Nate that Vincent knew, however, but he wouldn't be telling Claire—or anyone else—about it. Three years ago Nate had become the illusive Sam Steele, feared captain of the *Revenge*. He'd taken over the title from Samantha Bradley, Blake's future sister-in-law, in order to protect her identity when someone suspected that she was, in fact, Steele.

Not that anyone knew for certain what Sam looked like—Samantha had made sure of that by letting a different member of her crew assume the role when they made port or attacked another ship. That way the pirate's true identity was never certain. It was a brilliant bit of thinking, and it was what had enabled Nate to assume the role and the reason he'd kept the same tradition.

By doing so he'd not only deflected any threats to Samantha, but he'd acquired a new ship, one built by Samantha and her husband, Luke Bradley. It wasn't just anybody who owned a Bradley ship, the fastest in the Caribbean.

But it wasn't divulging information about Nate that Vincent was after; it was gaining more.

"He won't get it, Vincent. I meant what I said."

"Then, my dear, we have a problem. While I don't pretend to understand your past together, I do know Nate. If he doesn't want you to have it, he won't let you keep it."

Claire sighed. She'd already presumed that. And Vincent was right—they had a problem. A big one. She peered at the little man who was watching her closely.

"He doesn't need this treasure, he has this ship. I need this treasure more than Nate does."

"Be that as it may, it's as you said. This is his ship and it's his commands we follow."

Claire leaned forward. "Just let me examine it. I haven't had a chance to yet. Once I've studied it, I'll give it to you."

"Something tells me Nate wouldn't want that either."

"Then don't tell him!" she argued, anxiousness rising in her voice.

"I won't lie to my friend, Claire. Not for you or anyone else."

"Even though he lied to you about this treasure?"

Vincent nodded. "Yes."

Claire slapped her palm onto the table. Her hand tingled, but it was nothing to the rage brewing inside her. Nate had money, clearly he didn't need the treasure to put food on his bloody table, and yet he was going after the one thing Claire needed. She couldn't let him get away with that. She wouldn't.

"What has he ever done for you to earn this kind of loyalty?" she demanded.

Vincent's back went straight. "He's stood behind me since the day I met him. He's treated me as an equal, unlike most, who tend to look at my size and see nothing but half a man. Nate keeps to himself, I'll grant you that, but he's never faltered. When he says something, you know you can count on it."

"Count on it?" Claire spewed. "The man lies, Vincent. He's lied to me, to you, and likely to everyone else he's come across. He can hide it behind his charm, but at his heart he only cares about himself."

"I'm sorry, that's not the man I've sailed with for six years."

Claire balled her hands into fists and shoved away from the table. She nearly tripped over her own restless energy, which seemed to consume the room. What could she say, she wondered, that would make a difference to Vincent? That would convince him to lie to his friend in order to help out a stranger?

The truth, she thought, with a tightening in her belly. If Vincent valued honesty that much, then the only thing Claire could think of that would make any difference was the truth. She pressed a hand to her stomach. Well, some of the truth, at least. Claire had learned the hard way not to lean on anyone, as they usually betrayed her in the end, but looking at Vincent, at his large brown eyes and the sincerity that bloomed within them, seeing the way he'd refused to betray Nate, Claire was tempted to lean on him.

"Tell me why this matters to you."

"Look at me!" she cried, waving her hands at her clothes. "Isn't it clear why I need this treasure?"

"Claire." Vincent's smile was sad. "If I thought it was only money you were after, I would give you some of mine. But I think this is about more than a map and treasure."

Perhaps she was tired, or simply too weary of always fighting. Regardless she found herself softening toward Vincent. Sighing, she sat back down, emotions weighing heavily in her chest.

"When you and Nate were together at the orphanage, you loved each other, didn't you?"

Claire shifted in her chair. "You get right to it, don't you?"

Vincent smiled. "You and Nate have a lot in common. Neither one of you is forthcoming with information. While asking directly hasn't helped where Nate is concerned, I thought I could try it with you." He shrugged. "The worst you can do is tell me to shut up."

"I assume you've heard that a time or two?"

"More than I can count, my dear," he said with a roll of his eyes.

She liked him. Granted she'd only met him, but there was an easiness about Vincent, a natural way about him that inspired trust. It was that, and the fact that she'd been so long without someone caring about her, that eased her wariness. She didn't trust easily, and she wouldn't give Vincent everything, but what harm could come from talking to him a little? Besides, making Vincent understand was her last hope to getting the rest of the map.

"I loved him as much as a young girl of fourteen knows how."

"Fourteen?" he gaped.

"I knew him a few years prior to that, but it wasn't until I was fourteen that I realized I loved him."

"I'm assuming he felt the same."

"You'd be assuming wrong."

Vincent angled his head. "Nate is not a man prone to displays of emotion. On deck, he's constant. Whether we're engaged in battle or floating still, his demeanor is always the same. But tonight was different. I'd never seen him so riled," he added with excitement.

Claire had been wondering what Nate needed a ship for. Now, she knew. If Nate engaged in battles, he was likely a privateer. Most merchant sailors didn't engage in battles often and most didn't have new sloops.

"That was his anger you saw."

"And that's foolishness talking, but," he said, holding up a hand to ward off her reply, "I won't argue. At least not tonight."

His grin was catching and Claire felt her mouth curve.

"You are persistent."

"Comes from being raised with five sisters."

"No brothers?"

Vincent's smile turned to a frown.

"One. He left when I was a young boy. He wanted nothing to do with me. I didn't measure up, so to speak."

Claire remembered Vincent's comment of only ever being seen as half a man. That his own brother had felt the same must have been devastating to Vincent.

"I'm sorry," she said. "But he was wrong. From what I've seen so far, I'd say your brother missed out on knowing a very honorable man."

To her horror, Vincent's eyes gleamed with tears. "My dear, I've never heard nicer words. Thank you."

Warmth spread through Claire. She hadn't expected it, certainly hadn't gone looking for it, but she felt in that moment she'd made a friend.

"My mother died when I nine. She took a bad cold, which led to fever and a cough that wouldn't go away. I didn't know what it was, but I knew when she got to coughing, coughing so badly it wouldn't stop, that she was very sick." Claire took a trembling breath. It wasn't easy to talk about, even this many years later. "She died the day before my tenth birthday."

"I'm sorry."

Claire sniffed. "We buried her on my birthday, near the garden she loved so much. Later that night my father did his very best to try to give me a birthday. He cut a piece of cake from one that had been brought by a neighbor and he sang to me, though he cried through most of it.

"The days were awful after that. We were both so sad and lost without her. We went about our life as best we could but we soon fell into a pattern of picking at our food and staring at nothing. At day's end we'd sit in the parlor, but there were no words said, and hours later we'd go off to bed, again in silence, only to repeat everything the following day.

"The whole first year after her death was like that. But then, the day after the anniversary of her death, he brought home the map. Vincent, it all changed after that. He had a purpose in his eyes again, and seeing the life come back to him was all I needed. At first I didn't care about the map or the treasure because that wasn't what was important. All I'd wanted was my father back and the map had given me that.

"Only his excitement extended to me. Soon we were weaving stories about that treasure and the adventures we'd have looking for it. Vincent, that map gave us life, and when we talked about it, I believed we'd find the treasure."

"But Nate had a piece of that map tonight. How much of it did you have then?"

"More than half. The problem was the right side—the part I now have," she added, tapping her chest, "was missing. Without that piece . . ."

"You couldn't be sure where to look."

"We were guessing. Good guesses, we weren't silly enough to go off completely blind, but yes, without the rest we couldn't be sure."

"But it was enough to get you both excited?"

Claire laughed. "I think my father would have looked

with even less than what we had." She sighed because that was the sad truth. Once her father had found the map, he'd been unstoppable.

"You know the treasure came from Nombre De Dios, but do you know what happened to it after that?" she asked.

"Only that the *Santa Francesca* sailed from Nombre De Dios with a treasure that had no equal. It was supposed to be the richest load to ever leave Mexico and it left in the middle of the night, the day before it was set to, all to protect it from pirates."

"Exactly. And it was found three days later, its hull cracked open on the rocks near Cartagena. No treasure was found, not even so much as a coin in the water."

"So pirates got to it first," he said.

Claire shook her head. "It wasn't pirates," she sneered. "Pirates wouldn't have bothered with a map. With what was on the *Santa Francesca*, they wouldn't have trusted each other with burying it."

"You say that as though you've had entanglements with some."

"I have. I've seen, more than once, the ravage and bloodshed pirates leave behind. They're vile, the lot of them."

Vincent frowned, seemed to consider, then shook his head. "Then who took it, if not pirates?"

"Nobody."

"Nobody? Somebody had to have taken it or it would have been with the ship."

"Not," Claire said, holding up her finger, "if the idea had always been to crash the *Santa Francesca*."

"Holy hell. To what purpose?"

Claire leaned over the table. The same excitement she'd once shared with her father—the one that had vanished as time wore on and hopelessness had crept in—once again coursed through her. She may not have found the treasure, but she'd spent enough time to have figured some of it out.

"Think about it, Vincent. Even though the *Santa Francesca* left at night, she'd still be a target. Pirate and privateer ships cross these waters all the time. She'd be spotted easy enough, especially by those hungry enough to hunt her down. But if she ran aground, then what? The treasure could be transferred to any vessel and nobody would be the wiser."

Vincent frowned. "But if the treasure could be on any vessel, then doesn't it stand to reason that it's long gone? I mean, there's no way of knowing where it went or on what ship it left. Is there?" he asked, angling his head.

"I've researched the area. There were three ships in those waters about the same time. Unfortunately, they scattered in three different directions, and though I've looked in the most likely places, it was too broad an area to do a thorough search. With this"—she tapped her chest again— "I won't have to guess any longer."

Vincent shook his head. "Claire. There are no guarantees."

"I know that. If anybody knows that, it's me. But I feel it and my father did, too. This map leads to the treasure." And with any luck at all, some clue as to what had happened to her father.

"How is it you had a father and yet were in an orphanage?"

Claire sighed. When her father had first put her in the orphanage, she'd been angry. As the weeks turned to months, her anger had grown with each passing day that he didn't come back for her. But then, after first one year, then two, her anger had been replaced by the fear that she'd never again see him.

"My father, when he realized he'd need to go past San

Salvador to search, left me at the orphanage. He promised to come back for me once he found it."

"San Salvador? That's where you and Nate are from?"

"Yes."

Vincent nodded, then squeezed her hand. "But your father never came back, did he?"

"No, he never did."

"Claire, I'm sorry and I understand your desire to find the treasure, but—"

"No you don't. You don't know what it's like to be left behind. I have no family, no money and"—she once again pointed to her clothes—"no dignity. I can't hold my head up, I can't simply be Claire Gentry. You told me the treasure couldn't only be about the money and you were right. Yes, I have plans for the treasure, for what it can provide. But besides that, I can't buy myself a home, I can't let my hair grow again, and I can't ever be a lady. I can't do anything but live hand to mouth and hope nobody discovers I'm a woman!"

Vincent allowed her the time to gather her emotions before he continued.

"And the reason Nate knows of the treasure?"

Claire sighed. "I told him about it. Not at first, but later once we'd become close friends. I didn't have the map, you see, but I'd looked at it enough times to have it committed to memory and I shared that with Nate. He promised me we'd find it one day."

"And you think he's been looking for it all this time?" Vincent shook his head. "He hasn't. When we were on Blake's ship, Nate never went off looking for any treasure."

"You said he's had this ship three years?"

"Yes."

Claire sneered. "And in those three years you're telling me he hasn't looked?"

Vincent's frown was her answer.

"Among my many regrets, I wish I'd never told Nate about the map," she said.

She met Vincent's gaze, prayed he'd understand why the treasure was so important to her. But as his silence grew, so did Claire's fears that Vincent would stand behind Nate.

"I'll help you," he said finally.

Claire's heart filled as fast as her eyes.

"You will? Really?"

"Yes."

Smiling, she turned around, dug the map out of her undershirt. When she faced Vincent again, she had the paper clasped between her fingers. In a move she wasn't prepared to halt, Vincent snatched it out of her hands.

"You said you'd help me!" she sputtered.

"I will. I am. But you've said yourself you need money. Nate has that and a ship. Who better to help?"

Claire couldn't believe her ears. Vincent was betraying her trust? Already? At least Nate had waited years to do that.

"You let me talk, led me to believe you were on my side, that you cared, that you understood. And now you turn against me? You're as heartless as he is!"

"What? I most certainly am not!" he argued, his hands fisted on his hips.

But Claire was through listening. How many men had to lie to her before she learned her lesson? Well, no more.

"I don't need you, Vincent. Not you, and you can be bloody sure I don't need Nate either."

She spun, desperate for an escape. She hadn't forgotten they were at sea, but she couldn't remain in his cabin for one more second. She raced for the ladder and had made her way up three rungs before the hatch opened and Nate's shadow fell over her.

Claire lurched to a stop. Fire burned in her gaze. Its fiery blaze was enough that Nate looked down to ensure the ladder hadn't turned to ash.

"Going somewhere?" he asked.

"I'd say anywhere there isn't a lying man, but then I don't believe such a place exists."

Nate looked to Vincent. His friend held up his hand and the map within it. His expression wasn't as happy as it should have been. No doubt Claire had taken a layer off his hide.

"Get out of my way," she snarled.

Nate stepped aside, let Claire pass. The loathing she directed at him as she met him on the ladder stung Nate. He rubbed the back of his neck.

"She's angry as a stirred-up nest of bees."

"Well, perhaps if you hadn't promised her, back in the *orphanage,* that you were going to search for the treasure together, she wouldn't be so angry at you for going after it now."

Nate shut the hatch and climbed down into his cabin. "A lot has changed since I made that promise."

He shoved aside dirty dishes, grabbed a quill, and pulled out parchment from underneath the small steel trinket he used to keep it in place.

"Have you ever given a thought to cleaning?" Vincent asked, a look of disgust on his face.

"No," Nate answered, which was the truth. He never bothered much with his cabin, not until the cook started complaining he was missing dishes.

While Vincent looked at the newest piece of the map, a

partial drawing of the Spanish Main, which included the islands of Nevis, Saint Lucia, Barbados, as well as a series of words on it, Nate drew and wrote down what Claire had once said was written on other side.

He added Hispaniola, Port Royal, and a few other islands he'd been to over the years. Like Claire, he'd never committed what he knew to paper, but that didn't mean he'd forgotten it. On nights when he'd had idle time, he'd written it out, studied it, then burned it.

"At half-mast . . . with a marked waterline . . . thrice to fail . . . alone at peace?" Vincent shoved the parchment aside. "Even with the islands marked, this makes no sense!"

"It's more riddle than map, Vincent. The map had been ripped in two, with half the words on each half of the map. Now that I have all the map, I'll have the complete sentences."

"And because it has markings of the Spanish Main, you're convinced it's here?"

"Yes."

When Nate was finished with what he remembered, he took the other piece from Vincent's fingers and set both halves side by side. Though they didn't match in size—the newly acquired piece was much smaller—Nate figured it would be close enough to make sense of it.

He frowned as he looked from one side to the other. Then his hand slammed onto the table. Vincent jumped in his seat.

"What? What's the matter?"

Nate hung his head, although he shouldn't have been surprised.

"Claire. She never told me everything." He met Vincent's confused gaze. "She's still holding a missing piece of the map."

Seven

Nate decided to let it be for the night. Trying to discuss the map further when they were both already angry would be futile. Hopefully the morning would bring a calmer approach to their situation.

He relieved the man he'd awoken to take the helm then took his position behind the wheel. The lights remained unlit and the deck was dark. Nate glanced over his shoulder. Nothing had changed since the last time he'd checked. If he was being followed, there was no sign, but then if he was being followed, he didn't think James would be foolish enough to come after him with a deck full of glowing lamps. And he didn't think James could foresee which direction Nate was heading.

Come dawn, however, he'd know for certain. And if there was a ship following? His gaze rolled across the deck. A man accustomed to darkness, he didn't find it difficult to locate Claire. She hadn't crawled back under the lifeboat to rest. She was at the bow, leaning against the bowsprit. If James had managed to trail him, then Nate would do whatever necessary to protect his ship and everyone on it. And that included Claire. Regardless of old wounds, he wouldn't see harm come to her.

Nate had no idea what she thought he did on his ship, but he did know one thing. If they needed to defend themselves and she were to discover he was a pirate, and Sam Steele at that, it had best be after he had the complete map, or else he'd never have it in its entirety.

He'd always wanted it. Been obsessed with it really. Since he had his own small fortune, he couldn't explain why it mattered as much as it did. He'd built himself a house and was ready to leave piracy behind him. But not until he had the treasure.

Nate's gaze lingered on Claire. After all these years, here they were together, looking for the treasure. It wasn't in the manner they'd spoken of, but nonetheless time had brought them to it. Nate couldn't help thinking how it could have been different, how much more exciting it would have been to go after it with the bond of friendship they used to share solidly in place.

She'd been his first friend, and long before he'd fallen in love with her, he'd loved her for that gift she'd given him. He'd felt whole around her. He'd felt as though he mattered, that at last there was one person in the sorry world who cared what happened to Nate Carter. While it had wounded him to lose the woman he'd loved, it was the friendship that he'd mourned most of all. And if the smarting in his heart was any indication, he missed it still.

He watched her turn from the bow, and though he couldn't see her gaze, he felt its sharp edges. After she'd faced him a long while—enough, he figured, to damn him to Hell—she disappeared beneath the lifeboat. Nate sighed. Things could have been so different.

Damned if he was sorry they weren't.

Claire closed her eyes, wished dreams could take her away from the pain that never seemed to leave her. The pain of losing her father, then Nate, then her horrid marriage. The pain of being poor, of being forced to live the way she'd been. Of being alone.

She tugged her bag closer, wished with all her might it was someone she was holding, rather than something. She was angry with Nate, resented him for what he'd done to her, but in the deepest part of her heart, she wished he'd have looked happy to see her. That he would have admitted his mistake and taken her into his arms. That he would've said he still loved her.

Instead he'd tried to escape her, then he'd insulted her, and finally he'd taken the only thing she had left in the world, the map. She remembered the way he'd been with her in the orphanage. He'd been shy at first, then he'd seemed to find reasons to be near her. His smile had been timid, but his eyes, those vivid green eyes, had drawn her in. As they'd gotten to know each other, she'd been further captivated by his gentleness and patience with the younger children, by the small gestures he made to make her smile and feel special.

Wildflowers were picked and left where she was sure to find them as she tended her chores. Despite his own duties, he'd always been nearby to help her with a heavy load of laundry or with emptying the dirty dishwater. She'd fallen in love with him over time, then had dreamed of a life with him. Never, not even in her worst nightmares, had she ever thought it would come to this.

* * *

Dawn broke with a breathtaking spill of color, as though a barrelful of pinks and purples, soft yellows, and oranges had been upended on the horizon. With the wheel braced and nobody yet awake, Nate shifted to the stern, looked out to sea. He saw nothing but endless water and sighed deeply. Damp morning air filled his lungs. Despite knowing what was coming shortly once Claire awoke, Nate could nonetheless appreciate the moment. For now, everything was right.

Looking through the glass, he took his time, moving it slowly across the horizon. If he was being followed, he wasn't going to miss it by being sloppy.

There. His heart picked up speed. There, barely more than a speck of white, off his port side. Since he hadn't seen James's ship last night, he couldn't be sure if that was his. Hell, it was so far away he couldn't be sure of anything. Nate shoved the glass closed. For now, he'd do nothing. They were heading for Port Royal. Since they weren't heading for the treasure, and because he wasn't about to waste time slowing down on the possibility it was James, Nate kept his course.

But he'd watch. Nobody had ever caught Sam Steele unaware and unprepared, and Nate didn't mean for that to change.

Soon as his crew was up and about and the morning meal was out of the way, Nate went to the bow. She'd been there not long after he'd spotted the other ship. Other than going below to eat, it's where she'd remained. Her hat was on, covering her hair and most of her face, but Nate knew she wasn't staying at the bow to avoid contact with his men and with it the chance they'd discover she was a woman.

No, that wasn't the reason for her stance at the front of his ship. It was simply as far away from him as she could get without jumping overboard.

Though his men continued to see to their duties, they looked at Claire and cast Nate questioning looks as he moved in beside her. Nate braced his forearms on the gunwale. He'd half expected her to walk away when he approached and found himself with the unusual desire to delay the reason he was there. Normally Nate preferred to talk directly and get to the matters at hand. But with the wind brushing his face, with the sea sparkling like a fistful of jewels, Nate didn't want to tarnish the moment with business. There'd be time for that.

"Was it everything you'd imagined?" he asked.

She threw him a sidelong glance, her brows furrowed in confusion.

"Was what?"

"Being at sea, being on a ship. We used to talk about what it would be like. If it would give us a sense of freedom or if it would make us feel trapped." He took a deep breath—the crisp morning air felt wonderful in his lungs. "From the first time I stepped onto a ship, I felt freedom, that I could go anywhere, do anything."

Claire squinted against the brilliance of the water. "Surely you didn't come here to resurrect the past."

"Surely you're not scared of discussing it," he challenged.

Claire sighed heavily. "I don't mind the sea. It has its fine points. The endless horizon, the sunrises and sunsets are a sight to behold most days."

"No sense of freedom?"

Her mouth pinched. "I've chased freedom for years. I've yet to find it."

"Why n—"

She spun, met his gaze. Despite her words, there was no vulnerability in her eyes.

"Surely you've realized by now you don't have a complete map. Let's not pretend you're here for any other reason."

He studied her closely but she gave away nothing. And that wasn't the Claire he'd known. Her face had been her best quality and it had always been full of expression. Joy and sometimes impatience at the younger children, warmth and shyness when she'd been with him. Where had that gone? Where had that Claire gone?

"Have it your way," he said, though he refrained from adding, "for now." He was damn curious to know what had happened to her and knew he wouldn't be able to stop thinking of it until he learned the truth. Besides, he deserved at least that much. "I'll get Vincent and we'll discuss terms."

Her chin shot up. "I have what you need."

His grin came slow. "As do I. Shall we?"

She strode ahead, a woman with a purpose. She moved effortlessly over the deck, easily dodging any obstacle in her path. Nate's eyes slid over her backside again and ignited a spark of desire low in his belly. Despite her loose trousers, he appreciated the movement within them. But he should have been paying better attention to where he was going as he barely dodged some rigging before it strangled him.

"Mind the lines," she warned cheekily.

Nate ignored the muffled laughter of those men close enough to see what their captain had nearly done. He called to Vincent, who was about to go down the main hatch. The three of them stepped into Nate's cabin and took their places around the table.

"What's your offer?" she asked.

He raised a brow. "My offer? I have a ship, a crew, and most of the map."

"Most won't get you the treasure," she countered.

"Exactly," Nate said. He stretched his legs out before him. She was bolder than she'd been as a young girl, but that was fine. Nate was more stubborn than he'd been as well. "We're going to have to work on it together."

Her nostrils flared. "I don't want to work with you."

"Yes, that's clear. I see no other choice. I won't give you the map I won and I don't suppose you'll hand over the last bit I'm missing."

The map had four sentences on it, though Nate hadn't realized that until last night. Claire had only ever told him that the map was in two pieces, with half the sentences on one side and the rest on the other. Which was why having only half the map wasn't good enough. What he'd discovered last night was that there were, in fact, four sentences. The clue he'd won had all four. But Claire had only ever told him three.

"No, I won't."

"Isn't sharing the treasure better than never finding it?"

She crossed her arms. "You don't need it."

"Perhaps not. But I intend to have it." His eyes challenged hers. "I hold most of the map, a ship, and the means to go looking for the treasure. Are we going to strike a bargain or not?"

"And if I say no? Will you let me off the ship?"

"With that last sentence in your head? No."

"I'm not the only one after it."

"You're talking of James. A shame for him we shifted direction overnight. By the time dawn broke, we weren't much more than a speck on his horizon. Before long we won't even be that."

Studying him, Claire said nothing.

"Surely part of a grand treasure can't be such a disappointment?"

"How do I know I can trust you? What's stopping you from going back on your word once I tell you the last of the clue?"

"If I have to trust that you're giving me the right sentence and not something your clever mind thought up, then I guess you'll have to trust in my word."

Vincent, who'd stayed quiet this long, finally spoke up. "Claire, I give you my word. We won't betray you."

Claire's gaze cut to Vincent. "I already know where your loyalties lie."

Vincent went scarlet.

"You're simply going to have to take a chance, Claire."

Claire glared at Nate, then heaved a sigh. "Fine. But I'll be wanting my weapons back." She smiled. "Since we seem to be passing around trust, I don't suppose that'll be a problem?"

Nate chuckled, moved to the chest in his room, and pulled out her pistol, blunderbuss, and dirk. He set them on the table before her.

"My share is half?"

"We'll divide what we find between us. That includes the crew."

Her mouth gaped open. Red the color of the richest rubies poured into her face. "Your crew has no part in this!"

"The ship doesn't sail itself, Claire."

"But that's unfair! I have to share this treasure with men who haven't spent a moment looking for it when I've spent years?"

"I can't very well ask them to help us locate it, load it, and then deny them a part of it."

She snarled, stormed to the window. Nate watched her

stand angrily, her arms crossed over her chest as she stared out at the sea that undulated on the other side of the glass. He couldn't help wondering if, just once, she'd stood at the orphanage window looking for his return.

They'd spent most free moments together then and he'd known, despite being only sixteen, that she was the woman he wanted. Though they'd stolen many kisses and spent many times in each other's arms, Nate had never compromised her. But there had been times when that resolution had been hard to adhere to. Her kisses had been as hungry as his, her hands on his neck and back creating a need to feel them everywhere on his body. He remembered holding himself back until his body shook.

He'd left to find work and make enough money to earn them a reasonable start. It was the memory of her kisses that had kept him going. When his back ached from ploughing fields, her taste had kept him moving long after his body had had enough. And when he'd gone back, his money tucked solidly in his bag, it was her kiss that had him running the last mile.

But she hadn't waited. He'd arrived to learn—from one of the younger girls when he hadn't been able to locate Claire—of her pending marriage. He'd never learned who, only that he was wealthy. Then he'd run as fast as he could back the way he'd come. He'd run until his lungs burned and his legs screamed for him to stop. But there'd been no outrunning the ripping pain in his heart.

He hadn't thought her capable of such betrayal. But then, maybe he hadn't known her as well as he'd thought. Just as he really didn't know this Claire either. The one he'd left had long red hair, hands that were gentle, and a voice that could both soothe and seduce. She'd been soft in every way a woman ought to be.

Well, she certainly wasn't soft anymore and neither was she gentle. There was steel in her gaze now and a fierceness to her voice that he would never have believed possible if he wasn't at the receiving end of it. Her hands weren't gentle anymore either. He'd seen the dirt under her fingernails and thin white scar lines that spoke of hard work, harder than she'd had at the orphanage. He'd felt the strength in them when she'd fought him.

"The crew doesn't have to come." Vincent's words pierced through Nate's thoughts.

Claire turned from the window.

"We don't yet know where the treasure is, Vincent," Nate reminded him, "and we need a crew to man the ship."

"Well, then, I propose this. We determine where it is. If it's close, we'll drop you off while we fetch Aidan. Both of you," he added before Claire could protest. "And if it's further, we'll get Aidan first before seeking the treasure."

Vincent turned to Claire. "Going to Port Royal was to be a joint commission. We were not only going to see Blake and his wife, Alicia, who live there, but we were also to pick up Aidan."

"Who is this Aidan?"

"Aidan was taken in by Alicia's sister, Samantha. Aidan's been dying to sail since he was a young lad, but Samantha refused until he'd had some schooling and was at least sixteen. Well, his birthday is next week and he's through waiting. Since Samantha, Luke, and Aidan are visiting at Blake and Alicia's, we're to pick him up there."

"Who's Luke?"

"Luke is Samantha's husband. And he used to be an infamous pirate before he was pardoned. Have you never heard of Luke Bradley?"

Claire scowled. "It would be impossible to keep every pirate's wretched name in my head."

"Luke is Samantha's husband," Nate warned.

"You frequently associate with pirates?" she asked.

Nate's eyes narrowed. "He's also my friend."

"I imagine as long you don't turn your back on him for very long, you're safe enough."

Nate leaned forward, his blood simmering. "Your opinions of me are clear enough but I'll not hear my friends disrespected. Not on my ship."

He locked his gaze with Claire's long enough, he hoped, to get his message across. Her mouth pinched, but she said nothing more on it. He nodded, turned to Vincent.

"Sounds fair enough. But if you tell Blake and Luke what we're up to, they'll want to come as well."

Claire threw up her hands. "The crew, Blake, Luke, Aidan. Can you not think of anyone else? After all, there must be more friends and relatives you can call upon. We haven't divvied it up among the whole Caribbean yet."

Vincent grinned. "It's not as bad as all that. Besides, if this treasure is as grand as you two think, there'll be more than enough to go round. And we'll need people we can trust to haul it out. They don't come any more trustworthy that Blake and Luke."

"Are you in agreeance?" Nate asked Claire.

Nate knew she wasn't happy about splitting the treasure with the crew, but he also knew she was smart enough to realize it was her only choice.

"Fine," she said with a deep sigh as she took her seat at the table. "If that's all decided, then let's get on with it."

Nate went to one of his drawers, pulled out the two pieces of parchment. He dropped them in front of Claire.

She looked at them both, but it was the newly acquired piece that kept her attention. Her hands trembled as her fingers skimmed the words. Her eyes shone when they met Nate's and he was glad he wasn't called upon to speak, because he wasn't sure he could have managed it.

"It's all here."

He cleared his throat, nodded.

Her smile was beautiful and his gaze hungrily stared at it while she brought the piece Nate had written closer.

"I'll need a quill."

Vincent chuckled when Nate didn't move. "I'll get it," he offered and he passed it to Claire.

She wrote the last missing words—the first part of the first sentence as it happened—then leaned back in her chair and read the complete map.

> *"Where the black flag flies at half-mast*
> *stands a bold shore with a marked waterline*
> *at the turn, thrice to fail*
> *a lone piece, alone at peace."*

"That's it?" Vincent demanded, his dark brows drawing together.

"What did you expect, 'the treasure will be under the dock in Port Royal'?" Nate asked.

"Would have been bloody simpler, wouldn't it?" Vincent grumbled. "Besides, there's no mention here of the *Santa Francesca*. How do you even know this leads to her treasure?"

"There were markings on the map," Claire said and once again took the quill. She took a few moments, the quill sure and steady in her hands, as she added details to the piece Nate had created. When she was done, she pointed to the markings she'd drawn.

"These markings aren't there by chance. Look a little closer." She turned the map for Vincent to see and pointed to the first marking. It was near Nombre de Dios.

"What? It looks like a scribble."

"Or perhaps an *S*?"

He frowned, leaned closer still.

"I suppose it could be," he agreed reluctantly.

"And here." She slid her finger to the left. "What does that look like?"

"A triangle?"

"Not a triangle, an *A*."

"And if you examine it, you'll see every letter that spells the name *Santa Francesca* is hidden somewhere in that map of the Spanish Main."

Vincent arched his brows. "Really?" He kept studying it until he shouted, "There! That's an *N*, isn't it?"

Claire smiled. He'd found the third letter hidden next to Panama.

Vincent leaned back in his chair, a frown once again on his face. "Where do you propose to look?" He read the clues again. "Almost every island in the Caribbean has at least one bold shore," he said, referring to the steep coasts that allow ships to approach.

Claire felt as confused as he looked. "With the map I'd had, I was looking for a place where pirates thrived—"

"Again, that doesn't narrow it down," Vincent reminded them.

"I realize that. But now with the rest, it no longer reads, 'Where the black flag flies,' it reads where it 'flies at half-mast.' "

"Meaning pirates have died there?"

"Perhaps. It could also mean a place where pirates aren't welcome," Claire explained.

Nate nodded. "Makes sense. So we're looking for ports that have at least one bold shore and that either aren't friendly to pirates or pirates have died there."

"You both have lost your minds. This isn't a treasure hunt, it's a hopeless endeavor."

"It's real enough and it's out there. We have only to find it."

Vincent turned to Nate. "What if you can't find it? The crew won't be happy to wait indefinitely while you make sense, the galleon we—"

"Vincent."

Nate's harsh warning snatched Claire's attention from the map. She looked up in time to see the apology in Vincent's eyes and the scowl on Nate's face.

"What galleon?" she asked. Then her jaw fell to the floor. "You own a galleon as well?"

Fury swirled in the bottom of her stomach and spiraled upward. If the blasted man owned this ship *and* a galleon, he had no business looking for the treasure.

"Sit down, Claire."

For a moment Claire was stunned. She hadn't realized she'd stood. But now that she did, she remained that way.

"No, I won't. And I won't be told what to do, not by a lying bastard like you."

Nate stood then as well, and he loomed over her, his eyes sharp. Claire kept a firm hand on both sides of the map. A fact Nate didn't miss. Not if his frown was any indication.

"You need to decide and you need to decide now. You either trust a *lying bastard* enough to go searching for this treasure together, or you don't." His smile was as thin as the compassion in his eyes. "Either way, I'm going to look for it. And as my memory is very good"—he shifted his gaze to the map, chuckling when Claire's hands spread to hide it—"I don't need the map or you any longer. Am I clear?"

"You're going to take it without me?" The hell he would, she thought.

"I'm simply laying out the facts. I have a ship, and the complete map." He tapped his temple. "I won't undertake this venture with you jumping down my throat every chance you get. You've already made it more than clear what you think of me."

Claire sputtered. She couldn't believe Nate had such nerve. "You expect me to be happy that I have to share this with you when you clearly don't need it?"

He snatched the map from under her hand, growled when she stretched to take it back. He rolled up both pieces and handed them to her. "If you can figure out this map and get there before me, the treasure's yours."

Answering was impossible due to the storm of emotions blowing within her. How dare he! How dare he dangle his riches before her knowing she had nothing. And he knew it. Hell, anybody looking at her knew it. And he had the audacity to use it against her!

Search for the treasure without him? She would in a heartbeat if she could, but she'd lost everything in the game. She was destitute. If she let Nate go off to find the treasure, he would. And he'd keep it and then where would she be? Claire braced against the table, hung her head. She had no choice.

And oh, how she loathed that.

Being poor in and of itself wasn't so bad. She could feed herself and live by her own rules. But being controlled by anybody left Claire with a bitter taste in her mouth. She'd lived that life in the orphanage, and again in her brief marriage. She'd promised herself she'd never live that way again and yet here she was.

Nate made it sound as though she had a choice, but they both knew she didn't. She either had to hold her tongue in order to acquire a share of what she felt was rightfully hers or she'd lose it altogether.

There wasn't a choice to be made.

"Have you made your decision?"

Go to Hell, she thought, *and take all your money with you.* She couldn't believe she'd wished, just last night, that he'd take her into his arms. Well, she wouldn't make that mistake again, but it didn't change her predicament.

She nodded.

"Perfect," Vincent said, his face being the only one of the three around the table that looked even partially happy.

"Be sure, Claire. Once we set out, there's no turning back."

She met his hard gaze with one of her own.

"I'm not going anywhere."

"Fine then," Nate answered. "Let's get to work."

Eight

Work was exactly what it turned into and it ate through all of that day and most of the next. Vincent and Nate took turns at the helm and on deck. Claire spent most of the time in Nate's cabin trying to decipher the map. She continued to sleep under the lifeboat. She and Nate had formed a kind of truce as they worked on the map, but that didn't mean she was comfortable sleeping in his cabin, even if it was when he was on deck.

It was simply too intimate a thing to consider. It was already unnerving spending so much time with him after all these years, talking to him and remembering—despite her efforts not to—the times they'd shared. Sleeping in his bed, something she'd dreamed of often after he'd left the orphanage with the promise of returning, would make fighting the memories almost impossible. And she would fight them. Giving in to them would weaken her and she wouldn't allow that to happen.

Dusk had fallen outside the small window. Thin trails of black smoke wove upward as Nate lit the thick candles. Claire watched his face warm with the glow of flame and felt a tug in her belly. *No, no*, she thought. *No.* She forced her gaze back to the map, but no sudden inspiration came to her. It was getting harder and harder to keep up her hopes with the daunting task at hand. There were so many possibilities, and they simply didn't have a specific enough point to begin their search.

"Having the complete map was supposed to make things easier," Claire muttered. Her eyes burned from studying it and she closed them momentarily. The relief was immediate and wonderful.

"Perhaps," Vincent said, sliding the map from under Claire's fingers, "we should concentrate on the reason the treasure was never recovered."

Claire blinked her eyes open. "Because nobody's had the map."

Vincent humored her with a grin. "I realize that, dear, but I don't mean recently. What I am referring to is if the Spanish wanted this treasure badly enough to crash a perfectly good vessel for it, then create a map and hide it, why didn't they ever go back for it?"

"Or why did they bury it to begin with?" Nate added, taking his usual seat across from her. "Once the treasure was off the *Santa Francesca*, they had nothing stopping them from taking it directly to Spain."

"There's always the threat of pirates," Claire reminded them. "Pirate attacks aren't limited to ships known to carry treasure. They aren't exactly a discriminatory lot after all."

Vincent coughed. Nate smiled, his eyes filled with

humor when they met Claire's. "That would depend on the pirate, I suppose," he said.

"What I mean is that perhaps if we knew why they buried it to begin with, we'd have a better idea of where to look," Vincent stated.

"How in blazes are we ever going to know that?" Nate asked him.

"Claire, you said that you knew of three ships that were in the area about the same time the *Santa Francesca* left Nombre de Dios. What else did you learn?"

Claire sighed, tucked a leg underneath her, and leaned back in her chair. If they were taking this route, it was going to be another long night.

"It made sense to me, once I learned the treasure was never recovered near the wreck, that it must have been moved. I talked to several people, both in Nombre de Dios and in Cartegena, and they all agreed that they'd heard of at least three ships around that evening."

"At least three? There could be more?"

Claire looked at Nate. "I know that doesn't sound very assuring, but since most claim that there were only three ships, and were in fact able to name them, that's what I've used as the basis of my search."

"And they would be?" Nate asked.

"The *Maiden of the Sea*, which was last seen close to Havana. The *Emmeline*, which was reported to have gone past Santo Domingo, and the *Fernando*, which made its last known stop at Barbados."

"Perfect. Not only does this still not tell us why they hid the treasure," Nate reasoned, "but it also leaves us with three completely different routes."

"Only two, as it happens. The *Maiden of the Sea* was

taken by pirates not far from Nassau. The handful of survivors swore the treasure was never on their ship."

"Well of course they'd say so. You don't think they'd have told them where it was buried, do you?"

"From what I learned, the sailors on board were flogged. The cat-o'-nine-tails was reputedly well used that night and more than one man died from the abuse."

"A man would confess to almost anything to escape that," Vincent muttered.

From the horror on his face Claire knew he was picturing the hide-made whip that had nine knotted ends, each of which carved into the back of whoever was being flogged.

"Which is precisely why I tend to believe them."

Nate scrubbed his face. "All right, that brings us down to two ships and two routes." He looked at Claire. "There are lots of islands near both Santo Domingo and Barbados that have bold shores."

"I know," she agreed with a tired sigh.

"Let me see that again," Nate said and Vincent passed him the map.

Claire watched Nate as his fingers traced the islands and his lips moved as he read the words. Though men tromped about above and their muffled voices carried through easily enough, Nate's cabin was quiet and still.

"This," Nate said, tapping the map. "Where it says 'bold shore.' What if it doesn't mean what we think it does?"

"I don't follow," Claire said, though she unfolded her leg and sat straighter.

"What if instead of a steep cliff, it actually means to be bold, or brazen."

She frowned. "Brazen?"

Vincent looked at her, raised his shoulders in puzzlement. "I've no idea," he said.

"Can you not think of a port that is dauntless and arrogant?"

"Tortuga?" Vincent suggested.

"Not Tortuga. Pirates are more than welcome there. But there's a little island that once fought off a pirate attack. The natives were outnumbered dreadfully, but as they were fierce warriors, not only did they fight for their lives and won, they also took down half the pirate crew in the process."

The name came fast to Claire's mind and she grabbed the map, saw where Nate had drawn it in. She pointed to the island that lay southeast of Santo Domingo. "Isla de Hueso."

"Isla de Hueso?" Vincent repeated.

Nate smiled and his eyes sparked, drawing Claire into his excitement. "It wasn't called that at the time, but it's since been given that name. The point, however, is from that moment on, they flew a mutilated pirate flag from their shores."

"To warn other pirates away," Claire said. "I've never been there, but I've heard of it."

"Out of curiosity, does it also have a steep cliff?" Vincent asked.

"The island," Nate explained, "is shaped like a bone, which is how it got its name. The two ends are heavily treed and very rocky, but I wouldn't go so far as to call them bold shores. They aren't very steep and the rocks go out a ways, making mooring a ship there tricky.

"The middle part of the long two sides of the island, after you get past the rocks and trees, have sandy beaches and the town rests on a small rise between those beaches."

"If the pirates were run off, what makes you think we'll fare any better? Especially when they realize what we're after?"

"You have to remember that was almost one hundred years ago, Vincent. The island is barren and has been for near a hundred years."

His eyes flashed with understanding. "What happened to the natives?"

"Well, they weren't inhospitable to everybody and were more than happy to welcome visitors who stopped by to do some friendly trading. The problem, according to the stories, is that one such group of visitors brought along with it smallpox. It killed off most of the tribe. Those that survived left for fear of contracting the disease. It's been abandoned ever since."

Excitement skimmed over Claire and drew gooseflesh on her arms. It all made such perfect sense.

"If it is on Isla de Hueso, then that means the treasure was on the *Emmeline*, since Isla de Hueso is on course to Santo Domingo," Claire reasoned. "It's a likely spot to hide treasure and all the clues fit. If the island was feared to carry traces of the disease, then what better place to hide a fortune than an island nobody dares stop at?"

"Exactly. Besides, if the island was uninhabited, and it would have only recently been if the dates are accurate, then there would be nobody to witness them hiding it there."

"But why *did* they hide it and why haven't they come back for it?" Vincent argued.

Nate shrugged. "Could be any number of reasons. I'm inclined to believe that they suspected they were being followed and panicked."

"From what I've been told, the *Emmeline* never made it to Spain."

Nate arched a brow. "She sank?"

"Then how did the map come to be?" Vincent wondered.

"According to the stories, when the *Emmeline* stopped

in Santo Domingo, she wasn't anchored very long. I agree that they believed they were being followed and panicked. I think they hid the treasure then headed to Santo Domingo. I found a few people who'd been told stories by their grandparents. Apparently the sailors who'd come ashore had made a point of saying they had no cargo, that they'd already been plundered by pirates."

"But you don't believe that?"

"No, Vincent. I think it was a ploy used in hopes it would keep anyone from going after them. But in case it didn't work, they made the map. They hid half of the map on Santo Domingo that day and the other half—"

"Was taken by the pirates that looted and sank the ship once they left Santo Domingo," Nate finished.

"Yes. Add nearly one hundred years and the passing around of that map and here we are."

From the corner of her eye she saw Vincent shake his head, clearly not as convinced as she was that this treasure was real and that they'd finally deciphered its location, but that didn't matter. What mattered was the truth that rang in Claire's heart as surely as the moon that shone through the window. She finally knew where the treasure was!

"Are we on course for Isla de Hueso? How soon can we get there?"

"We'll change our direction immediately."

"And the ship that's following?"

"As she's not gaining ground, she's obviously a bigger ship that can't keep up. But don't worry, I won't lead her to our treasure. If she comes any closer, we'll turn round and sink her. She won't take what's ours."

Claire nodded.

"I'll go change our heading," Vincent said.

With the absence of Nate's first mate, the cabin suddenly

felt close and intimate, and it brought into sharp reality exactly what Claire was preparing to undertake. She and Nate would be alone on a deserted island for days while the ship went to Port Royal. Her stomach fisted. Her heart began to race.

Nate braced a foot on a chair, leaned on his thigh with both forearms, and looked her in the eye. She smelled the wind on his clothes, felt the whisper of his breath on her cheeks. She'd once looked into those pretty green eyes and seen, or believed to have seen, honesty and love. She didn't know, or trust herself to interpret, what was there now.

"If you'd prefer, I can have one of my men join us on the search."

Because his offer surprised her and because she wasn't sure of his motivation, she chose to make light of his words. "Are you scared of me?"

"I thought you might be more comfortable if it wasn't only the two of us."

His voice was deep and manly and made her very aware that despite the fact that she wore men's clothing, she was a woman beneath the fabric.

"I'm sure it will be fine. Besides, you've given me back my weapons."

He arched a brow. "Planning on using them, are you?"

"Not unless I have to."

His smile was as beautiful as his eyes. "Keep them close, Claire. You never know what may happen."

James snapped the looking glass shut and smiled. Finally things were going his way. The ship had changed its course, and unlike the last time when he'd realized they had changed direction, this time he wasn't left scrambling to make the necessary adjustments.

It had been pure luck that they hadn't lost Nate's ship that first night. He'd awoken to see it off his starboard side, nearly out of view completely, and had yelled and cursed and kept at his men all day until they'd gained some ground. Not a lot. Not enough to create a threat. Just enough to keep them in sight.

Giving his first mate clear instructions to maintain the current distance between the ships, James went below. Sunlight poked its way through the glass in fat fingers and illuminated the room. James strolled to the table and, with a sharp popping noise, yanked the cork off a bottle of rum. He poured himself half a tankard, replaced the plug, and took a seat.

From underneath his charts he slowly pulled a piece of paper, thin from the foldings it had seen over the years. It had both the color and the fragility of a freshly baked pie crust. James carefully set it before him. It was an account from his great-grandfather, written in precise script.

It was dated 1570.

I had never seen anything that compared to what I saw that night. There was so much of it. Barrels, chests, satchels. Anything, it seemed, that could be filled, was. Men, so many I lost count, transferred it from the holds of the Santa Francesca *into those of the* Emmeline. *I half expected she would sink then, for she was loaded as I have seen no other. We worked in darkness, each of us dripping with our efforts. We were tired, we ached, yet we did not slow.*

We knew the value of this treasure and we also knew the importance of what we were doing. Fool everyone and get the treasure to Spain. We all wanted it to arrive, for to leave it behind at the mercy of pirates, or worse, the British, was unthinkable. In Spain, in the hands of our king, was the only place we wanted this treasure to be.

As we watched the Emmeline sail away that night from that little spit of land, and as we all jumped back into our boats to go home, we all believed it would.

It wasn't until later that we learned she'd never arrived in Spain. I was sick thinking all that treasure was somewhere on the bottom of the ocean, or worse. It ate at me. I could not sleep, it was a chore to swallow any food and that which I did churned in my belly. Possessed by a fierce need to know, a need to know what had come from our soil remained with our people, I left Nombre de Dios, and my beautiful Isabella.

It took many months, but finally I learned that the Emmeline had stopped in Santo Domingo. She'd already been plundered by pirates when she'd arrived had been the tale. At first I believed them and my heart was heavy with the loss. But there were too many other tales, those of a torn map that had been left behind, those of a treasure hidden to keep it safe. The men from the Emmeline were lost, and those of us that had loaded it knew it was wise to keep our part in it a secret.

Yet I knew there were some of those men, like myself, that never stopped thinking of it. Nor had stopped looking for it. As I lay here, age and disease taking my body much before I'm ready to let it go, I wish I had found it. I tried. Every opportunity that arose, every spare minute I could spare I devoted to the treasure. Sadly, as my breath rattles in my chest, all that I have accomplished in regards to the Emmeline's treasure is the word of another old man.

I met him several months ago, before my health started to fail me. He was an old crippled man, given to long ramblings that more often than not didn't make any sense. He would speak of his children as though they were born into the world yesterday. He would speak of God and in the same breath, the devil. A devil with a pistol and a cat-o'-nine-tails.

He wouldn't always remember me from one visit to the next but that was of little consequence. I'd been told, in my search for the truth, that there was a man who claimed to have been on board the Emmeline. *Though they dismissed it as nonsense, I didn't. Not after he showed me the scars on his back and certainly not when, after several attempts, I finally witnessed another moment of sanity.*

The clouds that normally turned his blue eyes to gray had cleared. When he'd looked at me, when he'd spoken of the horror he'd seen, when he'd described the treasure, the casks and satchels exactly as I'd remembered them, I knew he had been on board the Emmeline.

I visited him daily from that point on, but his moments of madness were coming in far greater number and lasting far longer. Days would pass when I couldn't understand a single word he spoke. And when I'd all but given up, was ready to go back home, he had one last moment of clarity.

"The key," he'd said, "is in the last. Pay attention to that and you'll find it."

Where was it? I implored. He grabbed my hand, and as his eyes began to cloud for the last time, he managed to say, "Where there's nothing to fear . . ."

> *Sadly I never deciphered what he meant. But I write these words with the hope that one day, one of my own will.*

Well, James thought as he took a long sip of rum, none had yet. His grandmother, the only child of Isabella and Roberto, had never even tried. She'd married an Englishman, luckily after her father had died, but had honored her father's desire for his blood to locate the treasure. Since she also had only one daughter, she'd waited until her grandson, James, was old enough to receive his great-grandfather's words.

Like his ancestor, James was driven to find this treasure, though not for anything as noble as country. He'd thought he'd carried the advantage, knowing that the treasure had been moved to the *Emmeline*, but it hadn't helped in his search.

There were clusters of islands throughout the Caribbean, and the area between Nombre de Dios and Santo Domingo was no exception. James gently slid the letter aside then pulled his charts closer. His fingers swept the islands between the two ports. Where any formation of islands closely resembled a line, he'd gone to the last one of the line. Sometimes, he'd search the first, as the last depended on where one's starting point was. He'd never found anything. Of course, since it wasn't hidden in plain sight, he really couldn't do much as he had no way of knowing where to look. Without the map, all he could do was search some caves.

His great-grandfather's words, about a place where there was nothing to fear, didn't help either. Pirates, weather, sickness, lack of food, lack of money. To James's way of thinking, there was always something a man could fear if he were so inclined. As for himself, he shrugged, took another sip of rum. All he could do was make plans and follow them through. Not that he didn't fight to protect what was his, but he didn't lose sleep over what he couldn't change or prevent either.

Still, that didn't change the fact that, to most, there was always something to be fearful of. How could a place exist where there wasn't anything to fear? He leaned back in his chair and considered. Since Nate had changed his heading, James could only assume it meant he'd figured out the map. Heading south, he thought.

"Where are you going?" he said, his eyes running over the chart again as frustration began to beat an impatient drum through his veins. "Where is it?"

The names of the islands rattled through his mind while his eyes drifted over them. He'd been to them all. And had left with nothing. Even this blasted one, he thought as his finger tapped Isla de Hueso. Useless scrub of land that nobody bothered to . . .

"Wait a minute." He sat up straight, gazed hungrily at the map. "Nobody lives there. There's nothing to fear." Which of course he'd realized before now, but with Nate heading in that direction, it gave James reason to consider it again.

As far as islands went, it was the safest. Not a lot there, he mused. Ruins, two nice beaches. Enough fruit to keep a belly from starving. But it wasn't last. Not that it was in a row either. Isla de Hueso was mostly surrounded, by a half-day's sail, by other scraps of land smaller than it was. All nothing more than shoots of tree-covered rocks that bulged out of the sea.

He slid his great-grandfather's letter closer again, and when he reread the words, he shook his head at his own stupidity. It didn't say *on* the last, it said *in* the last.

His hands thumped the table in celebration. It was on Isla de Hueso. It was the only thing that made sense. It was the only place they could have hidden such a treasure without being seen. Dammit, why hadn't he figured that out before now?

He didn't know what was in the last, or where the last was, but he didn't need to. Nate had the map. Nate would know that part. The key, James figured, was in Nate having the time to find the treasure. Then James wouldn't need the map. He could simply sail in and take the prize.

Yes, he thought as he chuckled through the last of his rum. Let Nate do the work, think the spoils were his. He didn't need to know any differently.

At least not yet.

Nate sat heavily on the thick mattress in his cabin and groaned. How had things become so complicated?

He'd gone to Nevis determined to get the final clue to put the complete map together, to find the treasure, and to finally put the past behind him. Then he'd planned on telling Vincent that the house he'd built on Santo Domingo wasn't simply a base to use when they needed time ashore. That it was where he wanted to stay.

He loved the *Revenge* and had been more than happy to take the ship along with its captaincy. Having never had a real home, or one he could call his own since he had considered Blake's ship his home at the time, he'd cherished the *Revenge* and what it represented for him.

But it had been three years since he'd assumed the role of Sam Steele and he was beginning to want more. More than plundering and amassing wealth, though as someone who'd grown up with nothing, he didn't think there was such a thing as too much wealth. As the riches had accumulated, it hadn't changed the fact that something was missing.

Stability.

He was tired of always moving, of not having any roots. And as long as he was Sam Steele, he wouldn't have any. His taking the ship had protected Samantha but she was safe now. Nate had left enough witnesses to his plundering that there could be no doubt that Sam Steele was not Samantha Bradley, who happened to be one of the best ship makers in the Caribbean.

Nate had always planned on giving the ship back to Luke when he was done as Steele. He'd planned on going back to Santo Domingo and settling into his home.

He hadn't planned on Claire.

Nate sighed, and buried his face in his hands. Claire was going with him. She was going to be around him constantly. They'd eat, work, and sleep side by side. It was the latter that made his hands sweat.

She'd been on his ship for days now, and knowing she was close, after so many years without her, wore on his resistance. He found himself watching her on deck, watching that silly hat she wore flutter in the wind. Watching her face hunt the horizon. Watching the way her mouth moved when she spoke, the way her voice filled with passion when she was angry. He watched far more than he should and he yearned even more than that.

Nate scraped his hands over his face and looked out the window. He should have been excited, should have been ready to face this last task because it meant he was one step closer to saying good-bye to Steele. Instead he was wondering how in hell he'd be able to get through the next six days, the time it would take Vincent to sail to Port Royal and back to Isla de Hueso.

He wasn't worried about the treasure. Claire had it figured out, and though they were basing their search on a great number of assumptions, Nate knew it was right. Having near a week to find it while Vincent went to fetch Aidan was more than enough. No, that wasn't what was weighing on Nate's thoughts like a hundred-pound anchor.

It was his weakness for Claire. She struck something in him no woman ever had and it called to Nate in a way he couldn't explain. He only knew that, despite her broken promise to wait for him, despite his hurt, the minute he'd recognized her on the street, a part of him had been thrilled to see her. He didn't trust her. But he did desire her. Time hadn't lessened the want.

"That other ship is gone. We lost her about an hour ago."

Nate looked up, surprised. He hadn't heard Vincent come down.

"She change direction?"

"No. Just fell behind."

"I didn't hear the wind pick up."

"It didn't."

"Hmm." Nate wasn't sure what to think of that. If the ship didn't change direction and the wind hadn't changed, why had they suddenly pulled ahead?

"At least this way we don't have to worry about leading it to the island."

"I suppose so," Nate agreed.

"You all set for tomorrow?" Vincent asked.

"Yeah," Nate answered, coming to his feet.

Vincent leaned against the beam. "For someone who's going to be alone with his woman for days, shouldn't you look happier?"

"She's not my woman," Nate scowled.

"But she was once."

"We were at the same orphanage, that's all."

Vincent sighed, placing a hand on his hip. "For whatever reason you seem determined to lie to me, let me just say this. I know you cared for Claire just as I'm sure she felt the same way. Otherwise neither one of you would have been so quick to jump down the other's throat. Besides that, the air crackles when you're in a room together."

"Jesus," Nate grumbled. Vincent had spent far too much time with his sisters growing up.

"I mean it. You aren't seeing it because you don't want to accept that's the way it is. But I see it. Just as I see the reason for the house you've been building. When were you planning on telling me you were through being Steele?"

Nate sighed. "After the treasure was found."

He didn't miss the shadow of hurt that crossed Vincent's face.

"You think I didn't realize from the beginning why you were building the house? A man whose life is at sea doesn't need a fancy house."

"It's not that fancy. Why didn't you say anything?"

"What should I have said?" Vincent raised his palms. "If you want to give up your life at sea, that's your business. You can't possibly tell me you were waiting for my blessing."

Nate scoffed. "Not likely."

Vincent grinned. "Just as I thought. Besides, this will save me the trouble of killing you for it."

"Not that you could, but what is it you think you could kill me for?"

"For the chance to be Sam Steele."

"Jesus." Nate shook his head. "Why in hell would you want to do that? Samantha's safe. Steele can die now."

Vincent went pale. "Die? Not bloody likely! Maybe

you've been waiting for the right time to live in a fancy house, but I've been waiting just as long for a time to make a name for myself."

Nate had to sit down.

"You want to be Steele? Why? You thought *I* was mad when I took the title."

Vincent grinned. "I did. And you were. But it's not as dangerous as I thought it would be, and between this and Blake's ship, I figure I can handle anything that comes at me."

"You could," Nate agreed. "Of that I'm certain."

"Thank you," Vincent said. He bowed his head a moment. "I want this for me, Nate. I'm tired of being Vincent the dwarf, or Vincent the second in command. I'm the youngest of seven children and I've always felt like I came last."

"If I ever made you feel that way—"

"*You* didn't." Vincent met his gaze, shook his head. "You never did, but others have. And now if you don't want to be Steele, then I have the chance to be the leader instead of the follower." He sighed. "If that makes any sort of sense."

Nate rose, walked to his friend, and put a hand on his shoulder. He wasn't great with words but they pushed against his chest now and needed to be said.

"I can't think of a finer man to pass the title to than you. I'd planned on giving the ship back to Luke, which would have made Aidan angry after only joining us, but if you want it, then I say when we're done with the treasure, the *Revenge* is yours."

Nine

Nate finally gave up pretending. He threw the blankets aside and reached into the darkness for the clothes he'd tossed on the floor when he'd retired. Used to such a thing, Nate found them easily and dressed in the dark. Only after he'd slipped his feet into his boots did he light the candles. His cabin fluttered to life.

Unlike Blake, who'd kept an immaculate cabin, Nate wasn't so regimented. He kept his ship clean and in perfect working order. Planks were washed, sails were repaired as needed. And the galley was kept neat and tidy. The holds were precisely organized, and the barrels kept firmly tied to keep the load from shifting.

But his cabin, since he really didn't do much there other than sleep and chart his voyages, was very different. The table that occupied a solid third of the space, that held the plate of half-burnt flickering candles, was always in disarray. At the moment, other than the cluster of candles, it held enough dirty dishes that the cook would soon be screaming for them, ink, and a fancy metal anchor that held both parchment and the map in place.

Blake's wife, Alicia, had made the anchor after their first child had been born and Nate had agreed to be the boy's godfather. He picked it up, wrapped his long fingers around the steel, and in his mind saw the day he'd never forget. He'd come to Port Royal expecting to visit with his friends before the birth of their first child. They'd been eating breakfast when Blake had been called on to make a day trip at sea to deliver some goods. Nate and Vincent had urged him to go, ensuring Alicia wouldn't be left alone. Blake had left and hell if it wasn't three hours later that Alicia had doubled over in cramps.

Nate had sent Vincent for the midwife Alicia had been seeing, but by the time they'd returned, Nate had been bathed in sweat and Alicia was fine and holding her son. It was something Nate never wanted to repeat. He'd been lucky to remain standing as it was.

Smiling at the memory of how his legs had trembled, of how his heart had stumbled when the infant had slipped into his waiting hands, Nate set the anchor down. An anchor. Alicia had said he'd been one for her that day.

He'd once thought he'd been one for Claire as well, when she'd given up hope of her father ever coming for her. At least Nate liked to believe he had been. He'd sure done everything he could to prove it. And still it hadn't been enough. She hadn't trusted, hadn't believed in him enough to wait.

"Blake's damn lucky," he mumbled as he shrugged into his coat.

* * *

Someone was watching her.

Claire awoke with a start, her heart galloping. She reached into her boot for the knife as she bolted upright. She was promptly stopped when her head hit something hard.

"Ow!"

What in blazes? she thought as spots blinded her vision.

"Easy, it's only me."

As the last layers of sleep lifted, Claire's mind began to work properly and her surroundings soon became painfully obvious. She was on deck, that was Nate's voice at her elbow, and her clothes, as well as her blanket, were cold and wet. She raised her hand, felt the curve of slick wood. The lifeboat.

"What were you trying to do, have me crack my head open on the lifeboat?" she asked as she leaned on one elbow and waited for the white stars to clear from her vision.

"It's raining. You need to get out of the wet."

Because it wasn't the first time she'd slept through rain, it didn't surprise Claire that she'd done it again. Years of sleeping in the forest, despite her crudely made shelters, had accustomed her to sleeping in such circumstances.

"I'm fine, Nate."

"No, you're not. The wind is picking up, you'll get sick. Go dry yourself in my cabin."

She bristled at the order. "I won't wilt in the rain, and if I get cold enough, I'll go below with the crew."

His inhale was sharp. "How do you propose to get out of those wet clothes in front of the crew?"

Her eyes narrowed. "I have no intention of parading naked in front of your men."

"Claire," he sighed. "Do you really want a head full of cold when we're searching for the treasure?"

The wind picked that moment to reinforce Nate's argument. It raced across the deck and lashed her face. The sea spat; the ship careened on the waves.

"I can help here," she said as she crawled out from the boat.

He grabbed her arm, frowned when his fingers wrapped around her wet arm. His voice rose with the wind. "There's not much to be done. I awoke some of the crew and we've already dropped canvas. All we can do now is wait it out." His eyes held hers for long moments. "Please," he added.

It was the "please" that did it. And perhaps the fact that she'd begun to shiver. She nodded and was rewarded with a smile that heated her from the inside. He guided her to the hatch and opened it for her. Wishing him good night, she went down into his cabin, only realizing once she was inside that he'd followed her.

"What—"

"I'm just lighting the candles, Claire."

Soon there was the smell of smoke and a soft light bathed the room. He shoved some dirty dishes, ink, quill, and parchment into the far corner of the table before facing her.

Claire couldn't help noticing how handsome he looked with raindrops glistening in his dark hair. She began shivering for a reason that had nothing to do with the cold.

Nate pulled a shirt from his trunk. "It's not much, but it's dry."

After a few stunned moments, Claire managed to make her voice work. "I have more clothes," she said and held up the bag she'd been using as a pillow.

Nate gave it a dubious look and that was when Claire

heard the constant tap-tap of water dripping from the bag's bottom.

"Better hang those clothes up before they mold in there."

He set the shirt on the berth and suddenly smiled.

"Remember the time we went out to gather fruit and got caught in that storm?" His teeth flashed straight and white. "It came from nowhere. Do you remember?"

They'd only started back, their baskets full of fruit, when the sky had opened and dumped what felt like half the sea onto their shoulders. Her sodden dress had weighed her down and made the long walk back difficult. She'd slipped on wet leaves and gotten her shoes stuck in mud that had suddenly been everywhere.

Despite that, they'd had the time of their lives. They'd laughed when she'd fallen, covered in dirt, and then even harder when Nate, who'd thought himself better at keeping his balance, had slid down a hill on his backside when he'd lost his footing. When he'd challenged her from the bottom that she wasn't daring enough to follow him down, she'd promptly dropped her basket, gathered her skirts around her legs, sat herself down, and slid to his side.

"I remember you laughing like an idiot," she said through her smile.

He leaned against a post, crossing his arms over his chest.

"It wasn't all bad, was it?"

Despite how their relationship had ended, Claire couldn't dispute his words. An orphanage could be a place of great loneliness, but owing largely to Nate's presence, it had also been a place of great joy.

"No," she admitted, suddenly unable to meet his eye. "It wasn't."

"Get dry and get some rest." He gently brushed his

fingers over her cheek. "I expect to arrive at Isla de Hueso late tomorrow afternoon."

Her heart swelled along with the sea, and words failed her. She hadn't had anyone touch her with gentleness in far too long. Though he'd attempted to kiss her on the street in Nevis, it hadn't been real, not like what she'd felt just now. Unsettled by this turn of events, she said nothing, simply watched him climb the ladder and waited until the hatch closed behind him.

Claire took a deep breath, let it out slowly. Well, she wasn't cold any longer. Stepping to the bed, she looked down at his shirt and wondered if it was wise to put it on. He'd worried about her getting sick and was giving her the privacy of his cabin. They'd shared a memory that further threatened the wall Claire felt safe hiding behind, and now he wanted her to wear his clothes? She pressed a hand to her fluttering heart. If she wasn't careful, she'd find herself back where she'd been all those years ago. Falling for a man she had no business falling for.

Still she knew it wasn't wise to stay wet all night. Yes, she'd done it before, but only out of necessity, and as Nate warned, she'd usually come down sick a few days later.

Starting with her bag, she pulled out her extra clothes and hung them on the backs of the chairs that circled the table. She dumped what was left of her bag on the clean bit of table Nate had cleared for her. Lastly she peeled off her wet garments.

Not comfortable being naked, especially knowing there were men nearby and the hatch could open at any time, Claire donned the shirt first, then went about the process of hanging the clothes she'd been wearing. Soon every chair in Nate's cabin had dripping garments draped over them and Claire was left feeling very strange indeed.

Wearing Nate's clothing was a double-edged sword. On the one side it made her feel far too vulnerable. She hadn't fully realized just how much she hid—not only her body but also her identity—behind her clothing until she looked down the exposed length of her legs and her bare feet. Though the shirt fell past her knees, she felt naked and defenseless, despite the weapons that lay on the table within easy reach.

The other side of the imaginary sword was equally dangerous as it reminded Claire of what was missing in her life. She pulled the collar up to her nose and inhaled the clean smell. It didn't stink of dirt or smoke; it wasn't tattered and torn. It hadn't been mended over and over again because he couldn't afford to replace it.

Sighing, she sat heavily on the berth. She wanted it over. She wanted the treasure and she needed to get on with her life. She was tired of living from a bag and foraging for food. She hated waiting until night to bathe but neither did she dare do so in the daylight, not in the places she'd been.

She was tired of sleeping on hard ground, she thought, pressing her hand into the soft mattress beneath her. And if she were truly honest with herself, she was bone tired of being alone. Letting herself fall back, she stared at the wooden ceiling. Shadows cast by the candles frolicked on the planks. Shadows, Claire thought with a heavy heart. It seemed those were the only things keeping her company most days. Shadows of the girl she used to be, shadows of her past, and shadows of an elusive treasure.

Stop it, she chided herself. It wasn't always possible to ignore the regret that haunted her, but she determinedly cast it aside tonight. Growing up had taught her that regret changed nothing. It didn't change the past or her current situation. She had to concentrate on her future, on making it be everything she wanted and needed. And for that, she needed the treasure.

They reached Isla de Hueso at sunset the next day with the only threat to them being the churning black clouds and the impending rain.

Though the weather had improved enough to allow full sails, it had worsened the closer they'd gotten to Isla de Hueso. It was almost as though the island was staying true to its nature of not welcoming anyone who wanted to plunder its soil. The wind that had raged all night once again continued its assault. Rowing the longboat to shore was an ordeal that pushed every person on board to their limits.

Waves splashed over the sides, soaking all its passengers. The men at the oars growled with every stroke. Claire knew from their strained faces that they were working as hard as they could. She also knew that if it hadn't been for the ship that had followed them for a time, Nate wouldn't have risked rowing a longboat in these waters. But it made sense to drop them off while the sky roiled angrily and the rain that fell in sheets in the distance hid their location.

She and Vincent kept busy bailing, which would have been a useless effort had they been any farther out to sea as the amount of water that poured in was far greater than what they were able to throw out.

Overhead the sky was cold gray and the air no warmer. Wet and chilled, Claire jumped ashore with the others. Through her chattering teeth she helped unload supplies, crates of food, as well as whatever other provisions Nate had deemed necessary. He hadn't enlisted her help with any of that, and though she'd been annoyed by his slight, she had to admit that judging by the sheer quantity of supplies, he seemed to be well prepared.

"That's all of it!" he yelled over the wind as he set the last crate down.

Claire's hat had been jammed into her bag to keep it from sailing off to sea and her hair lashed about her head. Though it hadn't been declared, she noticed several crew members eyeing her differently and knew some of them had figured out she was a woman. She'd overheard two of them discussing it when she'd gone to the galley for breakfast.

They couldn't see why else their captain would go ashore with such supplies on a deserted island if it wasn't to be with a woman. They also had a good laugh over that, claiming she couldn't be much of a woman, not if they'd all believed her to be a man. Even after years of wishing differently, after knowing that her lack of curves had made her life easier, Claire couldn't stop wishing she were made differently.

Nate's crew piled back into the longboat. Claire's heart did a hard knock against her chest. In a matter of moments, she and Nate would be alone. There would be no crew between them on the island, no demands of a ship to keep Nate busy. No lifeboat for Claire to sleep under.

There was no denying, despite her lack of womanly assets, the attraction that remained between them. She'd seen it on his face when his hand had brushed her breast and she wouldn't lie to herself by claiming she hadn't felt anything. Because she'd felt a great deal. If Vincent hadn't come back at that moment, there was no telling what Claire would have let Nate do.

Well, she'd have to be stronger this time, she reasoned. There was too much at stake. Not only was there the treasure, but there was her heart, and since it had yet to heal from their first relationship, Claire knew she couldn't risk it again.

Feeling stronger with her decision, she plodded through the sand to where Nate and Vincent were talking, their heads bowed together in order to be heard over the wind. Grit flew up and pelted her face with each step she took.

"All set?" she yelled.

Nate nodded, slapped Vincent on the back. "Bring her in if you need to. There are enough little bays around here to tuck her into while you wait out the worst of it."

Vincent nodded. "Just as I could bring her into a little bay for a day or so to give you some extra time." His eyes danced from Nate to Claire.

"Oh, for the love of God," Nate growled. He ploughed through the wind to address his crew one last time.

"Don't waste this time, Claire."

"We'll find the treasure, don't worry," she shouted as another slap of wind hit her.

Vincent shook his head. "I thought he was the only idiot around here. You two care for each other. All you need is time together."

"Nothing is that simple."

"Claire." Vincent grabbed her hand, which was as chilled as his. "If he hasn't realized what's before his eyes by the time I get back, then you and I will just have to get married and be revoltingly happy to spite him. How does that sound?"

Claire grinned. "It sounds fine to me."

He smiled, his cheeks red from the wind. "I'll see you soon. Either way, Claire, you'll end up with a good man."

Claire laughed, kissed him on the cheek. The red on his cheeks flushed deeper.

"Godspeed, Vincent. Be safe."

"Just so you know," he hollered over the roar as he stepped away, "I sure hope it's me."

Chuckling, she watched him tuck in his head and trudge to the longboat. He had a few words with Nate before climbing in. Despite the waves that rose in white swells, Nate waded in the water and shoved them away. He watched them row for a bit, then turned to her, hands on his lean hips.

He had a sheathed sword hanging from his waist. The wind whipped his hair over his forehead; the waves rose up his thighs and darkened his trousers. His shirt snapped with each gust.

The gaze he locked on to her was as turbulent as the sea.

Everything that was woman in her warmed at the sight of him. Bold, manly, and purposeful, and any man standing next to him would pale by comparison.

And for the next handful of days they were going to be alone together. Claire expelled a troubled breath.

"What have I gotten myself into now?" she said.

Ten

Nate strode to her, water swishing within his boots. They were alone now and the realization unnerved him. Finding the treasure was going to be the easy part, he thought, as he closed the distance between them and her every feature beckoned.

The water behind him was filled with angry white-capped waves, but her eyes were the same blue-green hue as a calm sea. Though her face was red from the abrasive wind, he knew her skin to be smooth as any pearl. Even if he hadn't remembered that about her, he'd been vividly reminded when he'd slipped his hand down her undershirt.

Wind tossed her hair, making it look thoroughly ravaged. Hell, he thought as his groin tightened, it was that kind of thinking that was tying him in knots. He couldn't think of any part of her as being ravaged.

Not without wanting to be the one doing the ravishing.

And he couldn't think about that either. Regardless of

where her husband was, Claire was married. He needed to remember that.

"Let's get out of this wind."

"Agreed," she answered.

Now that he was beside her, he saw that her whole body was shaking. Damn. Because he'd packed the crates himself, he knew which one contained the blankets. Scooping that one off the sand, he tucked it under his arm.

He gestured to the top of the hill. "There's not going to be much of the town left by now, but it's a central point. We can make a camp in the trees up there. We're going to need a fire and I don't want it to be seen from the beach."

He took her hand. It wasn't a big island. Though it had become overgrown with the absence of people, it wasn't that far up to where the town ruins should be. He could easily dump this crate, get a fire going, and come back f—

"What about the rest of our supplies?" she inquired.

"I'll come back for them," he muttered. Once she was out of the wind, once her lips were no longer blue.

"Don't be ridiculous." She dug in her feet.

"Claire, you need to get warm and dry."

"As I'm the one trembling from the cold, I'll agree with you. Therefore I suggest we take these supplies into the cover of the forest before everything gets soaked."

Thunder rumbled across the sky, evidence that time wasn't on their side. In the distance the wall of rain was getting closer.

"I can get them later." He tugged on her arm.

Claire was having none of it. "We'll take them now. The sooner we get them off this beach and into some shelter, the better."

"I'll make the shelter. Once we have a fire going and you're warm and—"

She snapped her arm from his hold. "I've made my own way for some time now and that won't be changing today."

Before he could stop her, she had a crate in her hands.

"Shall I pick the spot, then?" she asked, though she didn't bother to await his answer.

She strode forward, seemingly unaffected by the burden she carried. A burden, he knew for a fact, that was quite heavy. Though irritated that she wouldn't listen, he couldn't help appreciating her effectiveness.

Since arguing at this point would do no good, Nate turned back to the remaining boxes and added one of the smaller ones to his load. There were two larger ones left and he assured himself that *he'd* be the one going back for them.

The respite from the driving wind happened the moment they entered the forest. While twisted vines and leaves the size of Nate's hand hindered their progress, it was warmer within the leafy arms of the jungle. Taking the lead, he forced the vegetation out of his way with the crates, mindful that the branches didn't snap back into Claire's face.

They made their way up the slight climb to the abandoned town. The smell of decaying vegetation rose with each step they took. Above their heads fronds rubbed together, giving Nate the image of large hands rubbing together in anticipation. Anticipation of what he didn't want to think about. Families and pirates both had perished on the island but it wouldn't be taking any more lives. At least not his and Claire's.

Wind whooshed down from a sudden opening in the canopy and it cackled as it swept over Nate's face before swooping back up again. A vine tangled around his ankle. Nate stumbled, then gave his leg a firm kick to free himself. He wasn't prone to superstitions but he couldn't help looking back to check on Claire.

She looked exhausted. Her hair was a mess. Her clothes hung wet and heavy on her body. She was breathing through her mouth and he could hear the effort behind it. Yet she kept his pace. She eyed him questioningly.

"If we don't get to the town soon, we'll stop anyhow. I think we're far enough away and the forest is thick enough to hide us."

She nodded and kept going. Nate didn't know where her husband was or why she was alone, but he couldn't help thinking that the man was missing something special.

The trees began to thin. Long grasses replaced vines, ferns, the tall hairy bark of palm trees, and the gangly lengths of the rubber trees. The ruins spread out before them. Severed walls of stone houses stood crumbling and broken. Moss clung to some, a green blight that appeared to be caught in the process of swallowing the rocks whole. Windows were hollow and dark. Grass grew in thick emerald blankets between the structures and within those that no longer had roofs. Bold trees pushed their way between the desolation, trying to reclaim the land.

Past the town lay a low stone fence and within it the crosses that marked its dead.

Claire set her box next to Nate's feet.

"It's sad, isn't it?" she asked when she saw where Nate's gaze focused. "They took the time to bury and mark their dead and yet left them forgotten."

Nate turned to her, stirred by the sentiment. He touched her cheek, waited for her blue-green eyes to lift to his.

"Just because a person leaves doesn't mean they forget." Her eyes widened, nothing more than a flicker, then she stepped back. "We should make camp."

He let his hand fall, but refused to let his heart follow. He wanted their friendship and he'd keep working until he had it.

"Not much here will keep us sheltered. All the roofs seem to have fallen," he said as he scanned the area. "Let's go in there." He gestured to the forest.

Not far into the trees they came upon a small area of ground that was mostly low-growing ferns and grass. He immediately set down his crates and opened the smaller one. He pulled out a blanket, tossed it to Claire after she set down her own box.

"Is that a sail?" she asked when he pulled exactly that from the other box.

He turned in time to see her set the blanket down. "What are you doing?" he demanded.

"What?"

"I gave you that to use."

"And I will," she agreed with a smile that made Nate's teeth ache, "after we're finished what needs to be done."

Ignoring his scowl, she began scavenging the immediate area for dry sticks.

"You didn't answer my question," she asked as she worked. "Is that a sail?"

Nate sighed deeply. The woman was insufferable.

"It's an old one, but it'll work for what I have in mind."

Claire dropped an armload of small sticks onto the ground.

"Which is?"

Nate dug into the box for the rope. "A lean-to. The canvas is large enough to act as roof, wall, and floor. It won't be very big, but it'll keep us dry."

He set the canvas and rope aside and looked around for the best place to set up their shelter. Finding the perfect spot, Nate then focused on clearing out the area. He yanked his sword from the scabbard and began cutting off small branches that were in his way. It took a moment for him to notice the silence. He looked over his shoulder. She was watching him, her face a mask he couldn't read.

"Is something wrong?"

"What? Oh." She shook her head, licked her lips. "No. Everything is fine."

Nate wouldn't have gone that far. Sleeping in such close proximity wouldn't be fine, not when even a little pass of her tongue over her lips had his blood humming. He tossed another branch aside, wishing his lust could be discarded as easily.

Nate threw down his sword. He needed air. Lots of it. The colder the better.

"We've time yet before it rains. I'll go back for the last two boxes."

Claire gathered hair from the palm trees, peeled bark off with her knife, and placed it all in a way she'd learned best guaranteed success. She worked the flint; blowing gently when the sparks caught on the hair. She fed the tender flame until wood began to pop. Then, with the area around the fire bare enough that she felt comfortable turning her back, Claire grabbed Nate's sword.

She'd learned after only a handful of nights living on her own how to make sleeping outside as comfortable as possible and she moved efficiently from fern to fern hacking off their tops.

By the time Nate came back with the first box, she'd cut off enough boughs to make an acceptable bed. Saying nothing, Nate looked from the fire to the ferns. A muscle flexed in his jaw when he looked to the sword she held in her hand.

"You've been busy."

Her eyebrows arched. "Did you expect me to sit idle while there was something I could do to help?"

"Not really. I've come to realize you don't usually do what's expected." He looked at the blanket that remained folded on the box. "I had hoped, however, that you were keeping warm."

"I'm not as cold as I was—the work helped. I think my shirt's mostly dry now."

His eyes slid from her face to her neck before he jerked them away.

"I'll, uh . . ." He grabbed the canvas. "I'll get to that shelter now."

She tried to take an end of the canvas, but he stopped her with an arm across her waist.

"I can make our shelter."

"And I can help."

"Claire—"

"Nate," she sighed. "I'm here and I'm capable and it'll get done faster than standing here talking about it."

She expected another argument and had more than enough rebuttals to keep at it all afternoon. Instead he surprised her by smiling. It was a dirty tactic as it sucked out most of her frustration.

"I suppose it was foolish of me to think you'd left your temper behind on my ship."

She felt her own lips twitch. "I assure you, it's never far away."

He chuckled. "I'll keep that in mind."

Working together, they accomplished the rest of the chores quickly. Soon the canvas was spread over the boughs, up the trunks of two trees, and anchored across the top using two poles made of long, slender shoots. The fire blazed close enough to their shelter to cast warmth, but far enough to keep from catching the canvas. Extra wood had been placed in the shelter to keep dry from the coming rains.

Nate stepped back, gave a nod she deemed meant he was satisfied, then tossed her a length of rope.

"To dry your clothes."

"Again," she muttered. They'd still been a little damp when she'd stuffed them back in her bag that morning, and once the rain hit, they'd be wet again.

"I'll leave you to it. I'll go get the last of our things. I won't be long."

It wasn't lost on Claire that he was still giving orders. But they'd worked together well, and if they were to continue doing so, she'd have to save her arguments for when they really mattered.

"All right."

Seemingly satisfied, he turned to leave but stopped before he left their camp.

"And use the blanket, Claire. Or I'll wrap you in it myself."

Nate didn't hurry back to camp. Instead he sat on the last box he'd come to get and stared out at the roiling surf. He didn't care that the wind whipped at his shirt and howled in his ears. He hardly noticed the first warning drops of rain that splattered on his back. All he could think about was him and Claire in that small shelter.

He closed his eyes, an immediate mistake when the first picture that came to mind was of him walking toward her in their small camp, and her wearing only the blanket he'd passed her. As he came closer, as the flames danced over her face, she lowered the blanket, revealing smooth and shiny skin. He swallowed hard, both in and out of the vision.

A wave crashed on shore, pulling Nate from the illusion in his mind. He opened his eyes, and while the picture of Claire faded, the effect of seeing her naked remained sharp and clear. Despite the cold wind, sweat dampened the back of his neck. His body was taut with need. He passed a hand over his face and took a deep breath. He wasn't sixteen any longer. He was older, wiser. He should be able to control his desires.

Yet he'd failed at that so far. When they were together. he felt himself as drawn to her as he'd always been. Her eyes, her mouth, they all beckoned him just as they had at the orphanage.

Even as a young man he'd wanted her. After some time of being at the orphanage, when he'd summoned the nerve to talk to her, they'd begun spending moments together. Talking as they tended to their chores, walking in their free moments. It had come slowly, Nate hadn't wanted to push, but they'd grown closer, formed a strong bond of friendship before he'd shifted that friendship into something more.

It had surprised him how natural the shift had felt. She was his friend and he'd loved her. Holding her, having her lips touch his, seemed a branch of that love. When he'd imagined them finally coming together as one, that, too, would be another branch.

As their kisses had turned from soft and sweet to wet and hungry, his need for her had known no bounds. When he'd left, he'd done it anticipating the moment when he'd race back and sweep her off her feet. When they'd have a wedding and he could finally claim her as his own.

He'd planned a very short engagement.

Instead she'd married someone else. Why wasn't that knowledge killing this endless desire for her?

"Because I'm a fool," Nate muttered. But if he didn't hurry, he'd be a wet fool.

He grabbed the last box and settled it against his hip. The sand tugged at his boots but no more than his own reluctance to get back. Had it been sunny and warm, they could have begun searching for the treasure immediately, but with rain beginning to spill from the dark gray clouds, Nate knew that wasn't a possibility.

Until the weather improved, they'd be confined to camp together. He'd have given everything for that not so long ago, but now the thought was tortuous. Regardless of where her husband was, Nate wouldn't muddy those waters by stepping in where he had no business being. Marriage to him was sacred. He may not have seen it in his own future any longer, but his belief in the union hadn't changed.

He made as much noise as he could coming back through the trees, allowing Claire time to get herself covered if she hadn't dressed yet. Though he wouldn't touch her if he came upon her naked—he was fairly certain—it was best not to tempt fate.

He needn't have worried. Her clothes hung from the line and she was sound asleep within the shelter he'd made. Nate set the box down next to the rest of their supplies, all stowed beneath the protection of the canvas.

The fire was well stoked for now, though the rain would likely douse it shortly. Nate gathered more wood before the rain soaked it too much. He kept himself busy as long as he could. But after another hour, when the rain was drumming against the canvas, he'd run out of things to do.

Sighing, Nate dug through a box and dragged out

another blanket. He was damn glad he'd thought of that ahead of time, that sharing a bed and a cover with Claire would be testing his resistance past its boundaries. He tugged off his boots, slid in behind Claire, letting her have the heat from the fire. He threw his blanket over his legs and settled into the boughs.

Claire sighed next to him, dug herself deeper into their bed, which resulted in her behind inching its way closer to him.

Hell.

It didn't look like he was going to sleep after all.

Eleven

How about there?" Claire asked, pointing to a handful of large rocks that protruded from the water almost two hundred feet away.

Nate cupped his hand over his eyes and squinted against the bright glare of the sea. Unlike yesterday, the water was now calm and rippled gently as it folded its way to the beach.

"Seems as likely a spot as the last few we've checked," he agreed.

Claire dropped her bag onto the sand, and blew out a labored breath. The rain had ended by early morning, but it had left behind a humidity so heavy it made everything difficult. Breathing took effort as it felt like a sack of sand weighed her chest and restricted her lungs. Her hair was a mass of riotous curls, some of which stuck annoyingly to the back of her neck. Her clothes, consisting of a thin cotton shirt over her undershirt and pants rolled to the knees, clung to her damp skin and itched with each step she took.

Had she been alone, she would have stripped to the skin and plunged into the sea. Unfortunately, she wasn't and the water wasn't much relief either as it was nearly as warm as the stagnant air. After being confined to camp yesterday because of the storm, she should have been happy to get started on their search. Instead she felt like a flower wilting in the heat.

"I'd give almost anything for some of that wind we had yesterday," Claire said.

"You should put your hat back on," Nate said. "It would keep the sun off your face."

By the time they'd stopped for their midday meal, her hair had been soaking wet under her hat and the extra fabric had felt as though it were adding degrees of heat to an already sweltering day. That had been hours ago, and she knew come tomorrow morning her face would be burned red and she'd regret having taken off her hat. Yet she couldn't summon the energy to care.

"I'll manage. We've survived the worst of it." She looked to the horizon and the descending sun. Another hour or so and they'd have to stop for the day. While the idea of working a whole day without turning up anything was disheartening, Claire was too exhausted to dwell upon it.

"Then let's get to it," he answered a moment before she heard his boots drop onto the sand and the splash of water as he waded into the sea.

Claire waited and watched. Seeing Nate in the water was a beautiful thing to behold. He was graceful and strong, sure of his movements. Of course, the fact that he'd taken his shirt off and his long back was bare for her eyes to linger on wasn't a hardship either.

When the water hit the middle of his thighs, he sprung out, arms pointed and back arched as he made a clean dive into the sea. He remained under until her lungs burned for him to return to the surface and draw breath. When he came up, he shook his head and sprayed water every which way. He looked around, then turned to the beach.

"I thought you were helping me with this," he yelled to her.

Claire grinned, then kicked off her own boots. She wasn't nearly as graceful about it as he was. When she swam, she kept her head above water, having never been taught to swim like a dolphin the way Nate could. However, she was able to keep her arms and legs pulling her forward until she made her way to his side.

"That's as pitiful a display now as it used to be," he said with a shake of his head.

"We used to swim together often and you never complained," Claire reminded him as she circled her arms and legs to keep afloat. Of course, for her it was an effort, while Nate seemed to be keeping his chin above the water effortlessly.

Nate grinned. "A boy who fancies a pretty girl isn't about to insult her."

Claire flushed at the compliment but didn't acknowledge it. Times had changed, and with the current state of her hair and the clothes she wore, nobody would ever make the mistake of thinking she was pretty.

"I swim fine," she said instead.

"Half the sea takes flight when you attempt to swim."

"Attempt to swim?"

"You can't call what you do swimming."

"Then what would you call it?" she asked.

His lips curved slightly. "Near drowning."

"Drowning, is it?" she asked a moment before she cupped her hand and sent a spray of water flying.

He turned his head, but not before catching half of it fully in the face. Laughing, Claire did it again.

"That's it," he growled. He took a deep breath and plunged under.

The water was clear and it wasn't difficult to see Nate glide beneath the water, but it proved impossible to avoid him. Screaming, she kicked when he reached for her legs. Her arms worked the water, water splashed into her eyes, and her legs thrashed to keep Nate away.

All her attempts failed, and soon she felt his hand curve around her ankle. Knowing what he intended, she took a gulp of air before he tugged her beneath the surface. Underwater, eyes open, he released her ankle and swam circles around her, each time pulling her back when she tried to surface. Finally he stopped, grinning at her. When she saw the lighthearted teasing in his beautiful green eyes, she was reminded of all the fun times they'd had, the laughing they'd enjoyed so much. It made her heart tremble to remember.

He kicked his way to the surface, leaving Claire to follow in his wake of bubbles.

"You always were a braggart," she muttered when she sputtered to the surface.

He laughed and swam close enough that she could see the water droplets hover on his dark lashes.

"And you never were any good at swimming. Come on, let's see if we can find anything."

They swam around the rocks, with Nate diving below to search between the stones while Claire scrambled up the rocks. Nate came to the surface, wiped his face of water.

"There are no markings, not even a hint of anything shiny on the bottom."

Claire shook her head. "I don't see a marked waterline from here either."

Nate turned around slowly. "I don't think it's hidden in sand, do you?"

"No. I think they'd have been more clever than that."

"No point in staying then."

By the time they swam back to shore and trudged back to camp, Claire was beyond exhausted.

"I saw some nests not far from here. I'll see about fresh meat for our supper while you change."

"Thank you," Claire said.

Nate's gaze lingered. "You're welcome," he said softly. Then he disappeared into the forest.

Claire exchanged her wet clothes for the ones that now hung dry on the line. They were dry, but not clean, she thought, and she wrinkled her nose. And they were stiff, she grumbled to herself as she pulled the fabric up her legs.

When she was dressed, she lay down on the bed and promptly fell asleep.

She awakened to the smell of meat and her belly's growling response. It was mostly dark, with only the glow of the fire to light their small camp. Nate was squatting beside the fire, turning a small spit over low-burning flames.

Claire leaned on her elbow. "Smells wonderful."

He glanced up, released the spit, and poked at the coals. "I found some turtle doves and was able to catch a few before the rest took flight."

"Can I help?"

"They're done. I was mostly keeping them warm while you slept."

"You could have woken me," she said as she climbed from the bed and settled before the fire.

"You looked too peaceful." He took down the spit, slid the meat off onto a plate. Using a knife and fork he'd packed, he cut the meat and put some onto another plate.

He handed one to her. "Besides, if tomorrow is going to be anything like today, it's better if you're well rested."

He picked up his plate and set it on his lap.

Famished, Claire dug into her meal. She was almost finished when she looked up and realized he hadn't eaten at all.

"Why aren't you eating?"

He set down his plate, ran frustrated fingers over his face. "I'd hoped to find the treasure today."

She knew he was lying; it was in the frown that creased his forehead and the thin set of his mouth. What she didn't know was why. Hadn't they, despite the lack of treasure, had a great day? Hadn't they laughed and teased as they once had? He'd smiled as they'd frolicked in the water, and for those few moments, it was exactly as it had been between them all those years ago.

To Claire it had been a wonder. She hadn't laughed and played that way in so long she'd lost hope that she still could. She'd forgotten the sheer happiness that could come from being carefree, if only for a few stolen moments. Did he regret what she'd already tucked away in her heart to hold on to when the treasure was found and she was once more alone?

It seemed so, for when he picked up his plate again, instead of eating, he tossed his food into the fire.

"I guess I wasn't hungry."

It was one of the longest nights of Claire's life. She watched the fire burn itself out, watched the coals turn from red to black. The forest quieted, other than the occasional swish of a leaf. She hadn't dared move, nor had she spoken when Nate moved in the bed behind her. And she knew by his breathing that he'd been as awake as she. For the last while, though, his breathing had evened and his body had relaxed into sleep.

When the sky began to lighten, and Nate was snoring lightly, Claire eased from the bed. She felt dirty and was tired of wearing filthy clothes. Scooping up her bag as she went, Claire made her way to the beach. After ensuring that the horizon was free of ships, she dug out the bar of soap from her bag and waded into the sea. She scrubbed her clothes until there were no visible traces of dirt, then she spread them out on the beach to dry.

The sun crested over the horizon, instantly warming the air. With no ships in sight and knowing she'd left Nate sound asleep, Claire stripped to the skin and washed those clothes as well. When they were laid out next to the others, she slipped back into the water for the first full bath she'd had in far too long. Though she washed often, the opportunity to go completely naked and do a thorough job didn't often present itself.

Humming, she tilted back and floated. Clouds thin as a spider's web drifted in the sky as lazily as she did on the sea. Gulls soared overhead looking for their breakfast. With time yet before their search resumed, Claire lingered, enjoying the gentle lapping of the water, the occasional squawk of a gull. When the idea struck her, she didn't hesitate. She began to swim.

She'd watched Nate often enough to see how he did it, and she tried to mimic his movements. Arms arcing over her head, she stroked through the water. She concentrated on kicking harder, on pulling herself along with her arms. Still she didn't think she was swimming as well as he had, but after practicing for a while, she thought she was doing a better job of it. At least Nate wouldn't be able to tease her about drowning any longer. Not that she'd really minded because it was nice to have him tease her rather than be angry with her.

Satisfied with her efforts, Claire turned for the beach. Her heart jumped with a flutter of panic.

"How did I get so far out?"

She should have been paying better attention. The shore was far away and the clothes she'd spread on the beach looked like something a doll would wear.

Telling herself that all she had to do was what she'd been doing, she began to swim for shore. Only now she wasn't doing it for fun or practice, and she was no longer enjoying herself. All attempts to swim like Nate were lost when the wind suddenly gusted, mocking her efforts. She didn't seem to be making any ground at all—the beach was as far away as it had been five minutes ago.

Her breathing was becoming labored, and Claire's muscles began to burn. Fighting panic, she did what she could to make it to shore, somehow knowing through the choking fear that her attempt at swimming was worse than any she'd managed thus far.

The sea splashed in her face with each stroke. Saltwater rose up her nose and burned her throat. It was becoming more and more difficult to lift her arms out of the water. She turned onto her back. Pushing through the pain in her legs, she kept them kicking. She didn't want to die today, damn it.

There was much yet she wanted to accomplish. She wanted a home, a family. She couldn't die, not while she had nothing to her name and nobody who loved her.

"Oh, God, don't let me die like this," she prayed, kicking harder.

The wind eased a little, and it was all the encouragement

Claire needed. She flipped onto her stomach and with a driving determination repeated what she needed to do over and over again in her mind. *Up and over, up and over. Breathe. Don't stop kicking. You can do this.* The words became a song and in her head she had them marching to a rigorous rhythm. When the wind gusted again, Claire growled.

"You won't win, damn you. I won't let you."

Yet she knew there wasn't much left in her. Her strokes were getting slower and the energy behind them was waning at an alarming rate. Because of that, she didn't dare rest because she was afraid if she did, she wouldn't be able to get going again.

She hadn't wanted to focus on anything but swimming, and therefore she'd deliberately not looked all the way to shore. Seeing how little progress she'd made once had been disheartening enough. If she again saw that she wasn't accomplishing anything, it would be that much harder not to surrender. And she'd rather die trying than die surrendering.

She gave it her best effort. She truly did. But in the end, her arms simply gave out on her. Her lungs felt as though she were breathing in knives. Tears streamed down her cheeks and mixed with the salty sea. Her heart was full of anguish. She'd never felt so alone. Would she find a peace in the afterlife she hadn't found in this one?

She raised her head, needing to see the shore, needing to see it one last time.

It was closer. She was certain it was closer. She blinked through her tears. Yes, her clothes didn't look as small as they had.

Knowing her arms were spent, Claire turned onto her back and once again began kicking to shore.

The waves were no longer as strong and Claire knew she was making progress. She kept focused on a puff of cloud and never stopped moving her legs. When she couldn't even do that anymore, she let them drop, hoping she'd come far enough to touch bottom.

"Oh God," she wept when she couldn't feel anything beneath her feet. "Oh, God, no!"

She willed her body, biting her lip until the salty taste of blood mixed with that of the sea. She thrashed, yet her arms barely came out of the water. Her legs felt heavy and barely moved at all. Soon she was bobbing in the water, her mouth scarcely above the waves. Her head slipped beneath the water. She arced her neck, strove for the surface, and was able to draw in a quick breath before the water closed over her again.

Her lungs were on fire. Her muscles nothing but limp extensions of her body. Claire had survived many things in her short life—the loss of her parents, hunger, sickness, pirates, and a life no woman should be forced to live. She'd dug deep within herself in those times to push herself, to survive despite the odds against her.

She dug in that part of herself now. There wasn't much left, but she had to hope it would be enough. With the last of her strength she pushed her head out of the water. She spit the sea from her mouth then took a last breath. Before she went under for what she knew would be the last time, she spilled her breath in the loudest scream she could manage.

She could only hope it would be enough.

Nate was, by nature, a patient man. *Not today*, he thought, slapping aside another vine. Claire had been gone when he'd awakened. He'd thought she'd left to tend to her morning needs, but when she didn't return, he'd begun to worry. Worry soon gave way to anger.

She was after that damn treasure and they had an agreement, dammit, one he'd clearly been foolish to believe. She had no more intention of honoring it than the promise she'd made years ago to wait for him. In itself, that alone should have driven every other thought from his head.

Instead he was foolish enough to be concerned. She could get hurt or lost, and without him knowing in which direction she'd gone, he'd be incapable of helping. If she did get hurt and her injuries were serious, he may not get to her in time.

He flung a branch out of his way and stormed through the jungle like a bullet. By the time Nate strode from the trees onto the beach, he had a head full of steam. It didn't dissipate when he saw her swimming. But it sure as hell did when he realized how far out she was.

And that she was in trouble.

Even as he ran for the water, he saw her head slip under. His heart stopped until she came to the surface again. But then he knew a raw and biting fear when she thrashed to the surface and screamed. He heard the panic in it and barely took the time to throw off his boots before racing into the water. When the water was deep enough, he dove in. He kicked hard and pulled himself in long strokes before coming up for air.

When he did, Claire was nowhere to be seen.

Twelve

Fear, a blinding fist of it, gripped Nate's heart and refused to let go. He swam faster, harder than he ever remembered swimming before. He stopped only long enough to scan the surface. Nothing! He couldn't see her!

"Claire!" Nate shouted. His arms and legs circulated, keeping him afloat. The only thing that answered him was the raging of the blood pumping through his veins.

He dove under again, aiming for where he'd last seen her. Or rather, where he thought she'd gone under. He couldn't be completely sure, not without a landmark.

Nate had been in many battles over the years. They'd been attacked by pirates, and had attacked their fair share of merchant ships and scalawags alike. Each battle he'd approached with a sense of calm and even adventure. He knew how to keep his head despite low odds, despite the risks. Even wounded on Blake's ship, with a piece of the mast sticking out of the back of his leg, Nate had managed to run the swing gun. Nothing had shaken him.

Until now.

What if he couldn't get to her in time? What if the waves shoved her farther away from him? What if he'd been wrong, so consumed by fear that he wasn't swimming in the right direction? What if, before he could find her, her cold, lifeless body floated to the surface?

Oh God, don't think that, he told himself. He wouldn't be too late. He wouldn't. When he reached the point where he figured he was close, he took a deep breath and plunged under. While his eyes desperately scoured the area, his mind remembered every moment they'd spent together, from the orphanage to his ship to the island.

She'd been the best thing in his life back then, and the one thing he desperately wished for now. Married or not, he needed to know she was safe. That at least she was alive.

He looked until his lungs were bursting, then he kicked upward only long enough to draw another deep breath before going down again. He'd do it as long as necessary, he vowed, until he found her. Claire was beautiful and strong and it would kill him if her life ended now.

But he couldn't see her. *Dammit, Claire*, he yelled silently, *where are you?*

There! Oh my God, there! Though his lungs were ready to shatter, he kicked toward her. She was floating, head down. He grabbed her, turned her over. Her eyes were closed as though she were dreaming. Nate whimpered when he saw how pale she was. How lifeless. He pulled her tightly against him and shot for the surface.

"Claire, Claire!"

She didn't respond. He put a hand to her naked chest

and pinched his eyes closed when he felt no heartbeat. Scooping a hand across her shoulders, her chin supported by his forearm and her body resting against his chest, Nate kicked for shore. Though his breathing was ragged, he talked to her.

"Don't leave me, Claire. We have a treasure to find, remember?"

Each moment that passed felt like years. When finally he was able to touch ground, he fought and cursed the water that impeded his movement, that was determined to fight his progress. When it fell to his waist, he hefted Claire over his shoulder, digging it into her stomach. He hoped to God it worked.

Her body stiffened as water and air gushed from her lungs. Nate's knees buckled and he struggled to keep them both upright. He hadn't lost her! Claire drew in a ragged, gasping breath that was the sweetest sound Nate had ever heard. He ran for the beach, fell on the sand, and cradled her within his arms, holding her as tightly as he dared. He closed his eyes, pressed his lips to her cold forehead. His body began to shake as much as hers. She was alive.

She continued to cough, great deep coughs that wracked her body. Nate rubbed his hands over her back, cursed at the frigid feel of her skin. She was so damn cold.

"Let's get you warm." He set her gently on her back, swept her hair off her forehead. The coughing grew worse. Afraid she'd vomit and choke, he rolled her onto her side while he ran for the clothes that lay strewn on the sand.

Gooseflesh covered her from head to toe. Her color was tinged with blue. Trembles shook her so hard he worried she'd hurt something. Using the clothing he'd gathered, he covered her and tucked the garments tightly around her body. Her teeth were rattling. He needed to get her warm.

Gathering her and the haphazard coverings in his arms, he made his way toward camp.

"I'll get you warm, darling. You're going to be fine."

"I'm so c-cold."

And her voice was so damn weak. This wasn't the fiery woman he was used to, and the fragile one in his arms was scaring him to death.

"I know." He leaned down, gave her forehead another kiss, wished he could drain all of his heat into her. "You'll be warm soon, I promise."

He helped her dress, and the weakness of her movements made him shudder. He'd almost lost her. Why the devil hadn't he gone and looked for her sooner? And what would have happened if he hadn't checked the beach first? His hands fumbled as he slipped her shirt over her shoulders. He rested his head against hers.

"Don't ever scare me like that again."

He watched her sleep, grateful that the coughing had finally stopped. Though the sun was high in the sky and the heat in their camp had Nate feeling like his skin was going to melt off his bones, he had Claire covered with both blankets. She had color again, and in case anything changed, he sat close enough to see the gentle and constant rise and fall of her chest.

He buried his face in his hands. It still had the power to rob him of breath if he considered how close he'd come to losing her. Not simply to another man, but forever. He shuddered again, remembering how cold and still she'd been. How lifeless. He dropped his hands, looked at her. His heart was in turmoil. There were things he wanted to say to her, things he had no business saying to a married woman.

Claire stirred and Nate leaned forward, ready to give her whatever she needed, but she simply turned her head away from the fire and continued sleeping. He'd been afraid to leave her for any reason, but he could no longer put off a walk into the woods to see to his needs. He rose, hesitated a moment. When she made no further movement, he slipped quietly into the forest.

He'd just turned to go back when he heard her gasping for breath. His stomach fell to his feet and he ran, whipping branches out of his way as he leapt over ferns and shrubs. He charged into their camp. Claire sat up, eyes wide, her hands at her throat. Nate dropped before her, his hands taking hers.

"Claire! What's wrong?"

She was wheezing. Her eyes were dark indigo with panic.

"I can't—I can't breathe!" She clutched at her throat.

It took a moment for logic to penetrate the fear that wanted to cloak him. She was breathing, though it was ragged. She wasn't coughing, vomiting, or choking. Her color was good. A nightmare, he reasoned, as he forced himself to steady his own breaths.

"You can. Look at me." He took her chin and held it tightly. "Claire, breathe. In, out, just as I'm doing." He held her, one arm around her back, the other on her chin, as he showed her what to do. Slowly the panic ebbed from her eyes and her body eased. "There, you see? You're all right." And eventually he hoped he'd be as well.

She sighed heavily. "I'm sorry. I just suddenly felt as though as I were back in the water and I was swallowing so much of it, that . . ." She shook her head. "Well, you know the rest."

Yes, he did. And he'd better never see such a thing again. He'd rather deliver Alicia's next child—he shuddered at the thought—than go through what he had earlier with Claire.

"I imagine you'll have nightmares about that for some time." Nate knew he would.

"I didn't thank you properly," she said, easing back from his chest. "You saved my life."

He smiled, kissed her forehead, and lingered a moment.

"It was worth saving."

Now that she was awake and no longer in any danger, Nate became aware of just how intimate their circumstances were. He'd seen her naked—though in truth he couldn't remember what she looked like—he'd helped her dress, and now she was once again in his arms. Her hair smelled of the soap and the sea, a combination far more potent than any rum or brandy he'd come across.

Looking down, he saw her lips were once again a healthy coral color and they were so very close to his. Heat enveloped him, which had nothing to do with the sun.

"I'm sorry."

"Sorry you saved me after all?"

The uncertainty in her voice surprised him. Did she really think he'd rather see her dead?

"Never that, Claire. When I woke earlier and you were gone, I was mad. I thought you were going to search for the treasure without me." He shook his head, disgusted that while she was in grave danger, he'd assumed the worst.

"Nate, it was a reasonable supposition. Besides, it was my fault for leaving without telling you. The blame is entirely my own."

"What happened?" He held up a hand. "On second thought, you don't need to answer. I'm sure the last thing you want is to relive it."

She crossed her legs and clasped her hands in her lap. "It's all right, you have a right to know." She sighed. "I simply thought to go to the beach, wash my clothes, and have a bath. Then, since it was early and I was alone, I decided to practice my swimming. I'd hoped to improve, not kill myself."

Shame roiled in his belly. If he hadn't teased her about being a bad swimmer, she wouldn't have felt—

"Don't blame yourself. It was sheer stupidity on my part. I know I'm not a very good swimmer and I shouldn't have attempted to practice on my own."

"And I shouldn't have teased you."

She dropped her blankets, moved to his side. This time it was she who touched his face. "I like that you teased me again. It's been a long time."

Nate placed his hand over hers. She was right. It had been a long time. A long time since he'd held her against him. A long time since he'd heard her breath catch in anticipation of his kiss. And too damn long since he'd had her mouth under his.

He didn't know where her bloody husband was, and at the moment, as Claire's head leaned toward his, he didn't bloody care. If the man was any kind of a husband, she wouldn't be in this situation, wouldn't have almost lost her life today. Wouldn't be wanting another man's kiss.

And it was Nate she wanted. He saw it in the darkening of her eyes, in the way he heard her breath race. It was him she reached for. And it was her that sparked his blood, the only one who ever had. He'd had other women, and he'd treated them as kindly as he could, but they hadn't reached into his heart. He's shared his body many times. He'd shared his heart only once.

Nate lowered his mouth to hers. The moment their lips touched, something settled in his soul. He pulled her against him, felt her fingers anchor in his hair, heard her moan as he parted her lips with his own.

It was everything he'd remembered and nothing like he remembered. It was sunshine, pure and gold. It was the rarest of gems, sparkling and priceless. Claire fit. Her mouth, her body, everything aligned itself with Nate's. He swept his tongue into her mouth and thought to himself, *Yes, this is what I remember.*

Her mouth opened like a flower under his; her lips were petal soft. They seduced him, stripped him bare until he felt, knew, nothing but her. He couldn't feel the heat of the day pressing upon them. He knew only Claire and the desire for her that thrummed in his veins, that made him hard with need.

He drew back, filled his lungs with air. Claire, too, was out of breath, though this time the sound was a satisfying one. Nate shook his head, pressed a kiss to her lips, then another to her forehead. He pulled her tightly against him, heaved a sigh.

"Ah, Claire, why the hell did you marry someone else instead of waiting for me?"

Thirteen

It took a moment for his words to seep through the mist of desire, but as soon as they did, Claire jumped from his lap. All thoughts of wet kisses and warm arms around her making her feel safe fled.

"I did wait for you. I waited a year and a half, but you never came back!"

"I bloody well did," he argued as he came to his feet. "But when I came back, I found out you were betrothed to another man."

He looked at her and she saw the pain in his green eyes, knew his words to be true. He'd come? Her head spun with the truth. Her heart broke with it.

"Why, Claire?" he asked quietly. "Why would you marry another man?"

"It had been so long, I didn't think you'd come back."

His mouth hardened. "Had I ever given you the impression I wasn't a man of my word?"

"No, but—"

"Did you not believe me when I told you I loved you? Had I done such a poor job of showing you what I felt that you turned to another?"

Her eyes filled. "No, it wasn't like that."

"I told you that as soon as I felt I had earned enough to give us a fair start, I'd come for you."

"I know you did, and I believed you."

Nate laughed, though there was no joy in it. "Did you now? Because that's hard to believe from where I'm standing."

It would be, she realized, and she looked away. If she were in his shoes, she'd feel the same. She'd feel betrayed and angry, and if he tried to explain, would she listen? Would anything at this point ease the hurt? No. Shame pressed hard on Claire's heart. All this time she'd blamed Nate for her plight and all along it had been her own fault.

"When did you come?" she asked, looking into the dying fire. She couldn't bear to look him in the eyes.

"It doesn't matter, it doesn't change what happened."

"It matters to me." Now that she knew he hadn't broken his promise, that he had loved her enough to come back, she needed to know it all. Though it killed her to think of it, she needed to know by how long she'd missed him.

Nate sighed. "I came back on the summer solstice."

She pressed a hand to her stomach, suddenly feeling sick. He'd come back the day of the solstice. The day before her wedding.

She faced him then. "Why didn't you come find me?"

"To what purpose?" he asked, holding his hands out. "I couldn't bear to watch you give yourself to another."

"If you'd come, I never would have married him." The truth of that had sorrow burning the back of her still raw throat.

Nate angled his head. "Did you not care for him?"

"I hated him," Claire spit, letting her tears run unfettered.

He sucked in a sharp breath, his eyes widened. "Then why in blazes did you marry him?"

The truth was dangerous ground for Claire. Nate had implied once, back on his ship, that she was a whore for sailing the Caribbean with various crews. She wanted to believe he hadn't meant it, but if she told him why she married and what had happened afterward, would it only convince him that was indeed what she was? Claire was ashamed enough of what she'd done without having his disgust laid onto hers.

Claire wiped her cheeks, drying her palms on her pants.

"It was something I had to do."

"Claire, nobody *has* to marry anyone they don't want to."

His shoulders, so wide and strong, moved with his troubled breaths. His eyes were two emeralds set into a face that had no equal. Little white lines spread from the corners of his beautiful eyes. She'd never seen a more handsome man. And once, he'd been hers. But he wasn't any longer.

He was wealthy, she was poor. Once they found the treasure, Nate would return to his fancy ship while she took her money and went back to the place where her life had fallen apart. Though it helped to know he hadn't lied, that he had loved her, it didn't change the present. And it certainly didn't mean there was a future for them.

"We should get back to the treasure."

His eyes latched on to hers, and in them she saw that he wanted to understand her choices, but that he was struggling. His hands rubbed over the stubble that darkened his cheeks and chin.

"Not until you talk to me."

"Nate, we've already lost half a day. We need to get going."

He crossed his arms. "You didn't stop me when I kissed you."

"No."

"Are you sorry about that?"

She shook her head. She'd never be sorry she'd kissed him.

"Then why won't you talk to me? What happened to your husband? Where is he?"

Claire expelled a heavy breath. "I don't know."

He arched a brow. "You don't know where your husband is and you're kissing another man?"

"It's complicated!" she yelled, something she was immediately sorry for when her throat burned in protest.

"I'm not daft. I'm sure if you tell me, I can make sense of it."

Claire threw up her hands. "There's no point in telling you. It'll do nothing but hurt us both."

"You're sure of that, are you? You've been around me so much these last years you know how I think?"

His anger caught like wildfire and soon it was thrumming through Claire as well. She'd been forced into enough situations in her life; she wasn't about to get pushed into another.

"I don't pretend to know what you think and feel, but neither will I discuss this anymore. It's in the past, Nate, and that's where I want to keep it."

His eyes glittered. "One thing about the past you don't seem to be able to leave behind is this lack of faith in me."

He turned, and grabbed the shovels. Soon the jungle wrapped around him and he disappeared from view. Claire took a moment to steel herself before following.

* * *

They worked in a pattern established by exchanging nothing more than curt nods and crisp sentences. Every inch of shoreline, every jut of rock, was explored for some kind of marked waterline.

Claire didn't protest when Nate offered to be the one to swim out to the outcrop of rock and for that he was thankful. Not only did it save them from arguing, but he was still so angry at her that he didn't particularly want to be near her.

Taking a breath and plunging under the water, Nate looked through the bubbles his disturbance caused. Fish of the brightest colors swam nearby. Yellow, blue, some with a flash of red. They were bold and swam alongside him as he skimmed his hands over rocks and pushed fingers through the sand on which the rocks rested.

Underwater was silent and beautiful but he knew a sense of loss that he wasn't able to share it with Claire. Annoyed, he pushed to the surface and filled his lungs again before disappearing below. This time he concentrated harder on his task, but the only thing he got for his efforts was a nick on his palm from a sharp piece of coral. The only thing shiny he spotted was a shell or two.

He resurfaced with a flick of his head that sent droplets of water flying from his hair and landing with tiny little ripples in the teal sea.

"Nothing?"

Nate trudged ashore, where he'd left his shirt and boots. His pants were rolled to the knees but still dragged on his waist as he walked. He sat on the sand and rested his forearms on his bent knees. Squinting against the sun, he could already feel its heat dry the water from his shoulders.

"I can't help but feel we're wasting time looking at every rock we come across."

"I've been searching the shore, but I can't find any marked waterlines." She sat beside Nate, though not too close, he noticed. "Could it be it's been erased by time?"

He shrugged. "Anything's possible."

He looked at the horizon, at the endless expanse of sea, and hoped Vincent was faring better than they were.

"It's not a large island. Even with checking every bit of shoreline, we'll have gone all around in another day or two."

He came to his feet, wiping sand from his backside. "Then let's hope we find something before then."

Sweat dripped down Claire's back. Her feet itched from the heat but she didn't dare take off her boots or her feet would burn. The sand glistened white, but she knew it was anything but cool. Shore birds took flight as they approached, then swooped down and alighted on the beach behind them.

The sea was calm and the waves tumbled in sleepily. Humidity hung in the air, thick as molasses and just as sticky. Her eyes burned from searching for any kind of marker. She wasn't even sure what she should look for. A carving in stone, a crop of rock? It could have simply been a handful of stones that had been laid down on the sand and since been swept to sea.

In all the years of searching for the treasure, she didn't remember ever being this frustrated. Nor this discouraged.

Of course, that could have as much to do with Nate as it did with the treasure. He popped out of the water then, looked at her, and shook his head. He hadn't found anything.

Sighing, Claire moved along. They were approaching a rocky point of the island where a finger of sand jutted out from the knuckles of rock. Intrigued, Claire increased her pace.

It wasn't a long piece of land, nor a particularly wide one. It was perhaps the width of Nate's ship and twice its length. Claire walked onto it, then across to its tip. From the corner of her eye she saw Nate dive underwater, aiming in her direction. She smiled sadly. As much as she wanted one, she had no intention of asking for the swimming lesson he'd offered.

Claire stopped when sand met sea. Before her was nothing but water and glimpses of islands in the distance. Claire looked from her right, from where Nate was swimming toward her, to her left.

Rocks, hundreds of them piled high, rose from the sea as though a giant had used them as dice and dumped them on the ground to fall as they may. And there, among those rocks, she saw it.

"A cave!" she yelled. Her stomach soared and she jumped along with it. "Nate!" she called, waving her arms when his head came up from the water. "Nate! I found a cave!"

He hesitated only a second, then his grin spread wide and he dove under again. Soon he was back on the surface, using long strokes to close the distance. Her belly did a little flutter at the sight of such grace and strength.

He was at her side in minutes. "Show me."

She took his hand and pointed with her other. "Over there. See it?"

Claire's excitement shimmered on the air. He felt the energy of it transfer from her hand to his and up his arm. Still, he'd learned with time it was best to be cautious and he forced his own excitement back.

"I see it. And it's a good spot to hide a treasure, but don't get ahead of yourself, Claire. I don't see a marked waterline, do you?"

She released his hand. "You said yourself markings could have faded since then."

"And they could have, I'm not disputing that."

"Well, then, do you want to discuss possibilities, or do you want to see if the treasure is there?"

He grinned despite himself. "Let's go."

She was off almost before he finished his sentence. She eased onto the rocks, keeping crouched and using her hands for balance. Nate looked down at his bare feet and wished he had his boots with him. Not that he'd take the time to go back for them, not when there was the very real chance they'd finally find the treasure.

He followed her across the slick rocks while trying to avoid the sharper ones that could slice his feet open. They both slipped a few times, and each had a few scrapes along their forearms to show for their troubles. Nate knew she didn't feel hers any more than he felt his.

They made it to the mouth of the cave.

"Good thing it's low tide," Nate said, tracing the narrow, slightly gouged line on the rocks above his head, "or we wouldn't have seen it, let alone be able to get inside."

"Nate!" Claire said, grabbing his arm. "It's a marked waterline."

His heart raced, but he took a moment to look at Claire, with her eyes shining and her smile nearly as blinding as the sun. Regardless of their past or future, there was nobody he'd have rather shared this moment with.

"Ready?"

"Come on." She laughed and shoved at his back. "I can't wait any longer!"

There were enough gaps between the rocks to cast light within the cave. It wasn't bright, but at least they weren't moving in total darkness. Not a high cave, even Claire had to bend over. Nate had to bend nearly in half.

The cave itself was quite long, and if the light was any indication, it veered right at the end.

"Stay close," Nate said as he began to move, the water only deep enough to cover his feet. "There may be sharp drop-offs anywhere."

She didn't argue, enabling Nate to concentrate on the terrain instead of worrying about her. They moved slowly, looking into every crevice. Barnacles clung to the cave walls and shells crunched underneath their movements. A few cut into his feet.

"Nate, the map said 'at the turn'! This is it!" Light dimmed a little more as they made their way around the bend.

They rounded the corner and the ceiling of the cave rose to allow them to stand their full height. Before them, before the wall that marked the end of the cave, were three small chests.

"That can't be it," Claire said, looking around. "The treasure on the *Santa Francesca* was substantial. It couldn't only be three chests!"

Nate frowned. Claire was right, it didn't make sense.

He'd of course done some of his own digging in the last few years and everything he'd gathered had closely matched what Claire knew. The treasure was famous because it was one of the largest ever to leave Nombre de Dios.

"Doesn't seem right," he agreed. "But it did say, 'thrice to fail,' and there are three chests here. It's got to mean something, Claire."

He scuttled forward, pulling his knife from the sheath he kept tied to his belt. He tried to pry the chests open but the locks wouldn't give, and no amount of battering at them with his knife helped.

"We'll have to take them with us," he said. He tried to lift one but was barely able to get it off the ground. "I'll need your help."

They each grabbed an end and soon their labored breaths echoed off the cave walls as they made slow progress back to the mouth of the cave. They left the chest there for the moment and went back for the other two. Only after all three chests were at the mouth of the cave did they begin to move the first one to the beach.

"This better be worth it," Claire grumbled when her knuckles scraped the rocks.

Each taking a side, though most often Claire's dragged on the ground, they maneuvered one chest over the rocks and to the beach. They dropped it gladly as they were already exhausted and the sun was a scorching fire on their already overheated skin. Without taking time to do more than catch their breath, they went back for the others.

Nate grabbed his end of the second chest but Claire wasn't paying attention. Her eyes were on the inside of the cave. He grabbed her arm when she went to step in.

"What is it?"

"I simply can't believe that was all of it. The treasure should have filled this cave."

"It may not be the same treasure or it may be that it was here, and for whatever reason, three chests were left behind."

"Why?"

He sighed. "I don't know. Another ship was approaching and they didn't want what treasure they had found to be taken?"

"And so sacrificed the rest?"

"It's as believable as anything we've already heard about this treasure."

"I'll grant you that," she agreed.

"Come on, there's nothing else here."

Claire rolled her shoulders. "There's something here. I can't explain it. But I feel . . . there," she said and pointed to a spot inside the cave to the right. "Do you see that? Between the rocks, where the light is coming in? Something's shining."

Nate leaned over her shoulder. "Likely just a piece of shell or coral."

She angled her head toward him. "It won't be the first time we search for naught. I want to see what it is."

They crept back into the cave, and sure enough, within a ribbon of light was the unmistakable glitter of gold. Claire tried to reach into the gap, but couldn't get in past her knuckles.

"It's too small to get my hand in. Maybe we can move some of these rocks."

She curled her fingers around one and grunted as she pulled. Nate stepped beside her and grabbed the rocks on the other side of the opening. He felt them shift.

"It's moving," he said.

Claire reached in again.

The wall gave way.

Before he could pull Claire out of the way, rocks tumbled down and knocked them both to the ground.

Fourteen

She had time only to throw up her arms and use them to shield her head as the wall she'd been touching crumbled. Rocks bombarded her and she knew the sharp edge of them when they pushed her hard and she lost her balance. She landed with a hard splash on the watery cave floor and struggled to sit upright as more rolled over her and tried to hold her down.

Noise rumbled through the cave like thunder caught in a bottle. The silence after the stones had tumbled and splashed to a stop was deafening.

For a moment, Claire didn't move. Stunned, she looked at the wall that had let go, at the rocks that were spilled around her. Though it had felt as though the whole of one wall had crumbled, it was, in fact, only part of one. Nevertheless she considered herself lucky to have her head intact.

"Claire!"

More rocks went flying and Claire hunched down, once again protecting her head.

"Claire, are you hurt?"

There was splashing behind her and Claire realized more of the wall hadn't let go. It was Nate. Turning, she lowered her arms and saw Nate flinging stones as he freed himself of their weight. He had a gash along his temple and blood ran down the side of his face. But he was alive and so was she. She didn't move any farther, needing a moment to steady herself, but she answered Nate because of the worry in his voice.

"I'm all right," she answered.

He splashed to her side and his eyes scoured her face. He helped her move rocks, though most had landed beside her rather than on top of her, then he helped her up.

"Are you sure you're not hurt?"

His concern touched her, gave her the strength to lock her knees. "I'm sure." She wiped away the blood from his temple but it only ran again. "You're bleeding."

He looked down at her fingers that held his blood, then over to the wall. "Could have been worse."

Because she knew it could have been, she slid her hand into his and wove her fingers through his. Nate's attention turned back to her, his eyes softened, and his mouth curved.

"Had enough of caves?"

"Oh my, have I ever."

He leaned in and kissed her forehead. For a moment his lips held there, warm and sure. Claire wondered if he needed the connection just then as much as she did.

"Let's go." With his hand still in hers, he stepped forward.

"Wait!" Claire pressed her other hand across his stomach. "There it is."

Beneath the water something glinted. She dipped her hand into the warm water and closed her fingers over it. It slid smoothly into her palm. Pulling it from the water, she saw that whatever it was had a chain attached to it. The slim length of gold dangled from between her closed fingers.

She opened her hand.

Within her palm lay a simple gold cross. It wasn't enameled, and there was no shiny coat to make the gold glitter. There were no jewels that glinted from within it. Yet it stole Claire's breath and filled her throat with emotion. Slowly she turned it over.

Love Eternal

She closed her hand over the cross and pressed her fist to her heart. *No, not like this. Not like this!* She rocked to and fro, aware, if only vaguely, that a mewing sound was coming from her lips.

Nate lifted her chin. "You know this piece?"

She pushed her hand harder against her chest and tightened her fist. The corners of the cross dug into her hand but the pain was nothing compared to the agony that pulsed in her heart.

"Whose is it?" he asked.

She didn't want to answer, because if she said the words aloud, then they'd be true, wouldn't they? And more than life itself, she didn't want them to be true.

"Claire?"

She forced herself to swallow the truth.

"It was my mother's," she whispered.

Nate frowned. "How is that possible?"

Claire closed her eyes. "My father gave it to her when I was born and she wore it until the day she died. That day . . ." Her breath caught and she had to wait a moment before she could continue. "The day she died, we were all together in her room and she took it off, placed it in his hands. She told him to wear it until they could be together again."

Her voice broke as she remembered, as clearly as if it were yesterday. Her father had wept when he'd slipped the necklace around his neck. And Claire knew for a fact that he'd been wearing it the day he'd left her to seek the treasure.

Which meant . . .

"My father has to be here."

With the cross secure in her palm, Claire splashed to where the wall had crumbled. "If the necklace was behind it, he must be as well."

Another small slide of stones fell when she displaced a few of the larger rocks she could manage.

Nate's hand was firm on her shoulder. "Claire, there's nothing here."

"Go, if you want. I'm not stopping you," she growled. She grasped a rock and pulled. It didn't give. Bracing her foot on a boulder, she yanked hard. Nothing moved.

His sigh tripped down each ridge of her spine, and snapped her raw nerves.

"Either help or go away," she grumbled.

"What are you hoping to find, Claire? He's not likely to be alive and hiding behind these rocks."

She spun round. "I realize that! But I can't keep living with the thought that my father loved a treasure more than me."

"You know that's not true," he said.

"Do I? Then why, if he hasn't found it, hasn't he given up and come for me? And if he has found it, then why did he leave me in that orphanage? Why didn't he come back for his only child?" Tears ran now, fast and hot.

He wiped them from her cheeks. "There could be any number of reasons for that."

"But I'll never know for certain, will I?" She shook the cross at him. "This is the closest I've come to him since he left me at the orphanage. If there are answers here, I won't leave without them!"

He sighed and looked away. Then his body went rigid. Instantly he stepped before her, his long arms spread wide.

The bottom fell out of her stomach.

"It's him, isn't it?"

The sympathy he emitted when his eyes met hers was answer enough.

"Don't look, Claire. I don't know if it's your father or not, but you don't need to see this."

" 'This' could very well be the last of my family. Let me see."

The frown that pulled at his mouth told her he wasn't happy, but he conceded and stepped aside, giving her an unobstructed view of a skull drifting on the water.

Nausea came fast, a blazing trail up her throat. There was no hair, no skin or features to prove who it was.

"Finding the necklace doesn't prove this was your father," Nate whispered at her side.

It may not have, yet Claire knew it was.

She pressed the necklace to her lips, bent her head, and closed her eyes. There was no way of knowing how long her father had been there, if he'd died alone or if he'd been murdered. Had he found the real treasure only to have been killed for it? So many questions she'd never have answers to.

"There were times I hated him for leaving me, times my

heart bled because I missed him so much. Times I worried myself sick over him. I alternated between anger and worry, but Nate, I never stopped loving him. Never."

"I'm sure he knew that."

She opened her eyes and looked into Nate's.

"There's no guessing or wondering any longer. He's not ever coming back."

Nate drew her into his arms. His lips once again pressed against her forehead, and his hands splayed across her back. For a few moments they remained in the cave that had at first held so much promise. She'd never dreamed it would end in such hopelessness.

"Is this a sign, Nate? Are we to search endlessly without ever finding it as well? Will we also die for it? Is that the price we'll have to pay?"

He drew her back and looked deeply into her eyes.

"We've already paid, Claire."

They laid the third chest next to the other two. Nate fell onto the sand, legs spread wide and an arm flung over his eyes to keep the sun out. Sweat trickled down his temples. The gash he'd received from the rock throbbed but he no longer felt the sticky oozing down his cheek.

"I wish I had a cask of water," he mumbled through a throat that was gritty as the sand beneath his back and equally as hot.

"I'll get you some."

Nate sat up. "I didn't say that so you'd serve me."

"I know." She shrugged, then looked off to the horizon. "I need some time alone."

"I'm not that thirsty," he said.

Her eyes shifted to his. He'd seen her eyes sleepy with

desire, seen them flash with anger. He'd seen them turn to steel when she was determined. But he'd never seen them as stark as they were as she looked at him then.

"Stay." Kneeling before the chests, he pulled out his knife. "Let's see what's inside."

She shook her head. "I'll be at camp. You can tell me later what you found."

She walked away, her head hung low and her shoulders defeated. Nate flung his knife into the sand.

Hell.

She'd never minded her own company and had, many times, sought only that. She'd left Nate on the beach thinking time to herself was what she wanted, but as she sat brooding into the cold, black coals of last night's fire, she realized she'd been wrong. She didn't want to think of her father, of how he'd come to be alone in that cave. Had he suffered? Had he drowned? How long had he been there? Had he thought of her in his last moments?

"Did you ever," she asked aloud, "regret leaving me?"

Oh, how she wanted the answers to those questions. How she needed them.

Claire poked at the ashes with a stick she'd found nearby. Dust swirled from the charcoal remains. Ashes to ashes, dust to dust.

"Never to be seen again," she said.

Dropping the stick, Claire wept for what had been lost and what had been sacrificed. As the tears flowed freely, she raked through the memories, good and bad. The first doll her father had given her, the walks the three of them had shared, the telling of stories while she lay warm and secure in her bed.

She thought of the sickness that had weakened her mother's body before it ultimately took her life. To the final words he'd said to Claire before setting out for the treasure, to finding the necklace today and what was left of her father's remains.

Claire wiped her cheeks and wished she could wipe away the ache in her heart as easily. There was grief now where before there had been anger. In the prayers she recited, asking that her father find peace alongside her mother, there was also finality.

And loneliness.

Claire shoved to her feet. "I am so bloody tired of being alone."

While the birds sang from their perches, reminding Claire there was life around her, it wasn't the feathered kind she sought. She couldn't draw strength from the brightly colored parrots or the cooing doves. They couldn't hold her and, just for today when the world felt its emptiest, give her something vital and elemental to hold on to.

She looked down the trail they'd made that wove through tangled vines and swaying leaves and felt a sharp jolt low in her belly. Nate. It was dangerous ground to be treading, considering their past, but it was that same past that kept Claire from rejecting the thought outright. Circumstances had kept them apart, continued to keep them apart, but she knew for a fact that he desired her.

For the moment, that was all she needed.

The ruffling of leaves and the muted sound of footsteps approaching announced Nate's arrival before he rounded the last bend of the trail and strode into Claire's line of sight. His shirt, caught by the hook of a finger, hung down his back. His dark hair was dry and disheveled, as though he'd taken his hands to it in frustration. The gold skin on his face gleamed and the shine continued down the long expanse of his chest. Claire followed the color to the band of his pants that rode low on his hips.

Her breath escaped her.

He stepped into their small clearing, tossed his shirt onto his bag. Broad hands went to lean hips. Claire was glad to see the bleeding at his temple had stopped.

"I wasn't sure how much time you wanted." His eyes traveled her face before locking on to hers. "I can leave if you need more."

"I'd rather you stay, if you don't mind my company."

He gave a quick nod. "I left the chests. It didn't feel right to open them without you."

Claire shook her head.

"All right. Well . . ." His hands tangled in his hair, found their way back to his hips, then finally fell at his sides. He sighed.

Claire smiled despite the knots that tightened her belly. For a big man, he looked adorable when he was ill at ease.

"I'm sorry," he continued. "I don't know what to say. I feel anything I can manage will be lacking."

That he cared enough to worry about her feelings helped Claire move toward him.

"I'd rather we didn't talk at all."

His brows arched as she closed her arms around his back, then tilted her head up.

"Would you kiss me?"

He took a lung full of air, which pressed her breasts more firmly against his chest. His eyes turned turbulent.

"You know I want you, have always wanted you. But not like this . . ."

"I need you to hold me. I need you to help me feel something other than the loss that's weighing on me. Can you do that?"

Hell.

Nate had managed, in his years of pirating as Sam Steele, to avoid the noose. He'd never heard the rope snap taut, had never seen the last moments of struggle as man, or woman, fought the inevitable.

But at the moment, with Claire watching him, her eyes as clear as the sea, with her rising onto her toes so that he felt the heat of her breath on his chest, he imagined he knew very well just how that rope would feel going over his head and slowly closing around his throat.

Hell.

What kind of man would he be if he took advantage of her grief? He should be consoling her, fussing over her. Not, he thought with chagrin as his loins tightened, thinking of how well she fit against him.

She didn't wait for him to answer; rather she slid those clever hands up his back and dug them deep into his hair. She urged his head lower, though truth be told, there wasn't a lot of urging necessary. She may have been slight, but he felt every curve of her. Her smell wasn't a specific scent he could name, yet it had lingered in his mind for eight years.

His blood simmered. Her lips touched his and it was akin to setting flame to dry tinder. The fire roared in his ears and he had one last thought before it consumed him.

Lord help them both.

Fifteen

As a girl, Claire had been shy, sweet, and a little timid. The woman in his arms, the one that opened her hot and wet mouth under his, was anything but uncertain.

Thank God.

Her hands tangled in his hair, she pressed her body tight against his, and his arousal nestled perfectly in her softness. He tightened his grip and slanted his mouth more fully over hers. Her sigh whispered across his lips and charmed him down to his soul.

"Claire," he breathed. Then he slipped his tongue inside her mouth.

There was no comparing her taste as there was nothing in this world that could match the flavor of Claire. She was innocence, passion, and sweetness combined. Nate couldn't get enough of her. He swept his tongue around her mouth, learning every texture, every secret corner that had a little mewing noise coming from her throat. He loved that sound and he made a point of drawing it out of her several times before he had to take a breath.

"Claire," he moaned. He buried his face in her neck, felt her curls tickle his face.

Her hands hadn't left his hair and they threaded through his locks. It felt fine, but it wasn't where he wanted her hands. Lower would be good. Lower would be very good.

"I'm not sure what to do next," she said, as though she knew his thoughts.

Nate drew back, looked at her flushed face, the eyes wide with uncertainty.

"You were married."

Her color deepened and she lowered her hands, looked aside.

"Did you never . . . ?"

She shook her head. "But it wasn't like this. It wasn't—"

"Wasn't what?" he asked, gripping her chin and forcing her to look at him. "It wasn't what?"

Her eyes narrowed and he hated the bitterness he saw creep within their depths.

"It was fast, and it was meaningless. Is that what you wanted to know?"

Hell, yes, he thought as his muscles eased. That was exactly what he wanted to know.

"There have been no others?"

Tears filled her eyes. "No."

"Ah, Claire," he whispered. He pulled her into his arms but she wasn't compliant any longer. She was stiff and her lips no longer responded to his.

Hell if he was going to let her get away with it. Her husband may have been a selfish bastard but Nate wasn't. Though he knew it was wrong to feel glad about that, he couldn't help feeling a little smug. Claire may not have been loved the way a woman deserves, but by God, by the time they were through, she was going to know what it was to come apart in a man's arms. His arms.

He wasn't her first, and he couldn't help being bitter about that, but he intended to leave a lasting impression. And a damn sight better one than she'd had thus far.

"You can do better than that," he growled. He licked at her mouth, pressed against the seam until her lips parted. He swept in and plundered. He was relentless in his quest and probed and teased until she once again came alive beneath him. When her hands clutched at his shoulders, when her mouth was as hungry as his, he knew the sweetest victory.

"That's better," he said. Then he bent down and swept her into his arms.

Claire didn't know what to do. She'd only coupled with her husband a handful of times, and each time it had been dark, it had been fast, and it had been something that always left her feeling dirty.

But when Nate set her down on their bed of boughs, when he balanced on his elbow to look down on her, she didn't feel dirty. Even though she was dressed as a man, the hunger in his gaze, the gentleness in his touch as he caressed her cheek, made her feel pretty.

"I've waited a long time for this," he said.

"I'm sorry," she answered, holding his hand close. "I should have waited for you."

He pressed a finger over her lips, silencing her. "There are no regrets allowed in our camp tonight. There's only you"—he leaned down and kissed her forehead—"me"—he ran his tongue across her bottom lip—"and this"—he moved lower into her neck, licked at her ear. He closed his teeth around the lobe, drew it into his mouth.

A hot spear of desire shot to her center, and for the first time in Claire's life, she felt the slick moisture of it between her legs.

"Show me," she whimpered when his hand closed around her waist. "Show me what you want."

His eyes were a green storm when they met hers. "I want you, Claire. All of you, and I don't want there to be room in your head for anyone but me."

"There never was."

His smile was feral. His kiss possessive. His hands, suddenly, were everywhere. They snaked from her waist, up her ribs, to her shoulders. He shifted his body fully over hers, pressed his hips hard against where he most wanted to be. There was no doubt of his desire, no doubt of his need.

But he didn't shove down her pants the way she expected him to. He didn't grope clumsily for her breasts. Instead, he seemed content to rock against her as his mouth continued to mate with hers. Tension built in her belly. She felt restless, achy.

Nate's breath was hot on her neck. His hands tugged her shirt from her pants, found her undershirt, and pulled it free. There was no room for doubt or second thoughts. There was only Nate and his fingers crawling over her belly. Claire sucked in her breath. Her nipples drew taut.

"I need to see you."

He sat up, drew both garments over her head. The sun was warm on her skin but her skin pebbled with gooseflesh. She tried to cross her arms over her chest. She wasn't buxom, and if she herself regretted that fact, wouldn't Nate also find her lacking?

His soft "Don't" stilled the movement.

He had large hands, but they were gentle when he slid them the rest of the way up and cupped her breasts. There was no way she could fill those hands, and she closed her eyes, wishing it could be different.

"Look at me."

His eyes were intent. His hands kneaded her flesh. "Look at me when I love you."

His raspy tone sent trembles skittering along her spine. When his eyes lowered sleepily and his mouth softened, when his fingers plucked her nipples and drew them into aching peaks, she could do no less.

Claire gasped at the flood of sensations that rippled from her breasts. She'd never had them toyed with, never realized so much pleasure could come from them.

There was a sense of loss when his hands moved, but when she felt his breath brush her heated skin, her nipples drew even tighter. Then he opened his mouth, drew her in, and suckled.

Claire's back arched. Her hands dug into his shoulders as his mouth moved from one breast to the other and the sensitivity became nearly too much to bear.

"Enough, I can't—"

"This is only the beginning," he promised with a wicked gleam in his eye.

Then suddenly he was tugging her pants down and off and Claire lay naked, open to his hungry gaze.

"Dear God," he sighed, ending any thoughts she had to cover herself. How could she when he looked at her with such reverence?

He came to his knees, took hold of her ankle. Lips barely touching her skin, he made his way up her leg with his mouth. His tongue laved the tender area behind her knee before continuing upward. Sensing what was coming, Claire tried to close her legs. He stopped her easily with the flats of his hands. Then he spread her wide.

"I wonder, Claire, if you taste as sweet as you look."

Before Claire could beg for him to stop, his mouth closed over her core and his tongue slipped inside her body. Her hips rocked up, thrusting his tongue deeper. She felt his hands on her buttocks, holding her in place. She gasped. His tongue was exquisite. It licked, tasted, and stroked until Claire felt the promise of something she'd never known.

Her blood hammered. Her breathing was labored. Her hips, with a mind of their own, rocked against his mouth. Everything inside her tightened and she moaned. Nate growled, then closed his teeth over the tenderest part of her.

Claire exploded into a million pieces.

Her body shuddered and pulsed. Then every bone seemed to melt and she was weightless. She felt Nate set her down, felt his hand on her breast. Claire opened her eyes.

The smile that curled his sensuous mouth was a very satisfied one. "You taste even better."

He kissed her, his tongue mating with hers. Though she'd have thought her body incapable, he eased her back into passion and very soon the need had her squirming. Only this time, she wanted Nate as lost as she'd been. She had no idea how to do that, other than to mimic what he'd done.

Knowing how his hands felt on her body, she let hers glide down his back. Daring, at least in this area, wasn't something that came easily but she wanted to please him. She slid her hands lower until they cupped his backside.

He nipped at her lip, rumbled his approval. Emboldened, Claire repeated the motion, pressing harder as his kisses deepened. Soon the hazy edge of passion was clouding her mind. There was no room for timidness when need swamped her. Digging her fingers into his buttocks, she pressed against him.

"Yes, Claire," he moaned into her neck, rocking his hips hard against hers. "God, yes."

As he'd done, her hands slid into his trousers and she felt the glory of his skin. His buttocks clenched underneath her hands. She moved her arm and he accommodated by lifting his hips.

Hard and pulsing, he filled her hand.

He tipped his head back, sucked in a deep breath.

"Are you all right?"

"You can stop," he growled, "sometime in the next century."

Smiling, she wrapped her hand around his length, feeling it throb. It was the first time she'd held a man in such a way, and she wondered if most women found it as empowering as she did. She felt his life beating in her hand, felt the proof of his desire for her.

"Do *you* taste as good as you feel?" she teased.

Nate choked on a laugh, then flipped them both over. In a swift move he removed the last of his clothing.

"I won't stop you from finding out," he challenged.

Claire's heart hitched. Nate, sprawled in the sun, naked and gleaming, was beautiful. That he trusted her so completely with his body was humbling. Her heart filled and spilled with more emotion than she knew what to do with.

Figuring it couldn't be so much different for him than it had been for her, Claire knelt before him. Unlike her, however, she didn't need to force his knees open. He did it for her.

Oh my, she thought, there was a lot to him. And it was hard, hard enough for the tip to be purple. Thinking it may be hurting him, she started there first.

Claire's mouth closed over him, soft and sweet. Nate growled low in his throat and forced himself not to explode at the first brush of her tongue. Her movements weren't practiced and were the more powerful for it. He forced his eyes open. He wanted to watch her take him over and over until he died from the bliss of it.

Her hand was silk as it cupped him. He looked past her mouth to her breasts, which swayed slightly. He'd never touched such sensitive breasts. And hell, he thought as her teeth grazed him, he couldn't think about that, not with what Claire was doing, or he'd spill his seed into her mouth. Though the thought held merit, it wasn't her mouth he wanted to pour himself into.

He managed a few more minutes, but his toes were curling and sweat that had nothing to do with the sun beaded his forehead.

He flipped her over again, kissed her deeply. He ravaged her with his mouth. His hands found those sensitive breasts and cupped them hard in his hand. She gasped.

"Did I hurt you?" he asked, pulling back.

"No. I've just never felt—"

"Me either," he said. He shifted lower, drew his fingers across her core, and felt the hot stickiness of her desire.

She wasn't a virgin, but she was his. He plunged inside her to the hilt, rocked with her until she gasped his name, until she wrapped her legs around him. He withdrew, slid back in, slick and hot with her heat surrounding him.

He held her head between his hands, mated his tongue with hers. He felt it now, the flick of flame, the promise of release. Not yet, he thought. He wanted it to go on forever.

But she moaned, raising her hips to meet his thrusts. Hell, he couldn't hold it anymore. He lowered a hand to her breast and plucked the nipple into a tight peak. Hearing his name on her lips drove him harder. But he wanted her with him. He moved lower still, slid a hand between them to the tight bud of her arousal. He pressed into it, circled it.

And felt her clasp around him like a fist.

He moaned, buried his head into her neck, and gave in to the pleasure of knowing Claire was finally his.

Sixteen

Claire lay in a cradle of warmth and safety. She didn't have to keep her ears open for sounds of men approaching. She didn't have to worry that she'd be discovered or be caught unaware. She closed her mind to the palm fronds swaying around her and the sounds of parrots chattering from their roosts nearby. For the first time since she'd left her parents' home, Claire knew what it was to sleep deeply.

She woke, softly and gently as the whisper of a spring breeze. The warmth of the sun, diluted through the leafy canvas, fell softly onto her face. The air smelled of forest, rich with life.

Nate was pressed against her, his hand curved around her middle, and one long leg draped over hers. Claire had learned to rely on herself for shelter, money, and food. She'd been forced by circumstance to depend on nobody but herself and what she could do with her own two hands.

But with Nate breathing evenly behind her, with his heat curling around her, Claire knew it was going to be difficult to go back to that life. It was hard, it was cold, and it was lonely.

"You didn't sleep long," his murmur rumbled just behind her ear.

Needing to see him, she turned in his arms and smiled at the sleepy expression on his face.

"How did you know I was awake?"

"You stopped snoring."

Laughter bubbled from her throat. "Then perhaps I ought to count myself lucky I had my back to you. Otherwise I'd be accused of drooling as well."

His brows arched; his fingers trailed her neck. "I'm not opposed to a little of that, now and again. Under the right circumstances."

"Is that so?"

"Hmm." His fingers dipped between her breasts. His thumb brushed her nipple.

The reaction was instant. Her flesh responded to his touch, and it yearned for more. In a fluid motion, he rose above her, pressing her into the boughs. His mouth feasted on her, from neck to belly and every speck of skin in between. His tongue washed her and it set her ablaze. He didn't have to ask for her to part for him. When he slid down her body, she eagerly gave him everything he was after. For it was the same as what she wanted.

To be connected, and oh, as his tongue once again swept her away in a pool of desire, to be wanted with such hunger.

He took her, with mouth and hands, to the edge of the world. And once he had her there, he held her suspended.

"Nate, please," she begged. Her hands latched on to his slick back and her fingers dug in for purchase.

"Please what?" he asked as the proof of his passion teased her opening.

She may have wept, she may have pleaded. She wasn't sure. She only knew that when her body bowed, when everything inside her let go, Nate was there, taking the fall with her.

The sun was sliding its way toward dusk. Though it was bright yet, darkness would come soon enough and Claire wanted to be back at camp by then. She'd left Nate sound asleep and, once clear of the trees, had charged down the beach. She didn't relish what had to be done, but the idea of not doing anything was intolerable. Regardless of the past, her father deserved some sort of burial.

And so she picked her way over the rocks, which were cooler now, toward the cave. The tide was coming in and the sea was now halfway up to the waterline. When she dropped from the rocks to the entrance to the cave, the water rolled around her waist.

After her near drowning, it wasn't a comfortable feeling.

She peered in, and as she'd feared, it was darker now than it had been earlier as well. With the water filling and the sun lowering, the light had been cut by half.

But it was enough, she told herself. It had to be. Gathering her courage, Claire waded into the cave. It seemed to close around her when she stepped through the mouth of it. Her chest tightened and her loud breaths echoed off the stony walls.

Her father hadn't been found far from the opening, and Claire could only hope that that hadn't changed with the incoming water. Knowing the bottom was flat with no sudden drops, Claire moved as fast as she could. Her eyes searched the surface of the water because, she thought with a twist of her stomach, the skull would float.

Some light rippled beneath the surface. Fists of sunlight pushed their way through the boulders above her head. They helped her not only to see but also to keep going. Had it been darker, she wasn't sure she'd have had the courage to come inside. Even for her father.

Water licked the walls as she moved. A gentle wind breathed through with the light. A dripping sound came from somewhere in the darkness. Alone, she thought, as her father had been.

"Don't think about that," she scolded herself. Neither would she think about how the water was now riding under her breasts or how her heart was shaking.

She'd have to find it soon. Claire knew a cave full of water, especially one that had already claimed her father, was the last place she wanted to be trapped in.

Pushing on, Claire cast a glance back to the cave opening. It was half filled. Her whimper echoed off the walls and filled her ears. She couldn't go on. Already the icy fingers of panic were clawing in her throat. She plunged her hands into the water to help push her way forward and promptly felt something hard brush her fingers.

Her scream ripped from her throat. Hundreds of her yelled back with the echo.

"Oh, God, oh, God." Her hands shot from the water, fisted at her throat. Breathing through her mouth, she gulped in air even as the skull bobbed to the surface before her. She choked back another scream.

"Claire!"

She spun, her heart galloping in her chest.

"Nate." She said it on a long breath of relief.

"Are you coming out or do I have to come in there and pull you out?"

He wasn't happy. His tone was a sharp blade of annoyance but Claire didn't care. She'd never heard a more wonderful sound.

"I'm coming."

She looked at the skull, had to will away any sentimentality. For the moment, until she could get out of there, it was just a thing. *Just a thing*, she told herself. But her hands trembled violently when she took it between her palms.

He'd woken to find her gone, again. This time, however, he didn't believe she was simply tending to nature's needs. He'd had a feeling, deep in his gut, where she'd gone. Because he'd have done the same thing.

He'd rushed through the trees, earned himself more than a few slaps across the face from the fronds he didn't bother to shove aside. He'd had thoughts of her slipping off rocks, knocking her head, and drowning. Or simply getting caught in the incoming tide. His thoughts on that had been warranted when he'd skidded onto the beach and seen that the water was indeed rising.

Running past the unopened chests, he'd raced to the rocks. Only then had he slowed his steps. Then he'd heard her scream. He didn't remember climbing the rocks, or jumping into the water. The next thing he knew he was in the cave. She'd been all right, he reminded himself, but it had angered him to think she'd come back alone.

But when she'd waded to him, her hands held high and the skull clasped between them, her face gray as ash, he'd bit back his anger. He'd held it while they walked to the remains of the town and the graveyard beyond it. He thought he'd done a fine job of keeping it tethered when she'd refused his help and dug the small hole with her own two hands.

Though it cost him, and his teeth ached from the effort, he'd waited until she'd eaten and a fire roared to ease the darkness that had fallen. But damn it all, a man had his limits and Nate had reached his.

"Why the hell didn't you wake me? I'd have gone with you."

"I know that." She poked at the fire with a branch. The wood shifted and hissed.

He ground his teeth some more. "And?"

She shrugged. "It wasn't for you to deal with."

"So that's the way of it, is it? I can bed you but nothing else?"

Her gaze snapped to his. "You weren't complaining about that this afternoon."

"Did you think I cared so little for you that I wouldn't help you with such a thing?"

"You were sleeping."

"That's a sorry excuse, even for you."

Claire threw down her stick and leapt to her feet. "What is that supposed to mean, 'even for me'?"

He stood as well, went toe to toe with her.

"Only that you always have an excuse, don't you, when it's convenient? I was sleeping—therefore, you didn't bother to wake me. I waited too long, so you married another man."

Her mouth pinched. "That hurt me every bit as much as it hurt you. I'll not stand here and have you throw it in my face!"

"How am I to know it hurt you when you won't tell me anything of it other than he was a sorry sort in bed?"

She reared as though slapped, but managed to keep her eyes on his. Eyes which were shadowed with hurt.

"That's right," she answered coldly. "He was."

"Hell." Nate rubbed his hands over his face, took a deep breath, and fought to rein in his temper. "You could have at least trusted me enough to tell me where you were going."

"And if I had, you'd have let me go alone?"

"I don't know."

"At least you're honest about that."

"I've never lied to you. Never."

"And we're back where we started." She threw her hands wide. "I've lived with the thought that you broke your word to me. I believed it for eight years. Forgive me if it takes me more than a day to accept otherwise. Besides, it's not as though you're brimming with trust. You wouldn't trust me to sleep below decks without bedding half your crew in the process."

He sighed, stepped back. "I never thought you'd sleep with my crew. That was a way to strike at you."

"Well," she breathed out. "You hit the mark."

"Trust doesn't come readily for me either. I was young when I came to the orphanage but I vowed, once I stepped inside those doors, that nobody was going to hurt me again. A physical blow I could tolerate, but no other. I gave you more of me than I ever thought I could trust anybody with."

Claire looked down, properly chastised. "You never told me that."

He'd never told her any of it. She'd asked, of course, many times in those years they'd shared at the orphanage, but he'd been too mortified to tell the truth. Rather than lie, he'd said nothing. To this day, nobody knew his past, not even the women who'd run the orphanage at the time he'd arrived.

"It's why I never went looking for you. I was mad that I'd let you get close enough to me to hurt me like that. I felt like a fool for believing the words you'd told me."

Claire sat on their bed of boughs and looked up at him with sad eyes. "Was it so easy to believe that nothing we'd shared had mattered to me?"

Nate exhaled, looking out into the darkness. He'd never dreamed of telling his past to anyone but it seemed the time had come. He needed to bury it the way Claire had buried her father. And the only way he knew to do that was to exhume it first.

"I had reason to believe that nobody could love me." He took a deep breath, then another. "I never knew my father. Or," he added with a shrug as he turned back to her, "perhaps I did. Who's to know?" At her confused expression, he explained further. "My mother was a whore. There's no gentle way to put that, for that's what she was. She peddled herself on the street, in the taverns, on ships. She was always surrounded by men. It's possible one was my father and I never knew it.

"Our life," he continued, hating the way the memories were still so clear after all this time, "consisted of sleeping in strange beds. Well, she slept in a bed, I was always relegated to the floor. A few times, she made me sleep outside."

"How old were you?"

"Four."

"Dear God."

"No," he said with a forced laugh, "God wasn't around much. Least not in those days. Anyhow, that was our life, moving and living hand to mouth. Mostly she simply carried me along like baggage. I was always dirty, mostly always hungry."

Even now, he could remember what it was to be hungry enough to search through the streets, the refuse other people threw out, for a scrap, any scrap, of food.

"But one night, one night she came to me, for once not wreaking of rum or sex, and promised that this new man was going to make all our sorrows disappear. It was a line I'd heard before, many times, but a boy of four tends to cling to any hope that may change his fortune."

"What happened?"

"I was told to wait outside. Since it wasn't the first time, I occupied myself well enough playing with rocks to pass the time. But the night got colder and more time passed and still she didn't come outside to fetch me. I decided to go in, thinking I could at the least grab a blanket."

The vision was sharp. Time hadn't dulled the edge.

"He was laying over her, his pants still around his ankles. His hands were around her neck. She was dead."

Claire gasped, pressing her fingers to her throat.

"I don't remember much after that. He'd taken off his jacket and scabbard, left them on the table. Next thing I knew I had the sword in my hands, the man was draped over my mother, and I was covered in blood." He looked down at his hands, still seeing them bloodied.

"My mother, in her worst drunken states, often threatened to take me to the orphanage if I spoke too much or got in her way." He shrugged. "I figured it couldn't be worse than what I had so I took myself there."

His eyes met hers and he felt somehow cleansed by the understanding he saw in them. He realized then that part of the reason he'd never told a soul was he'd been afraid to be looked upon as some kind of demon for having killed a man when he was only four.

Claire came to her feet, wiping a tear he hadn't realized hovered on his eye. "I'm sorry."

"When I implied you were a whore—"

She silenced him with a kiss. A kiss that soothed as much as it inflamed.

"You knew I'd sailed the Caribbean alone. Given your past and what you already thought of me, what else were you to think?"

"You can forgive so easily?"

Her smile wrapped around his heart, drawing some of the shattered pieces back together.

"I've said some things myself I'm not proud of. Done things as well."

"Tell me about your husband."

Claire shook her head. "A mistake I recognized too late. I'm ashamed of my actions."

"I murdered a man, Claire. Hard to be more ashamed than that."

"You were young, scared. No court would blame you."

"Doesn't matter, does it? Not when you blame yourself."

Claire's eyes shone with her own share of condemnation. "No, it doesn't."

"Tell me."

"I can't."

He caught her arm as she turned. "Why?"

"Because I was an idiot and naive, and I wish it had never happened." Her eyes sparked when they met his. "And telling you the sorry tale won't change any of that."

His grip tightened. "No, it won't. But it will go a long way to explaining the past. I need to know, Claire."

Their eyes clashed. The air between them turned brittle. Claire gave in first.

"Let me go."

She yanked hard and he released his grip. Rubbing her arms, she paced before the fire.

"You remember Mr. Litton?"

"The man who gave money to keep the orphanage going? How could I forget? He worked me hard. Never let a visit go by without tracking me down and piling more work onto me. Said I was too bloody old to be there. I knew I was but I worked for free so I don't know what the hell he had to complain about."

"He worked us all hard. Said we needed to show him more appreciation."

"I hated him. Hated the way he looked at some of the girls."

Claire stopped her pacing and looked down into the flames.

"Did he touch you?" Nate asked, sick at the thought. Litton was old enough to have been her father. His jowls shook as much as his belly when he talked and his breath had always been fetid.

"He did after we were married."

Nate couldn't have heard her right. "You married Quinn Litton?"

Claire sneered. "You're not the only one ashamed of the past. Litton told me if I didn't marry him, he'd refuse to help the orphanage any longer. Nate, he practically owned the town. Without his money, those children would have been on their own, with nothing. I couldn't let it happen."

It sickened him to think of it, that Claire had had to face

such a thing. That Litton could even consider tossing children out like garbage.

"Of course you couldn't." And damn Litton to Hell for forcing her.

Her eyes hardened. "But it didn't matter, Nate. He did it anyway. No more than a month after we were married, he stopped giving them money. Without his help, the orphanage was forced to close and the kids were left homeless. Nate, the youngest was only three."

"Bloody bastard," Nate growled, remembering, too well, just what if felt like to be alone at such a young age. "Nobody did anything about it?"

"Who could? Most folks were indebted to him and too afraid to speak against him."

Nate sighed. "Something he'd know, of course."

She hugged herself tighter. "I was sick about it. I wanted to help the children so badly, but I had as little as they did. There wasn't anything I could do. And if I stayed in San Salvador, I'd never be free of him, so I left."

And if Nate hadn't tucked his tail and run and instead had gone looking for her, she'd never have married and given her innocence to another man. He'd never liked Litton, but right then, Nate could have killed him.

"Has he looked for you?"

Claire shrugged. "I wouldn't know, I haven't stayed anyplace long enough, and I don't look like I did either. Still, something tells me that he wouldn't. After all, not only didn't he love me, but he got what he wanted from me as well, didn't he?" she added disgustedly.

"You married him, gave up your innocence for the sake of those children. Claire." He took her chin and forced her gaze to his. "That he misled you is no fault of yours."

Her chin quivered. "I should have known better. Nate, we all hated him, knew he was a vile man. Why did I think he'd be true to his word?"

His eyes sank into hers. "Did you, though? Did a part of you not realize it could all be a lie?"

"Yes," she admitted on a sigh.

"Yet you did it anyway, because it was a chance you had to take. Claire, it's not in you to watch children suffer. I know. I saw the way you tended the young ones. You were more of a mother to them than they'd ever known. You gave of yourself to try to help them. From where I'm standing, I'd say that's the most honorable thing I've ever heard."

Nate took her in his arms, pressed a kiss to her forehead, and held her head against his chest. He'd loved her at sixteen, and at the time he'd believed he couldn't possibly love her more. He'd been wrong. His chest was tight with the depth of emotion he felt for Claire.

She'd been through so much. She'd lost her mother, was left by her father. She'd been lied to in the worst fashion by a man that Nate had every intention of going after once the treasure was found. Was it any wonder, he thought, that she'd learned to depend on only herself?

"I'm sorry. For all the beastly things I said to you, God, I'm so sorry."

She clung to him, cried against his chest until his shirt was warm and damp with her tears. They weren't only for the loss of her innocence, he knew. They were for the father she'd buried, for the children she hadn't been able to help. For the years she and Nate had spent apart.

There wasn't much he could do about the rest, but he vowed, as he held her in his arms, that they wouldn't be apart again.

* * *

Luck, James Blackthorn figured, was much like a temperamental woman. Sometimes she was with you, making life easier, and sometimes, when you needed her most, she wasn't anywhere in sight. He'd had his fair share of both lately.

She'd definitely been missing at the poker game and again later when his useless men had let Nate slip through their fingers. She'd come back to his side when James had figured out where Nate was heading but the treacherous bitch had abandoned him again.

Night had fallen. The sailor's moon cast a bright light on the water and guided them as they finished gliding around Isla de Hueso. There wasn't a damn ship anywhere.

He'd been so sure, thought he'd had it all figured out. Isla de Hueso was abandoned, and it was the only island in line with where Nate was headed that made any sense. Though he'd fallen back deliberately and lost sight of Nate's ship for a time, he'd done so confidently. Dammit, had that been a mistake?

"Orders, Captain?"

Horace had been James's first mate since James had been old enough to claim his inheritance and purchase the *Phantom*. Together they'd sailed the Caribbean intent on finding the *Emmeline* and any information about her. Since they clearly couldn't rely on such a quest to keep the ship afloat and the crew paid, and since piracy and privateering were too rough for James's blood—he wouldn't risk losing his neck and his ship to the scourge of the Caribbean waters—they sailed as merchantmen until such a time that the treasure was found.

It was close, he felt it. Logically, it made no sense. But

instincts had led him to stay with that old man until he'd had a moment of clarity and told him about the treasure, and instincts told James now that, despite the lack of a ship nearby, the treasure was here.

He took a deep breath.

"Sail us back to that beach we passed. We'll drop anchor there. Come morning we'll go ashore."

Seventeen

They decided the next morning to examine the chests before continuing their exploration of the shores. The sky was thick with puffy clouds, but none that threatened rain. They wouldn't have to worry about a deluge slowing them down.

"What do you suppose is inside?"

"It's treasure, true enough. Or they filled them with rocks."

He'd brought along a hammer and he used it now on the barnacle-crusted lock of the first chest. It gave after a few hits. Nate dropped the hammer, letting it sink into the white sand. With Claire leaning over his shoulder, he opened the chest.

A ruby the size of a plum lay within a cradle of pearls.

"Oh," Claire sighed. "Look at them all."

Diamonds, rubies, emeralds of the richest green. Coins of silver and gold. She dug her hand through them and they slid over her skin like cool silk. A necklace caught in her fingers and she pulled it free. Her breath left her lungs in a slow exhale. Amethysts and diamonds beaded along a string of gold flashed in the sun.

Nate grinned, and took the hammer to the next chest.

"There's more yet," he said and held out a handful of Spanish gold doubloons, each worth months of work to a common sailor.

In the third chest, among more of what they'd already discovered plus hundreds of silver pieces of eight, Claire picked out a snuffbox. It was made of copper and etched with swirling letters in a language she couldn't read.

"Why would a plain snuffbox be with this kind of treasure? Did it get thrown in by mistake, do you think?" She frowned as she studied it. Understanding crept over her like dawn on the horizon.

"The map said 'a lone piece.' This is the only thing"—Claire gestured to the chests—"that doesn't fit with the rest."

Nate took the box, turned it over in his hands. Seeing something in the writing, he tilted it to the light.

"What?" Claire demanded. "What do you see?"

"I know some Spanish. This word"—he ran his thumb over it—"it says 'tomb.'"

Claire let the meaning of that flit through her mind.

"The last bit of the clue says 'alone at peace.' A tomb would go with that. Do you think, then, they left the chests here, enough to satisfy anyone who'd perhaps put the map together and got this far, then hid the rest in a tomb?"

Claire sighed. There were more than enough jewels and coins to lift her from a life of poverty, yet disappointment tasted bitter in her mouth. Why, she wondered, did she always seem one step behind what she wanted most?

"Where's the blasted tomb then?" she demanded in frustration.

Nate's eyes rivaled the sparkle of the emerald she'd first seen when he'd opened the chest.

"We were practically standing on it yesterday."

"Yesterday?" Claire thought back. It wasn't in the cave, and as much as her father had died there, she certainly didn't think he'd died at peace.

"Oh," she gasped, then spun and grabbed his forearms. "It's in the graveyard. They buried it in the cemetery!"

Nate's teeth shone when he smiled. "Let's go find out."

With the snuffbox in one hand, he took Claire's hand with the other. They left the chests and raced over the sand, laughing like children when it tugged at their boots and nearly sent them sprawling. Nate's strength kept her upright, kept her close as they ran from beach to jungle. They worked their way under and over vines thick as her arm, past branches burdened with broad, serrated-edged leaves, and leapt over roots and shrubs. Their laughter was loud enough to scare birds from their roosts. Monkeys with soft brown eyes stopped grooming to watch them race by.

They didn't stop running until the jungle opened to the crumbling remains of the town and to its other side, where the gray slabs of the headstones rose from the ground.

When they crossed the low wall into the cemetery, they respectfully slowed to a walk. There was something about a graveyard, Claire thought, that demanded hushed voices. Even the wind accommodated it. The breeze that swept between the stones was gentle as angel's wings.

"I'll look over here," Claire said and slipped her hand from Nate's, veering right.

She was careful where she stepped, and when she read the names and the dates on the stones, she couldn't help being moved. Some had died so young. They were sons and daughters, wives and husbands. They'd lived, and the fact that someone had cared enough about them to mark where they lay proved that their time on the earth had been cherished. It had mattered.

And here she was, she thought with a grimace, walking among them looking for gold.

Disgusted, she left the rest of the stones unread. She couldn't, wouldn't, bring a shovel to this place in the hopes of getting rich.

"What is it?" Nate asked, talking louder once they'd stepped back over the low wall.

She gestured to the graves. "I can't bring myself to seek wealth among the dead. It's barbaric." She shuddered. "It's inhuman."

Her words had fear sliding its icy hands over Nate's skin. How many times, under the guise of Sam Steele, had he plundered a ship, taken lives, and stolen off with their cargo? His sword may not have always sought a battle, but it had never turned from one either. And it was that sword and his time at sea that had given him a greater wealth than he'd ever dreamed of, even greater than the one he'd imagined when he'd lain cold and hungry on the street and dreamed of a better life.

They'd confessed a great deal last night, and though a tremendous weight had lifted off his shoulders, one remained. Steele. Claire could forgive a four-year-old boy who'd been shocked to witness his mother's death and had taken a life in his grief, but he feared, especially now, that her forgiveness wouldn't come so easily for a man who'd willingly, and happily, agreed to turn pirate. He couldn't risk losing her now that he'd only found her again.

"Come," he said, taking her hand and holding it a little

tighter than he had before. He led her around the graveyard, thinking, if nothing else, they could walk the areas
they hadn't yet searched and enjoy the time together until
Vincent came for them. Nate wasn't happy to leave the
treasure, considering what it had cost them, especially
Claire. His hand curved around the snuffbox. They'd come
so close.

His foot caught on something, and before he could stop
the fall, he was facedown on the ground with grass tickling
his nose. Claire laughed and Nate flipped himself over, saw
the light shining on her face as she exploded in a gale of
laughter. He thought to himself that he'd gladly embarrass
himself over again to hear that lovely sound ring loud and
true.

Still, he had his pride, so he brushed himself off as he
came to his feet. Her mirth died as he was wiping the dirt
from his knees. He straightened, found her dropped onto
her knees.

"Claire?"

"It wasn't in the cemetery, Nate. 'Alone at peace.'"

Claire gestured to the rock Nate deemed must have
tripped him. But when he leaned closer, saw the letters *SF*
carved into it, he knew it wasn't any old rock. It marked the
treasure.

Excitement once again rolled through him. He couldn't
stop the grin that stretched over his face.

"You don't have any objections to digging here, do
you?"

Tears shone in Claire's eyes and she shook her head.
Nate's chest tightened just looking at her. He knew that no
matter what treasure they unearthed, nothing would ever
be more valuable than Claire.

"Let's go fetch the shovels."

* * *

Isla de Hueso had two accessible beaches, one that faced north and one that faced south. The *Phantom* bobbed just offshore of the northern beach. It certainly looked abandoned, James thought as he leveled his looking glass onto the pearly sand.

A handful of dead jellyfish lay rotting in the sun, their veil-like skin looking dry and crisp. Scattered clumps of seaweed lay here and there, making it appear as though the sand was growing mold.

Though James saw nothing to make him think that Nate or anyone else had been there recently, he hadn't changed his mind about going ashore. The only way to be sure, to cast aside any doubt that Isla de Hueso had been Nate's destination, was to go see for himself. If they found nothing on this beach, they'd move to the other. He wouldn't leave anything to chance.

He, Horace, and four other men rowed to shore. Once the boat was dragged onto the sand, James began his search. Sand was fickle and he didn't spend too much time looking for tracks on it. A good wind or rain, both of which they'd had in the last few days, would have obliterated most signs of human activity. Instead he searched the tree line.

A deserted island such as this one had thick and lush forests. Walking through the tangle of vines and shrubbery wouldn't be impossible, but it would leave its mark. As James strode down the line where beach gave way to trees, he paid close attention to both the forest floor and anything at eye level. He looked for broken branches, cut vines, and here, sheltered from the driving wind, he searched for signs of footprints in the moss and decaying layer of leaves.

"Captain? Over here."

They had spread out along the beach and Horace was nearest James. He didn't have to say it loud for James to hear and soon he was looking at what Horace had found.

"Looks like a path to me, Captain."

Indeed it did. Smaller branches, those that could be cut with a sword, had been severed. Tops of ferns lay askew where part of them had been trampled into the spongy ground. And it was there, on the floor littered with decaying leaves, dirt, and moss, that he saw the unmistakable indent of a boot. A very long boot. He smiled. He hadn't been wrong after all.

James held up a finger and held his breath, but no human sound could be heard. It didn't, however, mean that Nate wasn't still on the island. He simply wasn't close enough to be heard. A good thing, James figured, since he wanted to be much better armed when they found him.

He stepped farther into the trees, then crouched down. Another boot, this one much smaller. *The dwarf or the kid?* James wondered.

"We should bring more men ashore," Horace whispered.

James stood, nodding his head in the direction of the beach. Neither he nor Horace said a word until they were on the sand, standing next to each other.

Horace was equally as big as Nate. In fact, James's ship was outfitted with many men built like Nate and Horace and some small wiry ones as well. The small ones could climb rigging like monkeys and were fast and wily. Since he had no doubt he'd be taking the treasure from Nate, he was glad he'd had the foresight to hire both types of men.

It didn't take long to issue the order. If Nate was ashore, James didn't want him to know he had company until James was armed and ready. He wanted to keep the element of surprise for himself.

The two men he and Horace had come ashore with were sent back in the longboat to retrieve another twenty men as well as an arsenal of weapons. The rest of the crew would be told to keep a sharp eye out for ships. They hadn't seen any, but that didn't mean there wasn't one nearby.

Since Nate had to have known he'd been followed for a time, it would only be good strategy to have his ship drop him off and lead anyone who may be looking for them away from the island. It was a good strategy, but only if someone fell for it.

When they arrived at camp, Nate ignored the shovels they'd come back for and scooped Claire up into his arms instead. She squealed, wrapping her hands around his neck the way he'd known she would. The way he'd wanted her to. He loved having her arms around him.

"What are you doing?" she laughed. "We have a treasure to dig up."

"That one's not going anywhere. Besides, the one I have here is even better," Nate said; then he captured her mouth with his.

She was so sweet, so incredibly perfect the way her mouth opened under his, the way she responded with the same need and passion that burned in him.

He laid her down on their bed then covered her body with his until they were aligned in all the right places. Until her softness cradled his hardness and the jut of her nipples pressed against his chest.

He buried his face in her neck, kissed along her jaw, licked her ear. He whispered what he had every intention of doing to her body. She parted her legs, allowed him to settle in deeper. His hands cupped her breasts and his thumbs flickered over their perfect peaks. He slid down her body, lifted her shirt and undershirt, and opened his mouth over her.

Claire arched off the boughs, the sweetest moan he'd ever heard escaping her lips when he drew her nipple into his mouth. With his hands spread at her back, he held her, drinking in every shiver of desire that rippled through her.

Her hands held him there and he suckled, teased until she was begging and he was throbbing with need. He slid her trousers down her legs, sucked at the spot on her inner thigh he'd discovered drove her wild. His fingers found her wet and ready.

He shucked his clothes, mating his mouth to hers. Her kiss further fed his hunger. Her tongue was in his mouth, teasing and tasting. Her lips played against his. When she wrapped them around his tongue and sucked, a flash of lust gripped his loins.

He lifted her knees, spread them, and plunged hard. Again she arched, bowing under the desire and need that held her captive. He took advantage of her position and lowered his mouth to her breast.

"Nate," she gasped. Then she clutched around him, hot and sweet, and took him up with her.

Shouldn't we go find the treasure?"

"Hmm," he answered.

He was lying behind her and holding her tight with one arm. His breath tickled Claire's neck; his chest hair was fuzzy against her back. She smiled. It thrilled her to know she was capable of making such a big man lose control and that she herself was capable of such passion.

She poked him gently in the belly. "Aren't you excited to find it, after all this time?"

"I will be, once my brain starts working again."

She laughed, then twisted out from under him. Though he grumbled and reached for her, she scrambled away before he could pull her back.

"Come on, Nate." She grabbed her trousers and drew them on. "Let's not waste daylight."

He balanced on an elbow and his eyes gleamed wickedly. "Who said we were wasting anything? Seems to me that was a pretty fine way to enjoy daylight. And I don't recall you complaining."

She flushed. She couldn't help it. Talking openly in such a way about such a thing was new to her. "I wasn't."

Then, laughing, she threw him his shirt. "I'll go without you if you don't hurry."

He sighed heavily, but he got dressed. By then Claire was dancing from foot to foot. This was really happening! After so many years, so much heartbreak, she was finally going to find the infamous treasure of the *Santa Francesca*.

"I don't need to ask how you're feeling." Nate smiled as he cupped a large hand around her neck. "It's all over your face."

"It almost seems surreal, doesn't it?"

He kissed her lips, then her forehead. "It's real. Let's go get—"

He stopped suddenly, went rigid. He angled his head, his eyes boring into the trees. A flock of doves scattered noisily from their perch, their wings flapping in haste. Nate shook his head and pressed his hand over her mouth when she tried to talk. Claire, too, strained to hear, but there was nothing. It was deathly silent, which was never a good thing. Claire had learned from spending countless nights outside that the sound of silence was the scariest sound. It meant something was about that shouldn't be.

Nate's eyes met hers and in them she saw what she herself was thinking. If it were Vincent, wouldn't he announce himself, whistle, or make noise to let them know he was there? Wouldn't he call their names?

Without a word passing between them, Claire and Nate grabbed what weapons were at hand and ran.

Eighteen

It was nearly as satisfying to see the camp as he expected it would be to find the treasure. He hadn't been wrong. Nate, or someone from his ship, had been there. The question remained: Were they still on the island?

James felt the ashes. Cold. He looked round, saw the bed made of ferns and the canvas that protected it. One bed? What the hell? Nate and the kid? Shuddering, James turned deliberately from the bed and its rumpled covers.

The camp, he realized, looked well lived in. There were crates at the end of the bed, and there was a stack of sticks yet to be burned. It looked as though the inhabitants had merely stepped away, to return later. It certainly didn't look abandoned.

James opened the crates and poked through them. Among the supplies were mugs, plates, cutlery, and a small pot. He found coffee beans, bananas, a handful of eggs wrapped in a shirt. There were tools as well. A small ax, knives with blades of varying lengths, another strip of canvas, and a small length of rope. He raised his brows at the weapons and ammunition he uncovered beneath some clothes. James smiled. Nobody in their right mind left ammunition behind.

He sniffed the air, as though he could smell them. Of course the only thing that hung in the air besides the humidity was the sweaty smell of his men.

In another trunk, James found more clothing. He felt another spurt of satisfaction when he pulled some of them out. Judging from the size of the garments, it was likely that Nate was ashore.

"Aren't we going to look for them?" Horace asked.

"I'd rather we stay together, at least for the moment. They can't be well armed"—he gestured to the weapons he'd tossed out of the box—"but I don't want him picking us off one by one the way he did in Nevis either.

"Besides, judging from that"—he pointed to the clean shovels—"they haven't found it yet. Let's have a closer look. If they heard us and hurried off, or if they weren't expecting visitors, they may have left something valuable behind."

It was the kid, James realized, when he picked the soiled hat from a box. The kid from the game was with Nate. It made no sense to James's way of thinking, but there it was. The kid and Nate were hunting the treasure together, and from the kid's size and the tears he'd seen in his eyes when he'd lost the poker game, James knew he had nothing to fear from him. His crew was more than able to take Nate down. He threw a glance over his shoulder, saw his men pillaging the camp, and thought they'd better take Nate down this time.

James didn't take the food that remained but he covered

it. If they were here for long, they'd need it. He found the coat Nate had been wearing in Nevis. Could he be so lucky? he thought. But fate was feeling generous, and when James reached into the pocket, he felt it immediately. He sat back on his heels and grinned.

"Captain? What do you make of this?"

James rose, went to the man who stood next to the bed, and accepted the copper box he gave him.

"Hmm, looks like a snuffbox." He opened it, turned it over, and saw the inscription.

"What does it say?" asked Horace, who'd come to see what was found.

"It says, 'The glory is in the tomb.'" He pondered the words a moment, then shook his head and chuckled. "Do you suppose it could really be so easy?"

"Easy, sir?"

"Horace. There was a town here at one time, was there not?"

"Aye, sir."

James rubbed his thumb over the engraving. "Then doesn't it stand to reason there would also be a cemetery?"

"We're checking there first?"

James pulled out the two pieces of the map. Horace whistled, leaned in to see. James read the riddle, tried to match it with what his great-grandfather had said. The old sailor had talked of the answer being in the last. The last what? James wondered. And the map said "marked waterline," which meant they should search near water. Since they hadn't seen anything on the beach they'd come ashore at, it stood to reason there could be something on the other.

"We'll make way to the other beach. If we find nothing there, then we search for a cemetery." James pointed to some of his men. "You four, stay here. On the slight chance they don't know we're already here, don't do anything stupid like start a fire and announce our presence."

"Aye, Captain," they agreed.

The rest, Horace included, followed James out of camp.

Nate's stomach was a snake pit of nerves. He knew he had to get the hell away from camp, but to where? He had no way of knowing where their pursuers were going. If he went to the town site, they could be caught. If he took Claire to the beach, they could end up being open targets. He leapt a fallen tree, glanced back to ensure Claire didn't need help, then kept running.

His mind raced along with his legs. He needed to think of a plan, but he couldn't do it when he was rushing through the forest, ducking tree limbs and leaping rotting vegetation. After another few moments he saw something that would work. A tall tree with a gnarled trunk that split into smaller, crooked trunks perfect for climbing.

Nate tucked his pistol into his trousers and turned to Claire. Since he hadn't time to fuss with a sheath before leaving camp, there was no place to keep his sword but in his left hand.

"We can't keep running blind," he whispered. He had no idea if their visitors had heard them run, but they'd no doubt found their camp by now and knew there were others on the island. "Until I can think of something, we'll hide up there." He pointed to the sturdy branches with his right hand.

Claire, who also carried a pistol and sword, managed to climb easily with her weapons. Nate stayed below for a few moments. He stepped back to study the effectiveness of their hiding place. It was a heavily leafed tree but still

Claire was easy to spot. Damn. Hopefully their pursuers would be too busy running to look up every tree.

The only reassuring bit was that he and Claire would have the advantage of seeing their enemy first. And though they hadn't had time to bring extra shots, at least the pistols they'd taken were loaded. It would allow them to shoot and run. At which point they'd only have their swords. He hoped it bloody wouldn't come to that.

He settled himself on a branch one down from Claire's, which allowed them to talk quietly.

"I don't think they're following us, at least not yet. Do you suppose once they reach camp and realize someone's here, that they'll come looking for us?"

It was what he'd first assumed they'd do, but now that he had a moment to think on it, he wasn't as sure.

"If it were you, would you waste time searching an island for a few people?"

She shook her head immediately. "If it were me, I'd keep all my men together—there's strength with that. And once I located the treasure, I'd post men all around to safeguard it." Her eyes grew round. "We left the map behind!" She grabbed his arm. "Do you have the snuffbox?"

He shook his head.

"How could we have been so stupid?"

"Well, we weren't given the luxury of having time to pack."

"Nate, with the map and the box, they have everything they need."

"They still have to figure it out. It took us a few days to accomplish that. Vincent will be back by then."

"Are you suggesting we hide in the meantime?" she asked, the outrage in her voice increasing its volume. She took a breath, then spoke much softer. "Nate, there are things we can do. We can attack them at night. I know we're outnumbered but we can slow them down." Her spine stiffened and her chin angled upward. Her eyes glittered. "I won't sit back and hide while they take what we've worked for."

Nate could do nothing but smile. God, he loved her. She had such life, such passion in her. True, her temper was also fiery, but it made Claire who she was. Everything she did, from swimming to treasure hunting, to giving him hell, to making love, she did with a depth of passion behind it that amazed him. Even now, outnumbered and outgunned, she wasn't giving up. She wanted to fight back.

If he hadn't been afraid of falling on his head or having her fall as well, he'd have leaned in and kissed her, swept her mouth until that passion consumed them both.

"What are you smiling at?"

"You're beautiful."

She flushed, then fussed with her hair using her free hand. "You've spent too much time in the sun lately."

He angled his head. "That's the second time you've ignored my praise. You doubt me?"

She wouldn't meet his eyes. "I thought we were supposed to figure out what we're going to do."

"We are. We will. Surely that doesn't mean I can't pay you a compliment?"

She puffed her cheeks and blew out her breath. "Fine. Compliment taken. Now, what's our plan of action?"

He chuckled. Claire wasn't used to compliments. She certainly hadn't been in a position to receive any the last while. Nate intended for that to change.

"We need more than what we have. I'll go back to camp tonight. While I expect there will be some men there, I don't think they all will be. If I wait until they're asleep, I can take care of them quietly. I'm not worried about food or blankets, but we need ammunition and we need flint. I hate knowing all I have is the shot that's in my pistol and I want to alert Vincent that there's trouble. Hopefully he'll be close enough to see it."

"There's a problem with that."

Nate frowned. "What?"

"You said, 'I,' not 'us.'"

"That's right. I'll go."

She shook her head. "*We'll* go. What if something goes wrong? Or there's more men than you think? You need the extra help and you're a fool if you believe I'll cower in the tree like a frightened maiden."

"It's not cowering, Claire, it's sound logic."

She rolled her eyes. "Only to your ears. Would you ask Vincent, or your friend Blake, to stay behind?"

Nate set his jaw, knowing she'd trapped him.

"Of course not, because they're men. Nate, are we in this together, or aren't we?"

Had he really admired her passion only a moment ago?

She leaned as far forward as she could without falling. "I'll follow you or I'll go with you. But I won't be left behind."

He set his teeth, wishing he'd have had the time to bring along the extra length of rope from camp. Then he could have tied her to the damn tree.

James saw the chests the moment he stepped onto the sand and had two immediate thoughts. The first was, who would be idiot enough to leave such things in plain sight? The second, following quickly behind, was that those chests couldn't be all there was to the *Emmeline*'s treasure.

His boots sank in the sand but it didn't slow him down.

He dropped onto his knees before the chests. They'd been forced open, he saw by the broken lock, but the wealth within them had been left unprotected. Why? He plunged his hand between the gems, which were warm from the sun.

"That sure isn't anything to be left about," Horace commented. He remained standing and peered over James's shoulder.

"No," James agreed, letting the pearls, rubies, sapphires, and emeralds slide through his fingers.

"Is it a trap, do you think?" Horace asked, turning toward the trees.

James heard the pistol cock. The other men who'd come did the same and a wave of clicks echoed down the beach.

"I doubt it. I'm more inclined to believe they left it thinking it to be perfectly safe."

"They didn't expect trouble?"

"No. And it's a mistake that will cost them dearly."

Horace lowered his weapon and turned back to James. "Do you believe this is all there is?"

"Absolutely not. There's more." He took the map from his pocket and read it again. "Thrice to fail." Well, there were three chests and clearly it wasn't all the treasure the *Emmeline* had left with. "Marked waterline." Hmm. James stood and went to the water's edge.

"What are you looking for?"

"A marked waterline. Have a look around. It's possible they found the rest and this is all they've carried away so far."

"But the shovels were clean, Captain."

"Yes. And if the treasure was found in water, they could be, couldn't they?"

Horace nodded. "Aye, Captain."

James looked out to sea, but saw nothing except a few crops of islands. While Horace and the men searched the beach, he went back to the chests and pulled out the map. "A lone piece." All three chests were full. He turned to the snuffbox. It didn't fit with what was before him. Coins of gold and silver, gems the color of a rainbow. And a snuff-box? It could be the lone piece, he thought. He turned it over. The glory was in the tomb.

It could be a watery grave, if the chests were found in water. It didn't necessarily mean a real grave, in a cemetery.

"Captain!" Horace called. "Over here."

James clutched both the box and the map and ran to where Horace stood on a long finger of sand.

"Over there, Captain. A cave."

James grinned. "Great work, man. Let's go have a look."

As they neared its opening, he saw the line that had been worn in the rock from the constant slap and retreat of the waves. "Marked waterline," he mumbled as he stepped into the cool, dim cave. It wasn't large and he could easily see where it made a turn at the end. He hurried to the bend.

There was nothing around the corner but a wall of rock, just as James had expected. The items, the chests, had already been recovered. "At the turn, thrice to fail." He waded through the knee-deep water back into the sunshine.

"What now, Captain?"

James emptied his boots of water, then struggled to get the wet leather back on.

"I want these chests moved to the camp we came from, two men per chest. If they could carry them, so can you. Come on, men," he said, "we have a graveyard to find."

* * *

The sun moved across the sky as afternoon wore on. It changed the angle at which its rays cut through the canopy. Where before he and Claire had been mostly in the shade, now the shadows of waving leaves danced over Claire's red hair.

She shifted, grimacing as she did. She leaned to the left. She leaned to the right. She jerked first one leg, then the other. Nate did the same. Tingles pricked at his feet, and he shifted the sword from hand to hand to ease the cramps in his fingers. He, too, tried leaning to a side, anything to ease the discomfort in his backside.

Claire flopped onto her stomach, straddled the branch. Her cheek pressed into the bark, which couldn't be comfortable. She had her arms around the branch; the sword never left her palm. She'd tucked her pistol into the back of her trousers. She sighed, and her eyes met his.

"Nate, getting shot can't possibly be worse than this."

"I'm beginning to agree with you," he said as he shifted off his left buttock. "I was thinking if we're careful and stay inside the cover of the forest, we can scout the situation, maybe get a sense of just how outnumbered we truly are."

"Amen," she said.

They held their positions a moment longer, taking the time to listen and look. Nothing moved but the sway of the canopy and the occasional patch of leaves below as some creature scampered away. Satisfied, Claire followed Nate to the ground.

By the time dusk fell, they had a better idea of where they stood. Four men watched their old camp, no doubt hoping Claire and Nate would return. A three-masted schooner bobbed in the same bay where Nate and Claire had come ashore, where Vincent was to meet them upon his return.

They'd been careful making their way to the relics of the town, keeping well back from the edge of the trees. They'd heard voices long before seeing the graveyard and had tread very lightly once they had. Using the same trick that had worked thus far, they'd climbed a sturdy tree, only going as high as needed to get an idea of what they were facing. When James's voice rang out, Claire met Nate's gaze. She wasn't happy.

James hadn't found the treasure, but his men, at least a dozen, were scouring the graveyard, reading every stone. Since James had figured the puzzle well enough to get him this close, Nate had no doubt he'd make it the rest of the way. He tapped Claire's arm to get her attention. They descended the tree and folded back into the forest.

Claire's breath whispered in Nate's ear. "They'll find it soon, Nate. If you could trip over it, so could they."

He sighed. "I know."

"You haven't changed your mind about going to camp tonight, have you?" she asked, stepping back to look him in the eye.

He touched her cheek, suddenly needing the contact. He'd expected the time on the island to be dangerous to his peace of mind, to test the limits of his attraction to her, but now everything had shifted like sand in a storm. Things were getting complicated, and if they made the wrong move, it could cost them their lives. He really wished he could hide Claire away in a cave until this was over, but he didn't want her on her own. At least if she was with him, he could protect her.

"Once they're asleep, we'll get what we need and leave

James a warning while we're at it. Then we'll head for the beach where we found the chests. With the chests gone and their ship on the other beach, we should be safe enough. But we'll have to work through the night, Claire. We need to make a fire big enough for Vincent to see, big enough for him to change his direction and too big for James and his men to put out."

"I hope Vincent is close enough to see it," Claire said.

Nate rubbed the back of his neck, which suddenly felt tight. "I hope he's the only one that is," Nate added softly.

Nineteen

James's eyes kept darting to the sky. Despite his curses, his silent will that the sun remain another few moments, it simply refused to listen. The blasted thing was about to fall behind the trees any minute now. He spun to his men.

"What the hell is taking you all so long? Find that treasure!"

"Captain?" Horace wiped the sweat from his brow with his forearm. "We've been looking for hours, sir. The men need a break."

"I don't care what they need!" James yelled. "Haven't I been right alongside them the whole of the day? Do you see these?" he asked, showing hands blackened with earth. Beneath the dirt were at least six raw blisters that burned like the devil, making his mood more sour than it already was.

"I've dug up as many graves as anyone here and we'll

keep at it until that treasure is found. Someone fetch some lanterns!" he roared.

He looked out again, swore savagely at the sun that was determined to mock him. Pink, purple, and blue filled the sky with color, but all James saw was red.

"There's a treasure here and any man that wants a part of it had better keep digging. Whoever puts down his shovel forfeits his share."

James ignored the grumblings and curses and picked up his shovel. Around him he saw his men do the same. The breeze had abandoned them in the last hour and the smell of sweat and dirt shrouded the graveyard. He hoped whoever had run off for the lanterns hurried back. Digging in a graveyard in full sunlight was one thing, but the thought of doing it in darkness made James shudder.

Claire blinked her eyes open. Nate's handsome face looked down on her, and a tender smile curved his lips. The hand that caressed her cheek was gentle.

As dusk was setting, they'd eaten a quick meal of bananas and berries then settled to wait until James's men had fallen asleep. When Nate had offered his lap, Claire had gladly used it as a pillow. She'd been exhausted from the day's events, and as Nate had said, they'd be up most of the night working under the cover of darkness.

She sat and stretched her stiff muscles. Around them night creatures buzzed and chirped. The underbrush rustled with things best not thought about. The moon was out, though the fullness of it was already beginning to wane. Still, it was mostly full, which would hopefully be more of a blessing than a curse. It would allow them to work with some light since they wouldn't dare use lanterns—even if they did steal some from camp—but it would also illuminate them once they were on the open expanse of beach. With James busy in the graveyard, and with no need for his men to be about when their ship was on the opposite beach, she and Nate were betting that they'd be safe. Considering her luck with gambling lately, Claire wasn't sure that was a smart wager.

"Is it time?" she whispered.

"I was about to check. Stay here and I'll—"

She grabbed his forearm.

He smiled, bent down, and kissed her forehead. "Don't worry, I won't do anything without you. I only want to see if it's safe to move."

She nodded, releasing his arm. As he folded into the darkness, it struck Claire that she trusted him. Not only to keep her safe, because that was simply in his nature, but also to keep his word. She smiled to herself, pulling her knees to her chest. She was still smiling when he returned and knelt beside her.

"They're asleep and the fire's low, so I think they've been asleep for a while."

"They didn't post a guard?"

"They did, but he's nearly asleep on his feet."

"Apparently they don't consider us a threat."

Nate grinned. "Only because they don't know us very well. Are you ready?"

Nerves hummed underneath Claire's skin as they crept closer to their camp. Insects buzzing in her ears, she felt some bite her hands and the back of her neck. It was a silly time to wish she once again had long hair, but the thought came nonetheless.

Soon not only could she smell the campfire smoke but she could see its glow through the foliage. Nate took her hand, pulled her up against him, and spoke low in her ear. Despite the seriousness of what they were about to undertake, her body responded to the press of his. Blood ran hot where he touched her, which was along most of her front. Even with her shirt and vest, her nipples felt his chest and beaded eagerly.

"I'll take the guard first. Don't come into the camp until you see me."

She stepped back, took an unsteady breath, and agreed. With her pistol in one hand and the sword in the other, Claire crept forward. When she was near enough to hear their snores, she dropped to her belly and dragged herself as close to the edge of the clearing as she dared, gently nudging some broad leaves out of her way.

The crates were open, the lids resting sleepily against them. Their bed held one man; the other two men lay on opposite sides of the fire and made good use of the blankets Nate had packed. *They sure made themselves at home*, Claire thought bitterly.

Dirty plates and cups had been tossed aside, attracting something furry that skittered among them. Shivers ran up Claire's spine. She'd lived in the woods a long time, but she'd never acclimated to furry things that scurried in the night. Or daylight for that matter.

Something flittered past her ear and Claire shook her head. What the devil was taking Nate so long? Had something gone wrong? Had James or another of his men come back to camp and caught Nate unaware? She slid a little closer, angling her head to hear. Fire crackled and hissed as burnt wood broke apart. Sparks danced heavenward. The men snored on. Claire came to her knees. She was going to count to twenty, and if Nate wasn't in camp by then, she'd go look for him.

A shadow moved in the trees across the camp from her. Her heart jerked. She waited, her breath catching in her chest. Branches parted and Nate stepped quietly into the open. Blood pooled from a cut on his bottom lip and the same crimson color dripped from his sword. He bent down and wiped the blade on a leaf. His pistol remained tucked into his pants.

Claire pressed her pistoled hand to her heart, sighed in relief, and came to her feet. As was agreed upon, Nate stood watch while she, being the smallest and thus more likely to creep around undetected, looked for what they needed.

Glad now that James's men had left everything open and ravaged, she eased her way to the open crates. There wasn't much left in them. The food, which had been intended for only two people—and had already been half consumed before the camp was taken over—was now gone. Her clothes were still there, as was her hat, but Claire didn't bother with those. The blankets were being used and the extra weapons and ammunition were also missing. As was the flint. She turned to Nate and shook her head.

Claire pointed to the sleeping men, then her weapon. Nate's eyes widened and he made a rubbing gesture. He wanted her to concentrate on the flint, not the pistols. Though it would surely be risky to try to get close enough to the men to unarm them, Claire didn't like knowing she was in their camp and they were armed.

She moved through the camp on silent feet. The area around the fire was nothing but ash and dying grass. Swallowing the lump in her throat, Claire went toward the dirty dishes. Even expecting it, she nearly squealed when the rodent dashed over her boots. Shuddering, Claire knelt down. A quick glance told her there was nothing in the pile she was looking for. Gladly, she stepped away. Thinking it would make sense to keep the flint near the wood pile, she made her way there next.

Clearly they had kept busy during the day by gathering wood. The pile of sticks and branches was nearly half her height. She saw it immediately—the low flames shone off the dull gray of the flint. Expelling a deep breath, Claire tucked her pistol into her pants and reached for the flint.

"Ay, you! Step a—"

Claire spun in time to see one of the men who'd slept by the fire's last words gurgle out of his throat. Nate pulled his sword free, his worried gaze meeting hers for the briefest of moments before the other two men leapt to their feet, weapons drawn.

All Claire could think of was that the men couldn't be given the opportunity to fire their pistols. If shots rang out, the sound would send James and his crew running, and she and Nate not only would miss the chance to start the fire that would signal Vincent but would also likely wind up dead.

Claire tossed her sword into her right hand and charged the man closest to her, the one who'd been sleeping on the bed she'd made. Since the camp wasn't large, she didn't have far to run. He laughed, dropped his pistol, and reached down for his own sword. When he lunged upright, Claire was upon him, her blade coming down.

The swords rang out as he parried her attack. Vibrations spilled into her hand and up her arm. He immediately riposted, his aim straight for her heart. Claire jumped back to avoid being pierced.

"Think you can best me, boy?" the man taunted.

He lunged, coming in fast and hard. The tip of his weapon rippled with the fire's reflection. With both hands on the grip, Claire caught the attack with her blade, swept her sword down in an arc, and brought it up, nearly cutting the man's ear off.

He snarled, bent his knees, and came at her even harder. Prepared, she leapt out of the way then swung her sword at his back, catching it with the end of her blade. He raged, spun, and came at her like a bullet. Their swords met over her head in a position that left Claire at a disadvantage. He pushed down on the weapons, a snarl twisting on his lips. Her back arched. Claire planted her feet, leaning her much slighter weight toward her adversary. Her arm shook from the effort to keep the position. Sweat, both from effort and from fear, ran in rivers down her neck.

Despite keeping her feet on the ground, she knew she was losing the battle of keeping her balance. She had to do something. If she lost her footing, he could easily sweep his sword across her throat. Metal clashing upon metal filled the camp, telling Claire that Nate was busy with his own opponent.

The man's rancid breath spilled onto Claire's face. "Ain't nobody helping you, boy."

He laughed, leaned in with all his weight, and shoved hard on the blades. Claire's arm flew back. The sword slipped from her sweaty palm and she stumbled back. He caught her easily, lifted her up by the shirt front, and tossed her like a sack of sand. She hit the ground hard, taking the brunt of the fall on her hip. He was there before she could move. His fist caught her on the chin. Claire's head jerked, her teeth snapped shut. The pain nearly blinded her. She fell onto her side and curled into a ball. Her hands wrapped around her knees. One slipped into her boot.

"Get up, boy," he said as he grabbed her hair and hoisted her to her feet.

White stars impaired her vision, but Claire didn't need to see his face for what she had in mind. He pulled his arm back, intent on hitting her again. His feral smile died on his lips when Claire's knife plunged into his chest. He dropped her and she scrambled away the moment he released her. He looked down at the expanding stain on his shirt, at the knife that remained plunged to the hilt into his chest, and stumbled back. He fell, dead, on the very bed he'd been sleeping on only minutes ago.

Claire wiped her mouth with the back of her hand. The trembling didn't surprise her. She'd killed before, out of necessity, and it never failed to leave her shaken. She looked up, saw Nate engaged in his own battle. Claire grabbed her pistol. She had nothing left to help him in a sword fight, but she could pull a trigger if needed.

Nate's opponent wasn't as tall but his arms were equally thick. Though the man had a gash along his cheek and another angry one down his forearm, it didn't appear to be slowing him any. Nate threw a look her way and some of the tension went out of his shoulders when his eyes met hers. He immediately shifted his attention back to his adversary.

Across the low-burning flames their swords battled in flashes of silver in a constant rhythm that, if a person wasn't watching, could be mistaken for the steady beat of someone hammering on an anvil. Claire's muscles ached simply watching them duel. Both men's faces gleamed with sweat. Their feet shuffled back and forth with each attack and parry. She didn't see either of them blink.

Suddenly Nate's opponent lunged to the side, swept his foot through the still burning coals, and kicked the red-glowing pieces at Nate. Claire gasped as they pelted Nate's pants and shirt. He didn't seem to notice. Other than a narrowing of his eyes, Nate gave no sign that he felt anything.

"That's enough playing," he said.

In a move that was little more than a blur to Claire, Nate grabbed his pistol and hurled it. The metal connected with the man's face with a sickening crunch. Claire shuddered. The man dropped his sword, pressed both hands to his nose, and groaned in agony. Blood poured from between his fingers and underneath his palms. Claire almost felt sorry for him.

Nate, apparently, didn't. He simply strolled over, grabbed his pistol, and tucked it back into his pants. Then, using his sword, he pierced the man's belly and simply watched him fall. He'd barely hit the ground when Nate turned his back and strode for Claire.

"Do you have the flint?"

She gaped at Nate for a moment, disconcerted that he could walk away so easily, without so much as a hitch in his stride or a hint of remorse in his eyes.

"I, um, no. It's over there." She pointed to the wood pile.

"Get it. I'll get their weapons."

She nodded. Once she had the cool metal in her hand, she glanced at Nate. He'd gathered their pistols and at some point had also taken her bag from the crates because he shoved them in there now. Then he walked to the man Claire had killed and stood over him a moment. With a wet, slurring noise, he pulled her knife from the man's chest. He wiped it clean and came to her again.

"This is yours?"

She nodded and took it back when he held it for her. She tucked it back in her boot, knowing the first chance she had she'd wash it properly in water. With soap.

"He didn't hurt you?" Nate asked, lifting her chin with his fingers.

Claire flinched. Now that she had a moment to think on

it, the throbbing in her jaw came back with a vengeance. Nate's eyes narrowed.

"He hit me in the jaw." Claire wiggled it, then pressed her hand to it when a bolt of pain coursed up her face.

His gaze softened. "And you'd finally gotten ridden of Sid's bruise."

He moved her hand, kissed the area tenderly. It was such a contrast to the man who'd killed so easily a moment ago. She'd known before he could be cold. Hadn't she watched him leave James in the street after knocking him unconscious? Hadn't she witnessed how cutting his words could be? But this, the easy way he'd killed, wasn't anything like what she'd seen him do before and it made Claire uneasy.

What had Nate done since the orphanage to enable him to take a life and walk away without remorse?

Where the devil is it?" James muttered. He jammed the shovel into the ground, rested his arm on the end of the shaft, and dropped his head on his arm. His back was in agony. Standing straight was no longer a possibility. He feared he'd be forever stooped like an old man.

Around him piles of freshly turned dirt were everywhere. The constant scrape of shoveling continued, though the pace was much slower than what they'd begun at. The scoops of soil that flew out of the holes his men were working in were getting smaller and smaller as the night wore on. Lanterns flickered near each open pit, but the only thing found thus far were wooden boxes filled with bones. He knew because he'd looked. After a while, they'd stopped opening them and simply lifted the caskets. The weightlessness of them was enough to tell them they didn't contain anything of value.

He shook his head dejectedly and swallowed. He grimaced at the taste of dirt in his mouth. Leaving his shovel piercing the ground, James shuffled to where he'd had the fresh water brought. He didn't take much, just enough to get the grittiness out of his mouth. He turned as two of his men ran forward. They'd been sent to the ship for more candles. If they were going to dig all night, they'd run out of light before much longer. It surprised James that they hadn't found it yet. It was a substantial treasure; they should have found some of it by now.

"Sir!"

A boy who'd only been on James's ship for near a year and was eager to please held out a fistful of candles as he ran. He'd nearly reached James when he tripped and fell. The candles went sprawling and the thinner, taller ones broke into pieces.

James never went without his weapon, and he drew it now, pointed the tip of it until it nearly touched the end of the boy's nose. Tired and frustrated, he was more than ready to pull the trigger. The boy knew it as well as his eyes went large enough to swallow the rest of his face. James drew the hammer.

The boy closed his eyes and turned his head. James chuckled and pressed the weapon hard against the boy's cheek.

He saw it then, just a breath away from the boy's nose. A rock with what appeared to be markings on it.

"Get out of my way," he growled as he lowered the hammer and put away his weapon. The lad didn't have to be told twice. He leapt to his feet and began gathering the candles, muttering his apologies the entire time.

"Blast it, shut your damn mouth!" James roared. "And somebody bring me more light!"

Within moments three lanterns lit up what James wanted to see. His fingers traced the letters on the rock. *SF.* The *Santa Francesca.* Relief poured through him like a cooling rain. He'd done it! He'd finally done it.

"Two of you go fetch the men from camp. We're going to need everyone for this."

"Alone at peace." *Well,* James thought, looking at the rock, *not any longer.*

They'd already begun digging when the same two men that had run for camp returned, alone and pale.

"Well? Where are they?"

"Dead, sir."

James steeled his mouth. He didn't need to ask how. He knew. Nate. "All of them?"

"Aye."

"Dammit!" James spun around. "Horace, post some guards. Four of our men are dead and I won't have any more die while we dig this up."

"Yes, sir."

By the time the sky was lightening with the approach of dawn, they'd unearthed the treasure. Other than stopping to catch their breath, James and his men had worked relentlessly. No man felt his tired muscles any longer. With each chest found, they became more spirited and gained more energy. Whoops of joy filled the night as piece after piece was lifted out of the ground. They used ropes and the sturdy trunks of calabash trees as leverage to heave the heavier trunks and barrels from the hole. These were set next to everything else they'd found thus far.

There were dirt-smeared metal chests and strong boxes, wooden crates with frayed ropes tied around them, and what must have been hundreds of bulging leather satchels. And there were barrels. Loads of barrels filled with glittering coins.

Better still, there'd been no trouble from Nate and the boy.

James took a deep, satisfied breath. *What the devil?* Turning, he saw the smoke and glow of flames that seemed to encompass the whole of the beach where they'd found the other three chests. It hadn't been dawn lighting the sky, it was fire.

"Holy hell," he muttered.

"Captain!" Horace came running, his dirty hands pointing.

"I've seen it."

"They're signaling their ship, sir."

James studied the orange glow. "Yes, but to what purpose, Horace? To lead their ship to that beach or to steer them away from it?"

"Captain?"

James took a deep, contemplative breath. "The fire could be a trap. If we panic and sail our ship out, is Nate going to be waiting to attack us? We know his ship isn't here, we sailed around to be sure, but there are other islands nearby. They could be within easy hailing distance. On the other hand, if we run toward the fire, it's possible his men have already arrived and are laying in wait for us."

He looked at the rows of treasure, at the casks and barrels, and cursed. Here it had been he—James—that had thought to let Nate lead him to the treasure. He'd had visions of Nate doing all the work so that he could sweep in and take it. But what if that had been Nate's plan, to let James think he'd won when all along he'd been led into a trap?

After all, it wasn't Nate that was weary from digging all

night, it was James and his crew. He cursed again. Some of the treasure would need to be carried with the aid of a travois, of which there was no time to build. And if, by some miracle, they could load the treasure before Nate's ship arrived, they had no hope of outsailing it, not with the extra weight impeding their speed.

If he took his crew to the fire, was Nate simply going to slip into the opposite bay and blast his ship, which wasn't heavily guarded? Or was his crew already hidden in the trees, waiting to execute James and his men the minute they came into view? Nate had already killed four of James's men; killing more wouldn't matter to him.

But if James ignored the fire and tried to load the treasure, there was every possibility Nate could be there, or arrive shortly, and catch them with their hands full, unable to return fire. If he split his men, sent some toward the fire while the rest dealt with the gold, all he'd accomplish would be to cut his firepower in half, thus diminishing any odds of winning. If James took all his men to his ship to wait there, Nate could slip in, load the treasure from the other beach, and James would be none the wiser.

He was damned whichever way he went. Goddammit, he wished he knew what that man was planning!

"Sir? They're here for the same reason we are."

"I'm bloody aware of that," James growled, wishing a sound solution would come to mind.

"Then wouldn't it make sense to stay here? They won't leave without the treasure any more than we will. And if we wait for them to come . . ."

"Then we've shifted the control to our side."

Yes, James liked that much better. Let Nate walk into this clearing while James and his men were strategically placed. Let Nate wonder what James was up to for a change.

"I still think we need to know what we're facing. We'll send two men over there. I don't want them to be seen, but I don't want to sit here completely unprepared either. If Nate has thirty men ashore, I want to know that. If there's a ship, I want to know that, too."

And if Nate found his men and killed them? James shrugged. Losing another two wouldn't diminish his chances.

Twenty

Claire's stomach leapt to her throat a moment before Nate went rigid beside her. Clearly he'd heard the sounds as well, the footfalls below them. Though the fire lit up the sky, its light didn't carry far enough to where they'd chosen to hide, close enough to the beach to see the water come morning, far enough away from the flames for safety.

Since they hadn't been followed in the two days since James had arrived, it struck Claire as strange that she and Nate would be searched out now, when they'd lit a signal high enough to be seen for miles. Why wasn't James concentrating on the treasure? Surely he'd found it by now.

"Don't move," Nate whispered in her ear, then he leapt from the tree.

Claire gasped. She couldn't help it. What the devil was he thinking? She held her breath as men groaned and thudded to the ground. Foliage shook, twigs snapped, and bodies rolled in the underbrush. Muted curses bruised the air. Finally she heard an exasperated whisper. "We're here to save your backside, you big lubber, not kill it."

She closed her eyes, forcing her constricted lungs to open and draw breath. It was Vincent. Claire pressed her hand to her chest, steadied herself, then jumped. She landed on someone's back, clenched her hands to hang on, then yelped when she was shoved aside.

"It's bloody rainin' bodies," the man grumbled.

"Careful who you're touching, Joe. That would be Claire."

"Blimey, sorry, lass."

Claire was on the ground, having landed hard on her own backside. She scrambled to her feet.

"How did you get here so fast?" Nate asked. More shuffling as he walked closer. "We only just lit that fire."

Claire could see nothing more than the dark outlines of men. Five or six, it was hard to say exactly.

"Vincent wanted to surprise you."

"Hell, you say. It was Luke who practically had the anchor hoisted the minute I spoke of treasure."

Luke. Claire sifted through her memories. When she remembered that Luke used to be a pirate, she wasn't as happy to be rescued as she'd been a moment ago.

"Aye, and have you found it yet, mate?"

"It's complicated, and it's the reason for the fire. We need to find a safe place to discuss this."

"We can go to the ship."

"We don't have time. Come on, there's a cave nearby."

The cave, where she'd gone to retrieve her father's skull. Yet the reminder didn't bring a sharp jab of pain, or a flood of tears, just the quiet wash of regret. If nothing else, Claire thought as she fell in line with the men, the island had at least given her that, an end to the wondering and a chance to heal.

The tide was on its way out, but the water nonetheless came to their thighs. They'd grabbed a lantern from the longboat and Nate lit it now. The end of the cave where the three chests had been came to life and Claire was finally able to see the men clearly.

There were four altogether, not counting Nate and Vincent. There was a bear of a man with grizzly hair—the one she'd landed on—a younger one with a cap of blond hair, a serious-looking man with dark hair and dark eyes, and finally—and she had to stop herself from gaping—a mustached blond man with a black patch over his left eye, a small treasure trove of gold chains around his neck, two pistols tucked into his sash, and a sword hanging in a scabbard at his side. She didn't have to be told she was looking at Luke.

The dark-haired man stepped closer to Nate, a slow smile curving his lips. "That fire's big enough to bring in the Navy. You used to be more subtle."

Nate grinned. "Things change."

"Yes, I see that."

The stranger's eyes were warm when he met hers. He extended his hand. "Blake Merritt."

Claire wiped her hand on her pants. Running and hiding hadn't allowed her the luxury of bathing. She felt dirty, and she didn't even want to think of how she must look. "Claire Gentry."

Blake nodded, then released her hand. "Pleased to meet you, Claire."

"And you. I've heard much about you."

Blake arched a brow and looked over his shoulder. Both Nate and Vincent batted their eyes at him. Blake shook his head.

"I'm afraid to ask."

Laughing, Nate drew him in for a quick embrace that included some firm backslapping. "Good to see you."

Blake turned serious, but the affection in his eyes for his friend touched Claire.

"And you. Why the fire?"

"And where's the treasure?" Luke asked.

"Patience hasn't yet come your way, has it?" Nate asked.

"Never will either," the grizzly-haired man added.

Their bickering didn't affect Nate, but it did seem to remind him he hadn't made all the introductions yet.

"Claire, this is Joe. The lad there is Aidan and this is Luke."

She acknowledged them all with a nod, though the one she gave Luke was harder to summon. He seemed to know it, because his eye narrowed.

"You didn't find the treasure?" Vincent asked. He looked from Nate to Claire, his eyes dancing. "Were you too busy?"

"Careful," Nate warned.

"We found where it was, but before we could dig it up, we were interrupted."

"Pirates?" Luke asked. He almost looked hopeful. No doubt looking for some of his own kind, Claire thought ungraciously.

"No." Nate turned to Vincent. "James. The one that followed us in Nevis."

"I thought ye said ye'd lost 'im," Joe said.

Vincent shrugged. "We had. We hadn't seen them in two days before I left Nate here."

"And they're still here?" Aidan asked.

"Far as we know. They were in the graveyard this afternoon but we haven't been back since."

Nate explained about the camp, the chests, and the map they'd left behind. "I'm sure they've found it by now."

"And either they've left with it or they're still looking for it."

"With that fire," Blake said, "they'd be fools to wait here much longer." He looked at Nate. "Did you have a plan?"

Claire had been thinking while they'd been discussing, and though it wasn't well thought out yet, she said what had come to her mind.

"They don't know you're here. They won't know until daylight breaks and they see the ship, assuming they have someone looking for it. I say we attack before they figure it out."

"I agree," Luke said nearly the moment the words left her mouth.

Nate looked at Claire and frowned. "You're not going anywhere near a battle."

Her hand stilled. "You don't have a say."

"The hell I don't."

"That's right." Claire raised her chin. "You don't. I did fine earlier, didn't I?"

"He hit you," Nate reminded her.

"Well, he didn't kill me."

Blake chuckled. "Finally met your match, I see."

"Isn't that what I told you? Claire won't put up with his overstuffed head," Vincent added.

"Well, are we going or not?" Luke asked.

"We'll need more men and weapons," Claire said and gestured around to the seven of them. "This isn't going to be enough."

Luke sneered and pulled a pistol from his sash, caressing its gleaming barrel with his other hand.

"Missy, you've got the best pirates in the Caribbean right here in this cave so show a little faith, would you?"

"Pirates?" Claire gasped, looking from Luke to Blake,

then to Vincent. Luke she knew about, but Blake, Nate, and Vincent? She looked at the men she'd just met. She couldn't imagine that the big bear of a man was a pirate. Despite his size, he seemed too gentle. And the boy? They'd turned him pirate as well? Had they no shame?

And yet, didn't it make perfect sense that Nate was a pirate? He had a ship, he was wealthier than any merchant sailor, and he was certainly fiercer than most privateers. And it explained, as well, his mercilessness in forcing her to share the treasure. Pirates always got what they wanted.

In the corner of her heart it made her wonder if that was all their time on Isla de Hueso was to him, a means to yet another treasure. Why else hadn't he told her about his being a pirate? He'd had ample time and opportunity. Or did he think, in the end, it wouldn't matter because he'd be long gone before she ever discovered the truth?

She wished she could know the answer by looking at him but his face was unreadable. His eyes were as cool as the emeralds they'd seen in those trunks. Where was the man who'd made her feel pretty and desirable?

"You're a pirate?"

"Ye've done it now," Joe muttered to Luke.

"You're not going to swoon, are you?" Luke asked.

"I've never swooned in my life and I won't be starting today."

"Claire, it's not as bad as it sounds," Vincent said.

"Hell, man, who says piracy is bad?" Luke asked, looking utterly insulted.

Claire ignored Luke and focused on Vincent. "Yet neither of you troubled yourself to tell me."

Vincent, at least, had the good sense to look ashamed.

"There's an abandoned town which lies between the two accessible beaches. It's heavily treed to get there, but it opens nicely once you reach it. We found a marked grave next to the graveyard. I say we start there," Nate said.

His dismissal of her and her feelings hurt more than the combination of both punches she'd received of late. Ignoring the sting, she decided that she could be as cold as he was.

"We're short weapons, and Nate and I are out of ammunition."

Luke grinned. "We sent a man back with the longboat. He was to bring back men and weapons. He should be there by now."

"With my stinkpots," Vincent added.

Though Luke had said there would be a longboat waiting, Claire was nevertheless surprised to see it there. She hadn't expected a pirate to speak the truth. The boat remained slightly back in the water until Vincent waved them over.

Another ten men spilled onto the beach, weapons in each hand. Luke strolled to the boat and, though it seemed impossible, loaded himself with more.

"Claire, you'll go back with the boat," Nate said.

That he had the audacity to order her about was as infuriating as the order itself.

"I'll not cower."

"Can you even fire a pistol without killing those of us who are on your side?" Luke asked.

Claire spun to Luke, her mouth tight. "Do you have this little faith in your wife?" Claire demanded, her hand on her hip and the other grasping to hold on to her temper.

Luke grinned. "Not since the first time she pulled a knife on me."

"I like her already," Claire stated and turned her attention back to Nate.

"I know how to fight and I will. I haven't plundered and stolen my way to wealth. This is my one and only treasure and I intend to fight for it."

Nate's jaw clenched.

Claire didn't linger. She skirted around Joe and Aidan and went to the boat. She should have known Nate wouldn't be far behind. Claire ignored him as she worked her way through the pistols, muskets, and blunderbusses, testing each one for weight.

"We don't have time to argue," Nate growled.

"Then stop doing it, because I'm going."

His eyes narrowed. "When I give an order to a member of my crew, I expect it to be obeyed."

"And when I'm part of a crew, I expect to be treated as such. Those men are here to fight. I'm no different."

"I beg to differ."

His eyes slid down her body, warming her even while his words infuriated her. She yanked on her arm but his fingers dug in.

"You got what you wanted from me, now let me go."

Nate's eyes flashed, then his gaze narrowed. "I wasn't the only one," he reminded her. Then he dropped his arm and stepped back.

"Excuse me," Aidan said. "These are mine."

Nate looked as surprised as Claire felt when the boy took out a bow and a quiver full of arrows.

"You know how shoot a bow?" Nate asked. "That's new."

Aidan shrugged. "Friend of mine showed me. I've been practicing for almost two years."

Nate waited for the boy to leave. His gaze locked on to Claire's for a long, silent moment before he followed Aidan back to the group. Claire wiped her hands on her pants, waited for them to steady. She hated that anger once again stood between them, but Nate needed to learn that the woman she'd become could handle herself.

She took a musket, tucked another pistol into the back of her pants, and gathered with the men. When the weapons were unloaded, the boat was sent back again. Yet this time it wouldn't be returning. It would be lifted onto the ship, which, it was decided, was going to the other beach. There were enough men on board to defend her should the other ship attack, and if the fire signaled others, they didn't want to leave evidence that there were men about.

"What's in there?" she asked Vincent. He had a bag slung over his shoulder and he was holding it as delicately as if it were a babe.

"Stinkpots. I make the worst. I only had four ready, so they'll have to do. A bit of warning, Claire, you don't want to be anywhere near them when they explode."

Dawn cast its soft light over the treasure. The fire was burning down, or at least the glow of orange wasn't as bright as it had been. Had he misjudged? Should he have spent the last two hours loading the treasure instead of waiting here for what might not be coming? James slapped the bug that was determined to fray the last of his nerves. There was a slight satisfaction in feeling it squish against his cheek.

He wished the men who'd been sent as lookouts would return with news. Just then the leaves burst open and they stumbled into the open without warning. James's fingers itched to pull the trigger despite the fact that they were his own men. Stupidity deserved to be punished.

"We almost shot you," Horace grumbled.

"You'd better have news," James warned.

"A ship, Captain, and at least a dozen men already ashore."

So it was a signal, and not a trap. Dammit, had he known, he would have begun to load the treasure.

"Are we to haul it out, sir?" Horace asked.

James shook his head. "This changes nothing. The men are already ashore. They'll be here soon enough. Have your weapons ready; we're in for a fight."

Twenty-one

As far as strategies went, it was a damn solid one. But that didn't mean Nate had to like it. He wanted Claire beside him. He didn't care that it wasn't rational thinking; he simply hated that he couldn't see her. She had a task and he didn't doubt she'd accomplish it, but what if something went wrong? He couldn't protect her if he was too far away.

"Be safe," he whispered as he crouched in the bushes.

With the early morning light bathing the cemetery, Nate could see the treasure spread out on the ground. It was even bigger than he'd imagined. Casks, chests, satchels stretched to their limit. And judging from where the expansive hole was, he and Claire had been right about its location as well.

Claire. Nate closed his eyes for a moment. When this treasure was finally behind them, he was going to talk to her once and for all. A shrill whistle split the silence. Nate immediately began to pay attention. That was Vincent's signal.

From his position in the trees behind the graveyard, Aidan let the first stinkpot fly. It exploded, and gray and black fingers of smoke rose from the open pit where the treasure had been. Nate had figured there would be men hiding in there, and he was proved right when they began screaming and struggling to get out of the pit. They shoved each other in their haste to escape the burning in their eyes and the scorching in their throats. Before they had made it out, Aidan sent another pot sailing.

That one burst with a nasty green-looking vapor. Nate winced in understanding as the men around it screamed and clawed at their eyes. Those who had been hiding behind the low wall of the graveyard leapt up and began firing weapons blindly into the forest.

Bullets burst through the trees, ripped through leaves, and pierced tree trunks with muffled whacks. Nate ducked his head and grabbed his pistol. Lying low on his belly, he aimed and fired. As he reached for another pistol, an arrow whizzed through the graveyard. It pierced a man through the wrist. He immediately dropped his weapon and howled in horror.

Nate arched an appreciative brow. Apparently Aidan had been taught well. He didn't see James, but that was fine. He'd get to him, taking his crew down one at a time if necessary. Focusing his aim, Nate fired again.

The smell of burnt gunpowder filled the air. Nate's crew was coming through the trees now, pistols and muskets in hand. Their battle cries made the hair on the back of Claire's neck rise to attention.

Nate had a musket to his shoulder. The barrel caught the rays of the ascending sun. He cocked his head, took his aim, and squeezed the trigger. Before smoke had cleared the barrel, he was running.

She'd been stationed at the other edge of the clearing, where James would go if he decided to head to his ship. It wasn't James, but three of his men were coming straight for where she hid. Claire shoved branches and leaves out of her way, aimed for the ground before them, and threw with all her might.

They knew what it was, but before they could do more than scramble for a change of direction, poisonous smoke had them coughing and falling to their knees. Some of Nate's crew stepped out from behind her and ensured those men never made it to their ship.

James's men howled, and suddenly split into two groups. One of them stayed in the graveyard and the other charged Claire and her group. Her blood pumped with nerves and a healthy dose of fear. She drew her pistols and dropped to the ground when one man took a shot at her. The bullet zinged by. She rolled, brought up her weapon, and fired. Tossing the loaded one from her left hand to her right, she pushed off from the ground.

A man was nearly upon her. Claire pulled back the hammer, but before she could fire, there was a shot. The man staggered, then swayed. Blood bubbled out of his chest and dripped from the corner of his mouth. His eyes rolled even as he stepped toward her. He died at her feet. Claire looked round. Blake nodded, tossed his spent pistol, and grabbed another.

Within moments after that, it was too late for pistols or muskets as the crew of the *Revenge* and that of James's ship intertwined, and to risk a shot would put their own in harm's way. Claire searched through the bedlam of movement, saw Nate swipe his sword, and breathed in relief.

Swords sparked and the clashing sounds of blade on blade rang over the trees. Drawing her sword from its

scabbard, Claire jumped into the chaos. A blur of movement had her swirling about, sword raised. A man's blade
clashed against hers, sending a hard jolt down her arm.
Claire pushed back with a snarl and the blades shoved
apart. Moving quickly, she thrust at her enemy and succeeded in ripping a gash into his shoulder.

Curses spewed from his lips as he lunged for Claire.
Anticipating, she jumped aside, brought her sword down
hard on his, and knocked it out of his hands. She moved in,
prepared to deliver the final blow, but Luke beat her to it,
with a rap from the butt of his pistol to her opponent's head.
Luke didn't blink, but simply spun to another opponent. He
wasn't even sweating, Claire thought, as she herself had to
wipe the moisture from her brow.

An arrow whistled past her ear. Heart in her throat,
Claire spun. Aidan was on the fringe of the madness, and
even as she watched, he notched another arrow, closed one
eye, and released his fingers. The arrow sailed straight and
true and pierced a man in the neck. Any that tried to attack
Aidan were dead before they could reach him. It was a
good thing there wasn't time for pistols to be reloaded.

Claire swung, parried, and lunged until her arm
trembled and her breath was rasping through her lungs.
The sword felt as though it outweighed her, and each time
she brought it up, it didn't go quite as high as it had the time
before. There was no chance to look around, to see where
they stood. There was only attack or be attacked instead.
Grinding her teeth against exhaustion, Claire brought
down her blade.

Nate wasn't sure, but he thought they were making
progress. He'd taken down a few already, had the blood
on his sword to prove it. He'd seen many fall, by his hand
or that of his crew's, but he couldn't help wondering how

much longer they'd have to keep this up. Sweat poured down his back and his shirt clung to the dampness.

"Holy hell!" Vincent sputtered. His round face was pale and his eyes were wide. His little chest was heaving. "Where are they all coming from?"

Before Nate could answer, he caught sight of Claire bringing down her sword, only to have her attacker swing his own in a hard circle that ripped Claire's weapon from her hand. Nate's heart took a hard jolt.

"Run!" he yelled to her, but his words were lost in the din of battle.

Shoving men aside, he fought his way forward.

He was suddenly knocked aside when the dead weight of a man fell on him. Nate lost his footing and roared in helplessness as he fell to the ground. He'd barely hit dirt before he was rearing up again.

"Are you deliberately trying to get yourself killed?" Blake asked, grabbing Nate by the back of the shirt.

"Let me go! She's in trouble."

"She's handling it," Blake argued and jerked a hand toward Claire.

Through the haze of his fear he saw her kick out, land a hard blow to her attacker's knee. Nate flinched when the joint bent unnaturally and the man toppled over. As he howled in pain, Claire grabbed her sword from the ground.

Aidan ran up. "I'm out of arrows."

"Use yer sword, lad, and don't miss," Joe spit as he screamed and charged yet another man.

Aidan hadn't needed to be told. He already had it in his hands and he used it now to deflect and parry. Then he scurried back, lowering his weapon. The man he'd been fighting growled and attacked. Aidan raced forward, slid on his hip, and kicked the man's legs out from under him.

Jumping to his feet, Aidan disarmed the scoundrel, then, for extra measure, sliced the man's hand so he couldn't hold a weapon.

Blake shoved Nate's arm. "Vincent."

Nate spun. Vincent was surrounded. Four against one, not good odds when the one being circled was a dwarf. Vincent looked particularly small all of a sudden and a cold ball of fear dropped into Nate's stomach. He ran to help.

Blake was beside him and they hit the attackers with a series of hard strikes that left no room for counterattack. Vincent moved, using his smallness as an advantage. His sword rang out as he blocked a shot. He dipped, scooped up soil from the recently dug up earth, and threw it in a man's eye. The man cursed and shook his head to dislodge the dirt. Vincent charged him and sent him flying into the open cavity.

Nate swung hard at his new opponent but the man was equally strong and he blocked Nate's attack. He grinned and began hacking in return. Nate cut a quick glance, all he could manage and not get himself cut into pieces. That's when he saw James, who was almost upon Vincent.

"Vincent!" Nate yelled.

Vincent spun, but it was too late. In horror, Nate watched James's sword pierce Vincent's right side. "No!" Nate roared when Vincent staggered and fell, his sword sliding from his hand.

Suddenly Claire was there and she charged James.

Air brushed Nate's face, forcing him to pay attention. But it was hard. In his mind he saw Vincent falling, over and over, and he felt both fear and helplessness. Driven by that fear, Nate blocked, ducked, and evaded. He hammered at the man's sword until his heart felt stretched from the effort and the grip of his weapon was slick in his hand. But he'd have revenge. Nobody hurt the people he cared about.

Blake came from behind then and knocked Nate's attacker down with a blow to the back of the head. Nate staggered and wiped his mouth.

"Vincent." He ran for his friend, Blake at his heels.

Nate dropped to his knees, was sure his heart was right there on the ground next to them. Vincent's eyes were closed and his face was still. A stain of blood, the size of a small fist, had already soaked through his shirt.

Nate ripped open the garment to better see the wound, touched his fingers to the skin near the gash.

"Holy hell," Vincent cursed, his eyes opening.

For a moment Nate had been afraid he'd never see those eyes again. His hands were unsteady as he peered at the wound.

"You're supposed to avoid the pointy end," Blake teased, but Nate heard the emotion that rocked his voice.

Vincent winced. "I'll remember that . . . next time." He sucked in a breath. "Goddamn, Nate, quit poking at it."

The bleeding was minimal. Nate breathed a sigh of relief and balanced on his heels.

"You scream like a girl," he teased, using the exact words Vincent had used on him when he'd gotten a piece of mast stuck in the back of his thigh.

Blake laughed.

"Very funny," Vincent said, already trying to get up. "Did Claire at least get the bastard?"

Claire! Nate spun round just in time to see Claire's sword get knocked from her hand. She was done, Nate could see. Her face was running with perspiration. Her shoulders drooped. Renewed energy pumped through his veins as he saw her facing James, unarmed and exhausted.

Nate jumped to his feet, reaching for the sword he'd dropped.

"Claire!"

James laughed. "Claire, is it?" he asked with a lecherous grin. Then he dropped his sword and ran forward.

And sent both himself and Claire tumbling into the open hole.

Tangled up with one scoundrel, Claire fell hard on another. Pain bright as a lightning strike rocked her body as she was pressed between them. Though they were a jumble of limbs snarled together like vines, Claire didn't attempt to reach for her knife. She couldn't, not when simply drawing a breath equaled jabbing her chest with a thousand needles.

"Get off me!" the one beneath her raged. His breath was hot and sticky in her ear and his hands were anything but gentle as he shoved at her. Each jolt brought a gasp to her lips. Her eyes watered with pain.

James grinned. "I wondered why Nate would share a bed with a boy. Now I know why." Though her breasts were small, his hands grabbed them and squeezed. Her chest felt as though she were being sliced in two. A scream rent from her lips.

"Shut your mouth!" James roared and capped a hand over it. She tasted dirt and sweat. Her stomach pitched.

Then the man beneath her bucked suddenly, and agony consumed Claire. It shattered her like glass and the world went black.

Claire's scream chilled Nate to his soul. Had she been stabbed as well, or worse? Nate jumped into the hole, the last thing on his mind the treasure that had been pulled from it. There was room only for Claire. When he saw James over her, one hand fondling her while the other cupped her mouth, Nate knew a rage he'd never experienced before in his life. He used his sword mercilessly and didn't think anything of tossing a bloodied and dying James out of the pit.

Claire's ashen face was as still as Vincent's had been moments ago.

Nate looked for wounds even as he dropped his sword and bent down. Claire was suddenly thrown aside like a piece of driftwood. The man beneath her came hurtling toward Nate. Unarmed, Nate ploughed his fist into the man's face. The resounding crack was absorbed by the dirt walls of the hole. Blood poured from the man's nose at the same time his eyes rolled into his head and he fell back.

Nate shook his stinging hand, then gently took hold of Claire and drew her onto his lap. Her moan was the best sound he'd ever heard. It meant she was alive.

"Is she all right?"

Blake loomed over the pit, his face smeared with dirt.

"Alive. How are we doing up there?"

"It's over. Those that aren't dead are cowering. Luke and Joe are organizing your crew. They'll have those left alive tied soon."

Nate released a tired breath. "Thank God. Vincent?"

"Up and about. He got lucky."

That he had, Nate thought. *And thank God for it*.

"Help me get her up, will you?"

As gently as he could manage, he scooped Claire into his arms, taking a moment to press his forehead to hers. She was too small to be in such a battle. And two of the people who meant the most to him had been hurt.

"Pass her to me." Blake was sitting on the rim of the hole, his arms ready.

Nate blinked, then nodded. Easing up, he held out his

arms as far as he could. Blake curled his own beneath Claire and lifted her out. Nate followed immediately after. A quick glance showed James's men being gathered. The ground had more than a dozen bodies lying dead on its grassy surface and he could only be glad that Vincent and Claire weren't among them. He hovered as Blake set Claire down on the ground. Vincent knelt on her other side.

Nate began searching Claire for injuries. It terrified him when he couldn't find any. He'd heard of stomach injuries bleeding in the body and feared for Claire. If it was something like that, then there wasn't a thing they could do for her. A doctor was too far away and the ship's carpenter was good for stitches, perhaps even sawing off a limb if gangrene took it, but nothing as complicated as opening a body.

His hands trembled around from her back, went up one leg then the other. He skimmed his hands over her chest. Her skin was warm, and beneath his fingers he felt the steady rhythm of her heart. When he moved to her ribs, her eyes shot open like bullets.

"Dammit!" she cursed.

Nate hung his head, fisting his hands to hide the shaking.

"About time you woke up," he said, deliberately keeping it light.

"Is it over?" she asked. Though her face was tight with pain, her eyes were clear as the sea. He'd never seen anything as stunning in his life.

"It is."

She closed her eyes. "It hurts to breathe."

"Ribs?" he asked.

She nodded. "James must have cracked some when he landed on me." She opened her eyes. "How's Vincent?"

"A little sore," the dwarf answered from her side.

She turned her head and smiled. "Just a little?"

"Judging by the way he screamed," Blake teased, "I'd say it hurt quite a bit."

"To hell with you both," Vincent growled.

Nate forced a grin, cutting his eyes to Vincent's side. Vincent had his hand pressed over it, but Nate didn't see any blood seeping between his fingers.

"We'll get you two settled on the ship while we load the treasure," Nate said.

"Those alive are contained," Aidan said as he walked over. He frowned at Vincent's wound. "You all right?"

"He was just looking for a way out of working and got himself stabbed to do it."

Aidan smiled. "I suppose that's effective."

Nate looked at him. When he'd first met Aidan, the boy was thirteen and filling into the man he'd become. Standing tall and strong at sixteen, blond hair falling over brown eyes, face dried with dirt, there wasn't much of the boy left. And the man he was becoming sure knew how to shoot a bow.

"That was some work you did with the bow."

Aidan smiled. "They won't always work in a battle, but they did all right today."

"That they did. We have a camp set up through there." Nate pointed to the trees and the narrow path that led to their camp. "Bring someone with you. Take back whatever is useful."

Aidan nodded and left.

"Let's get Claire and Vincent to the ship, and we'll load the treasure afterward."

"And what of the other ship?"

Luke strolled forward, wiping his pistol with the sash that hung from his waist. He was as dirty as the rest of them, but unlike Nate, who felt he could sleep for three days straight, Luke looked ready to go at it again.

"What about it?" Nate asked.

"You don't need it, Luke. You build better ships than that one," Blake commented.

"Aye, I do, but it's a shame to let it sit here."

Nate crossed his arms over his chest. "You've obviously a plan for it. What is it?"

Luke grinned, tucking his pistol back into his sash. "I'll take her to Port Royal, sell her to the highest bidder."

"You already charge a bloody fortune for one of your ships," Blake argued.

"Aye. And they're worth every penny."

Nate shook his head. "I don't care. Take the ship and as many men as you need. We'll load the treasure onto the *Revenge* and head for Santo Domingo."

Vincent came to his feet, swaying a little. "I'm all right." He held up a hand as Nate reached for him. "Just got up too quickly. I thought we were heading to Port Royal. Alicia and Samantha are expecting us."

"Luke is going there anyway. He can bring Samantha, Alicia, and the children back with him. My house is big enough for everybody and it'll take time to sort through this treasure."

And then, he thought as his gaze lowered to Claire, there were some discussions to be had.

Claire refused to be carried. There was enough to do without being tended to and fussed over. Granted it felt as though she were being poked with a red-hot iron, but she didn't see how being carried and jostled about would be any better. At least this way, she was in command of her own steps, slow as they were.

"How are you doing?" Vincent asked. He was keeping pace with her, and from the glance she cut him, she saw he was as pale and weak as she felt.

"I'm panting like a dog, and every breath hurts, but otherwise I'm fine."

He agreed with a sharp nod of his head. "I know exactly what you mean."

They made it to the beach. Joe, who'd hurried ahead, dropped his load of treasure and helped Claire into the longboat.

"Easy, lass," he said.

She ground her teeth, scrunching her eyes against the pain. Water splashing drew Claire's attention. She looked up into Nate's gaze. There was a steeliness there, a determination that reminded her of what he was. A pirate. In enough pain already, Claire turned away.

Nate plunged the oars in, leaned back as far as he could, and pulled with all his might. She'd looked at him differently just now, and he knew it had nothing to do with her injuries. She was upset about his being a pirate. He wasn't sorry he'd ever become Steele and hoped when he explained it to Claire, she'd understand his reasons.

Claire's eyes were downcast now, her teeth firmly pressed into her bottom lip. She was in agony. Her hand curved around her middle, her face was pale. She was bent forward and he could hear her sharp breaths when a particularly fierce stab of pain hit her.

Nate sliced the oars into the water again, determined that somehow he was going to find a way to make Claire understand. Once she was settled, the treasure loaded, and they were on their way, he'd explain. Surely she must care enough for him to see his reasons. Hell, she'd better. Because the alternative, at this point, didn't bear thinking about.

Despite Vincent's heated arguing, Nate settled him in his cabin then trudged back to the main deck, two items in hand. Claire had refused to share the cabin with Vincent, claiming the fresh air would do her good. There was plenty of room and he could have made her a comfortable bed on the floor or the table if it was a hard surface she was after.

Nate had seen through that bloody excuse but he knew she wasn't up to arguing. Since it would only disturb her to have the lifeboat dripping onto her when they lifted it back on deck, she'd agreed at least to make her bed at the bow of the ship, near the windlass. He stepped around the guns and knelt at her side. Though she no doubt heard him, she kept her eyes closed. The slight only added to his irritation.

"I thought you could use this," he said, holding up a bottle of amber-colored rum.

Her eyes opened, saw the bottle.

"It'll take the edge off the pain," he explained.

Nodding, she agreed. "Thanks, I'll have some in a bit."

Nate snarled. He knew what the bloody hell she was up to, and he refused to allow her to cause herself any more pain. He set the bottle down with a jolt hard enough to draw her attention but not enough to break the bottle.

"I know you're used to doing things alone, but I'll be helping you with this whether you like it or not."

"Nate!" she gasped as his arm went around her back.

"Shut up and sit up. I'll not wait until you're alone to muddle through by yourself. I'm offering the help, so be grateful enough to take it."

Her lips flattened and Nate knew it was as much from pain as anger toward him. Good. He didn't care. As long as he could ease her suffering.

Her shallow breaths had him keeping his touch as gentle as possible as he eased her into a sitting position. Then he passed her the bottle.

"More," he ordered after she took only the smallest of sips.

Her eyes flashed but she brought the bottle back to her mouth and drank two deep swallows. Satisfied, he took the bottle she passed him.

She had a trickle of rum sliding from her lips and Nate's stomach clenched into a fist when her tongue slipped out to lift the liquid away. It hadn't been that long, he thought, since that very tongue had been in his mouth. Had been on his body.

Her irritated tone ripped him from his memories. "You can set me down now."

"Not yet. We're binding those ribs."

Her eyes shot teal fire. "I'm in enough pain, thank you."

"I've had sore ribs once or twice. Binding helps."

"I don't need it."

She moved to get away from his touch, but cried out when the pain sliced through her.

"You don't have a say in the matter," he growled. Keeping one hand at her back, the other went to the buttons on her shirt.

"If you move," he warned because he'd felt her muscles tense, "it'll only take longer and hurt you more. Besides, you don't want me to do this once the crew is back, do you?"

A blind man couldn't have missed the scathing glare she shot him. Ignoring it, Nate undid the buttons and eased her shirt open. Because he was a man, he took a moment to linger on the gentle curve of her breasts and the saucy nipples that puckered for him.

"You're lovely. It'll be a shame to bind them." Angry or not, the words spilled from his lips.

"I doubt anyone will notice the difference," she muttered.

His eyes slid to hers, and saw that she believed her words.

"I don't recall complaining."

"Just get it done," she said as a beautiful flush covered her body.

"You can't deny what your body feels, Claire." Nate took the length of cotton he'd brought up along with the rum. Keeping one end on her back, he circled the cloth around her torso. She kept her arms away from her sides and he knew it was costing her by the lines that carved around her mouth.

"I've learned that both the heart and the body can be easily tricked. Better to listen to my head."

"And what's your head telling you?" he asked.

"That men, and pirates specifically, can't ever be trusted to tell the truth."

He bit back a curse, then tied the end of the cloth into a tight knot. He eased her shirt back into place but she refused to let him help with the buttons. It killed him to watch her suffer through the task, but he kept his hands at his sides.

When she was done, he helped her lie down, despite her protests, then covered her lightly with a blanket. Her eyes closed again, but he refused to be so easily dismissed.

"We're going to talk, Claire."   .

"I've had as much pain as I can take for one day. Go away."

"Claire—"

"Go get my treasure, Nate. That's all I need."

As he stood and stared over her, he began to fear exactly that.

Twenty-two

Never thought I'd see the day," Blake chuckled.

"Oh, God, not you as well."

"Did you think I'd let this pass? After the misery you gave me over Alicia?"

"That was Vincent. I stayed out of it."

"Did you now? Which time? When you told me I should give her my cabin and sleep with the crew myself? When you offered to show her my ship for the sole purpose of getting me jealous enough to do it instead?"

Nate laughed. "Worked, though."

Blake took one end of a chest and Nate grabbed the other. They followed the others around the cemetery to the path that led to the beach.

"Shall I ask Alicia to start sewing some booties for the little Nates to come?"

Nate fumbled the chest, moving his foot an instant before the chest came crashing down on it.

Blake lowered his end, placed a boot on it, and laughed until he nearly fell over.

"Hell." Nate rubbed a hand over his face. Then again until his stomach didn't feel inside out any longer. "Hell, don't do that."

Blake wiped his eye with the back of his hand. "Scary, isn't it, being in love?"

"Who said that's what this is?" Nate asked warily.

Blake rolled his eyes. "You went pale as dawn, almost took out your foot at the mention of babes. If it wasn't serious, you'd simply have told me to go to Hell."

"Go to Hell."

"Too late." Blake grinned.

Nate sighed, then took hold of his end of the chest. "I've loved her since I was fifteen."

It was Blake now who stumbled. "Fifteen?"

"It's a long story, and one you've never heard. You will," he promised, feeling better about his past than he ever had, "over a cup of rum in the galley. With Vincent."

"Your past, Nate, isn't our business, no matter how much it would thrill Vincent to know it. Besides, you never knew mine until I met Alicia."

"Are you saying it's the women making us soft?"

Blake laughed. "Don't tell Luke that."

Nate knew better than that. Though Luke was happily married to Samantha, his pride was renowned, and he wouldn't take to being thought of as less than the fierce pirate captain he used to be. "Wouldn't dream of it," he answered with a chuckle.

"I thought we were loading treasure?" Luke asked when he came back for another load.

Blake and Nate looked at each other and grinned.

"We're coming," Blake chuckled.

Aidan suddenly burst into the clearing. "A ship, Nate, coming in to the other beach."

Nate scrubbed his face. He hadn't thought to send someone to look; he'd been too worried about Claire and Vincent. He was damn impressed the boy had had the forethought to do it for him.

"How close?" Luke asked.

"Close enough to know she's not friendly."

Luke grinned. "Black colors?"

Aidan shook his head. A smile hovered on his lips but didn't take full shape. "Possibly."

"Do we have time yet?"

"Enough to sail around to that beach before they drop anchor."

Luke slapped Aidan on the back. "That's my boy." He turned to Nate. "I'll take the other ship now," Luke said immediately. "Joe, Aidan, and I will go, lead them away while you finish with this treasure. They've no reason to think there's more than one ship here. They'll follow us easy enough, though I'll accept your offer and take a few extra men with me."

"Take whatever you need, Luke. I appreciate this. You're sure you can handle it if they decide to fire at you?"

"Bloody hell, Nate, I'll pretend you didn't insult me." Luke shot a look at Aidan. The boy's face was brighter than the fire that had signaled him. They both grinned and raced off. They grabbed Joe as they passed and dragged him along.

"It's scary, isn't it, how much Luke loves this?"

"Not as scary as it is to see Aidan gnawing to be a part of it. How does Samantha feel about that?"

"Scares her to pieces, but she loves the boy and she knows she can't stop him."

Nate watched Aidan's long strides carry him into the forest, where the jungle swallowed him.

"No, I'm sure she can't," Nate agreed.

Things must be really dire if he's talking," Vincent teased. "You're not dying, are you, Nate?"

Nate had decided to have their ritual of drinking rum before retiring in his cabin rather than the galley, figuring Vincent would be more comfortable lying down. Vincent was on his left side, propped pillows and rolled blankets at his back. Though he'd yet to regain all his color and bruises darkened the skin beneath his eyes, the wound didn't seem to bother him much.

"He must heal fast," Blake said from the chair next to Nate's, "if he's able to badger you like before."

"It's ingrained in his nature," Nate said.

"Damn right," Vincent answered.

Tired, Nate buried his face in his hands. It had taken hours to load the treasure, turning a long day into an even longer one. He really wanted nothing more than to sleep, but he'd come to the decision to tell his friends about his past and he would stick to it.

"I think he's scared," Vincent whispered.

Nate peered at him through his fingers. Vincent's head was resting on his pillow, his hands clasped loosely before him. A grin curved his lips.

"Only thing I've ever been scared of is your singing."

The grin shone in Vincent's eyes. "If you say so."

Nate shook his head. He lowered his hands, clasping them between his spread knees.

"I murdered a man when I was four," he began.

He told the story as he'd told Claire, only this time he added the truth about Sam Steele to the telling.

"When I saw the opportunity to be Steele, I jumped at it. I'd never owned anything before, and even though I had money, thanks in large part to you," he added with a nod to Blake, "I wanted more. A chance to lead, to own a great ship and to be in command. I wanted, just for one bloody time, to be in control of my own destiny."

"You didn't tell Claire about Steele, did you?" Vincent asked.

Nate scoffed. "Much as I enjoy Steele and have never regretted it, it isn't something you bandy about in polite society."

Vincent arched a brow and Nate knew he was referring to Claire's life and the fact that she posed as a man. She wouldn't, not by anyone's standards, be considered "polite society." A fact that didn't bother Nate in the least.

"Nate, if you love her, you have to tell her."

He thought of her coldness earlier, how she'd cut herself off from him. How much it had hurt. What he'd felt when he'd touched her.

"I plan to tell her, though I'm not sure if she'll listen, or if the damage can be repaired."

"Take it from someone who learned the hard way and almost lost the woman he loved because of it—tell her everything. There's no future between you otherwise and you'll always wonder, if you don't, if it would have made a difference if you had."

Nate turned to Blake and shot him an incredulous look. "That's awfully philosophical of you."

Blake grinned. "I've always been the smartest."

Nate shook his head. "Maybe the most egotistical."

"Actually," Vincent cut in, "that would be you."

"The hell it is."

"No, really, it is," Blake confirmed.

"Wait until Vincent becomes Steele, then you'll know what a big ego truly looks like."

Blake gaped at Nate, then nearly wrenched his neck turning to Vincent.

"You might want to close your mouth. I can see what you had for breakfast," Vincent chuckled.

Blake shut his mouth and turned to Nate. "Since when are you not going to be Steele? Since you found Claire again?"

"No. I was considering it even before then."

"He wants to settle down and live a good, respectable life," Vincent teased.

Blake grinned now. "I have a hard time seeing it."

Nate grumbled at his choice of friends. Blake roared, then faced Vincent.

"And you want to take over? Why? Samantha's safe."

"I'm not doing it for her any more than Nate did. I'm doing it for myself."

"He'll do a damn fine job of it," Nate said.

Blake pressed a hand to his forehead, a sure sign he was under duress. After a few long moments and deep breaths, he dropped his hand and shook his head.

"I brought you two aboard my ship as respectable sailors on a privateer's vessel and now look at you. Bloody pirates, the both of you."

Looking at Vincent, Nate grinned.

"Sounds fine to me. How about you?"

Vincent winced as he made himself more comfortable then smiled as well.

"I've never heard of a finer idea," he concurred.

* * *

The wind snapped the sails and howled its way down the deck. It ploughed its invisible fingers through her hair. Standing at the bow, Claire raised her face to it, let it wash over her. In the western sky, the bruise of color was breathtaking. Purple battled with pink for domination. Orange struck out, not to be outdone. Though the sun was gone for the day, it had made certain to leave its mark behind.

Too windy to risk lighting a fire in the galley for the evening meal, their supper consisted of fruit, bread, and water. She'd certainly had worse fare in the years since leaving her husband but she had no appetite. The crew members who weren't seeing to duties had spread along the gunwale, devouring the food that filled the plates resting on their laps. Claire did nothing more than shove it from the back of her plate to the front.

"You need to eat, my dear," Vincent said.

"I'm not hungry."

He nodded. "I wasn't either. But Blake and Nate hovered like women until I ate some."

Her lips twitched. "I don't imagine they'd like knowing you compared them to women."

His grin was mischievous. "No, they surely wouldn't."

"Here, I'll take that." He took her plate, bent, and set it on the deck. When he straightened, he wavered.

Claire reached out and grabbed his arm. Her own world spun when the sharp pain felt as though someone were slicing her chest open with a spoon.

"I'm all right." He steadied himself by grabbing the gunwale.

Claire looked pointedly where she knew he'd been stabbed but couldn't see anything with his large vest hanging off his shoulders. "Is it bleeding? Did you need to have it closed?"

Vincent shook his head. "It seems to have stopped. Or mostly so. Don't fuss, Claire."

She squeezed his arm before releasing it. "It's nice to have someone to fuss over," she said.

She'd tried remaining angry with Vincent but hadn't been able to hang on to her anger where he was concerned. She hadn't given her body—and despite her better judgment, her heart—to Vincent. It wasn't he who had explaining to do. It was Nate.

"Why don't you try fussing over Nate?"

She turned back to the sea. "The time for that is passed."

"Is that why you're both glum?"

"I'm not glum, I'm tired." Though she hadn't done anything all day but try to find a blessed position that didn't bring agony, she was bone weary. If she was honest with herself, she'd admit she wouldn't have slept much anyhow.

"I hope you'll let him explain, Claire. He may be a big lubber, but he's a good sort."

"I'd expect you to defend him. He's your friend."

"'Course he is, and like you, I don't have them in great number either. I don't like to see my friends hurting."

"It'll pass when they heal," she said, placing her palm over the bandaged ribs. She had to admit, while the pain could still bring tears to her eyes, the binding had helped a little.

"I'm just asking you to hear what he has to say," he urged, suddenly looking weary.

"I can do my own talking." Nate had come up beside them. He didn't look happy to know they'd been discussing him.

"I'll leave you, then. Good night, Claire."

Nate placed a hand on Vincent's shoulder. "Get some rest."

Vincent nodded and walked away.

"Is he all right?" Claire asked. "He seems fragile and weak."

Nate was watching his friend's progress as well and waited until Vincent had disappeared into his cabin before facing Claire.

"It's a stab wound. I imagine it's sore, but the bleeding is mostly stopped and there wasn't much there to begin with."

"He almost fainted."

Nate frowned. "Just now?"

"He set my plate down, and when he stood up, he swayed as though he were fainting."

"Dammit. He did that when it first happened as well. I thought it was only the shock of the injury." He looked back down the deck. "I'll keep him confined to that damn bed if I have to. I told him he shouldn't be about the ship."

It must be really something, she thought with a pang of envy, *to have such a strong bond of friendship.*

Nate looked back to her, then down at her plate. "You didn't eat."

Because she knew it would be agony to shrug, she didn't attempt to. "I'm not hungry."

"You're as bad as he is," Nate grumbled, then took a step closer and peered into her eyes. "How bad is the pain?"

"I could do with more rum if you can spare it."

He nodded. "I'll be back." He scooped up her plate as he passed then handed it to one of the men who showed interest in it.

Claire sighed. She'd never been one to depend on the drink to see her through her troubles. If she were, she'd have spent most of the last few years drunk. Still she knew

Nate's presence meant he wanted to talk, and she figured the extra fortification the rum would give wouldn't hurt.

Her thoughts were heavy when he came back and passed her a small tankard of rum.

"Finish it. Then maybe you'll be able to sleep."

"If I finish this, I'll be out for three days."

His hand cupped her cheek. "Then at least you won't be in pain."

She stepped out of his touch. "Not all pain is physical."

"No, but it can be healed. All I ask is that you listen, Claire."

Claire looked into the rum, nodding. And as he began to talk, she sipped.

"I'm Sam Steele."

She choked on her rum. It burned in her throat and on her tongue. She fought the urge to cough because she knew the pain of doing so would bring her to her knees. She took slow breaths, her eyes watering, until the desire passed. Taking an unsteady breath, she wiped at her eyes.

"Sam Steele?" she squeaked.

Nodding, he watched her closely and explained. His reasons were as just and fair as any that could explain a man's decision to turn to piracy. Bad luck, a need to rise above the past. But she'd had the same reasons, and though a ship had never been a possibility, the chance to turn pirate had been real. And it had tempted her, the gold and the silver, the fistful of coins. She'd made her life harder by not taking that road, but it had never been one she'd regretted.

She swallowed more rum. The warmth of it flowed through her veins. It may have helped dull the truth of his words, but there wasn't enough in her tankard to take them away.

"You're not sorry."

"No," he said without hesitation. "I'm not."

"How many lives were taken, Nate, for you to get rich?"

He flinched, then set his mouth into a hard line.

"That's all you heard, isn't it? Of everything I said, you're only concerned with the fact that I was a pirate."

"Not was, is. And Sam Steele is not any pirate. Many men have died at Steele's hand."

"Sam Steele wasn't always me."

"Which changes nothing. Once you sailed away and made certain everyone knew Sam Steele was back and that it couldn't conceivably be Samantha, you could have stopped. Yet three years later you're still doing it. For what, Nate? You're richer than you need to be.

"I had nothing either. I was alone and miserable. Piracy loomed before me many times, like a shining jewel I could reach out and grab. If I did, my misery would be over. One good plunder, I figured, and I could leave, go back to a life of respectability." She swirled her rum, drank a little.

"But I knew it wouldn't work. I'd lost enough self-respect marrying Litton, I wasn't about to lose the little I had left by turning to piracy."

Nate's eyes hardened. "Yet you thought nothing of trying to steal the map from me at gunpoint, or again later when you came into my cabin and took it off my person. Does the line of right and wrong only include piracy?"

Her chin shot up. "I knew it was wrong, but I didn't trust you with it. I knew you wouldn't give it to me, that you'd do everything to keep me from what I wanted most."

His voice softened. "There was a time I believed it was me you wanted most."

Claire gripped her tankard against the effect of his words.

"For a time you were."

"Ah. But no longer. I see." He tapped the gunwale with his fingers and sighed heavily. "You showed me different on Isla de Hueso. There was no pretending there, not for either of us."

Because he was right, and she wouldn't lessen what they'd done with a lie, she remained silent.

"Yet you wouldn't have lain with me had you known I was a pirate." He watched her. "I have no problem with who I've become, Claire."

No, she already knew that, and in some ways, she envied him for it.

He scraped his hands over his face. "Claire, the more I gained, the more I wanted. No treasure was ever big enough, no plunder too rich. I'm not an extravagant man. I've set most of it away." He turned to the sea, drew a deep breath. "I guess because I had nothing for so long, I always think something will happen and I'll be back where I started. I saved most of it." He faced her again, the sunset catching the shadows in his eyes.

"I'd planned to be done with Steele after the treasure was found. I already have a house to live in. We're going there now." He smiled. "I think you'll like it. It would make a nice home for us."

Claire's breath stuck inside her chest. They were the words she'd yearned for, but they were eight years too late. "Too much has changed, Nate. We're not those children anymore."

"No, and I've no regrets about that either, Claire." He placed one large hand over hers. "I built the house because I was planning to forgo Steele. I'd never dreamed you'd be back in my life, but now that you are"—his hand slid up her arm and curved warmly around her neck—"I want to share it with you."

He'd promised her that once, when they were younger and she'd believed him with her whole heart and soul. But it was as she'd told him—she wasn't that girl any longer. She'd been let down by too many people, had them break their promises to her at each turn, or worse, betray her trust. Claire placed her forearms on the gunwale, the tankard safe within her hands. She was determined to keep her heart as safe.

"There's no future, not with us. You could have come to me when you'd learned I was engaged, but you ran. You could have told me everything when we made love, but you didn't. We don't have trust between us and I refuse to put myself in a position where I'll be disappointed and hurt yet again."

Nate yanked his hand away. Cold air replaced the heat of his touch but it wasn't why she shivered. It was the stiffness of his stance and the fury in his eyes.

"You've been waiting for me to fail from the beginning. It's my fault you married another man, it's my fault you have to share the treasure, and it's my fault for being a pirate."

He shoved off from the gunwale. The air swirled angrily as he paced. Claire turned, and was blasted by the fierceness of his gaze.

"You're scared to trust your heart, so be honest enough to admit that. You expect honesty of me, yet you cower behind excuses."

She tossed what was left of her rum into the indigo sea.

"Where has my heart ever led me that was worth going? And if I frustrate you so much, you're welcome to leave."

He came at her so fast she'd barely had time to blink and suddenly he stood before her, drawing her chin up with the pressure of his thumb and forefinger.

"You think I'll fail you, like your father did, like Litton did, and like you believed I had. Well, I won't. If you want to run, run. But you'll go knowing it's of your own doing."

His mouth captured hers in a searing kiss. His teeth nipped, his tongue demanded. Claire's thoughts scattered. Every thought but that of him. In that moment, he was her world, her very breath. She let him ravish her mouth and ravished his at the same time. Heat exploded in her chest that had nothing to do with her injury. His tongue swiped at hers, swept her mouth. A strong hand held her back tenderly while his mouth plundered until her knees trembled from the onslaught and every bone felt as if it were melting.

He ended the kiss as fast as he'd started it. Claire stood disoriented a moment. Then her eyes cleared and she met the deep green of Nate's.

"That kiss was no lie." He stepped back. "When you've come to your senses about our future, you've only to find me."

Twenty-three

Claire had yet to come to her senses. He'd figured, by morning, she would. But that had been two days ago, and though she answered when spoken to, and did it so damn politely it made him want to plow his fist into something, she hadn't thrown herself in his arms and begged his forgiveness. Nor had she admitted to loving him.

Nate yanked on a rope, coiled it tightly, and wished women could be as easily maneuvered. What else could he do? They'd be in Santo Domingo tomorrow and it scared him to think what would happen. Once the treasure was sorted out, she could go anywhere. She was certainly independent and hardheaded enough to do whatever the hell she wanted. Save tying her up, there wasn't much he could do about that.

The hatch to his cabin banged open and every man on deck, as well as Claire, spun round. Only Blake's head and shoulders cleared the hatch; the rest remained in the cabin.

"Nate!" Blake's brown eyes looked wild. "We've got trouble."

Nate ordered a crewman to the helm and raced down the ladder of his cabin. Blake was at Vincent's bedside. Vincent appeared asleep. Yet there was enough of Blake's anxiety thickening the air to make Nate's stomach clench in fear.

"What's wrong?"

"I can't get him to eat. He's barely drinking. When he tried to sit up, he fell over. Said the cabin was spinning. And he's fallen asleep again."

Fear slid along Nate's spine. Vincent had been sleeping a lot. "It's been two days. He hadn't lost enough blood to be dizzy nor this weak."

"Not that we know of," Blake concluded, saying the words that had entered Nate's own mind. If he wasn't bleeding out, then that meant he was bleeding in.

"Jesus," Nate said. Feeling his knees weaken, he grabbed a chair and sank into it. He looked at the dwarf's still face, at the paleness that had taken over the normally bronze skin. Vincent may have been in his mid-twenties, but he looked young as a boy lying there.

At the end of the day, he and Blake remained at Vincent's bedside. Vincent had woken up, given them grief for all too brief a time, then had fallen asleep again. Nate had gone on deck, had informed the crew of Vincent's injuries, and had given his orders. By whatever means possible, they were to get to Santo Domingo as fast as possible, not an easy trick with a ship burdened with treasure. He'd stayed on deck long enough to see that every sail was rigged and working. Now, in the small cabin, silence reigned. It bounced off the walls louder than cannon fire. The candles that flittered on the table added light, but they didn't add hope.

Blake poured more rum into their tankards.

"The winds are high, we're making good time," Blake said.

Nate swirled the amber-colored liquid, then scoffed when he realized his thoughts were doing the same thing, going round and round and not accomplishing a damn thing.

"Will it be enough?"

Blake looked as worried as Nate felt. Lines creased his forehead and bracketed his mouth.

"I don't know."

"He's bleeding inside and I don't know how to fix it. If I did . . ." He bared his teeth and sucked in a breath. "If I did, I'd have opened him up, but I don't want to make it worse."

Though Blake nodded in agreement, it went unsaid that they were thinking the same thing. Could it get any worse than it already was?

"God," Blake said, pressing his fingers into his eyes. "I'm scared he won't hold on long enough for us to get him help. Alicia will be devastated if he goes without her saying good-bye."

Nate smiled despite the fist that squeezed his heart. "He has a soft spot for Alicia."

Blake met his gaze. "And she for him. And from what I've been able to see, he also has one for Claire. For a little man, he sure can get under the skin and stick there."

Because he needed time to fight back the surge of emotion that wanted to douse him, Nate took the time to drink. Then setting the tankard down, he looked to the bed where Vincent lay resting. Nate held his breath until he saw the covers rise and fall with Vincent's breaths.

"You wouldn't have it any different," Nate whispered and felt Blake's gaze shift to the bed as well.

"No," his friend answered quietly. "I sure as hell wouldn't."

By midafternoon the next day, Claire was beyond exhausted. Her shoulders drooped no matter how she fought to keep them straight. Her eyes felt as though they'd been washed in sand and her nerves were strung tighter than the ropes that held the sails. She hadn't seen Blake or Nate since yesterday and the fear and worry were eating her alive. She paced, cursed, prayed. She was ready to gnaw on the gunwale by the time Nate stepped from the hatch.

Every hand stilled, every pair of eyes latched on to Nate. He looked at his crew, shook his head slightly. "He's weak, but he's with us."

Claire pressed a hand to her heart, then bowed her head as tears filled her eyes. Vincent was alive. She'd cling to that, cling to any scrap of hope she could.

It surprised her when Nate strode directly to her.

"Vincent wants to speak with you."

Claire saw nothing in his eyes but weariness and worry, yet she couldn't help wondering if Nate held her as accountable for Vincent's wound as she held herself. He'd been hurt over the treasure and she'd been on enough ships to know that the weight of the treasure was slowing them down and could keep them from reaching a doctor in time.

"Thank you," she said when he held the hatch open for her.

His gaze lingered on her and she couldn't help herself. He was hurting and she hated to see the haunting look in his eyes. She took his free hand and squeezed it.

"It's a good sign he's talking, isn't it?"

Nate shook his head, sighing heavily. "I hope so. But I don't know."

He didn't acknowledge her touch and she dropped her hand. More guilt settled over her, pressing even harder on her already tired shoulders.

Nate waited until she'd stepped down then gently closed the hatch over her head.

It surprised her how bright the cabin was. Perhaps because the circumstances were so dire she'd expected it to be dim and gloomy. Instead, sun and its reflection off the sea beamed into the window and spread both its heat and its cheer into the room.

"Don't stay long," Blake said as he moved from the table that filled a corner. "He's tiring easily."

"I won't," she promised.

He took a chair with him as he stepped forward and placed it close to the bed for her. "Sit before you do yourself any more damage."

The look he gave her didn't brook arguing and she eased herself onto it. She managed to hold the hiss of pain until he'd left.

"Are you in much pain?"

Claire swallowed hard, pushing the agony aside as Vincent's face turned toward her.

"Only a little."

His grin was weak, but for Claire it was the brightest smile she'd ever seen, and she gazed at it hungrily, committing it to memory.

"You're a terrible liar," he said.

Because his hand was near her knee, she grabbed it, trying not to squeeze it too hard as feelings overwhelmed her. "Can I do anything for you? Do you need anything?"

He sighed. "There's so much I wanted to do."

Tears pricked at her eyes and she blinked furiously to clear them.

"You'll have the time."

"We both know different." He closed his eyes and rested a moment. "You need to help Nate."

"What can I do?"

"Blake has Alicia." He smiled again. "She's something, our Alicia. But Nate has nobody. He'll need you."

"Please." Claire brought Vincent's hand to her cheek. "I heard Blake say we'll reach Santo Domingo before nightfall. Don't give up."

"A doctor can't help me now."

Claire squeezed her eyes shut. Her chest ached with the denial she wanted to scream from her lungs until it changed the truth.

"I'm sorry."

"For what, my dear?"

"It should be me, lying there. You wouldn't be hurt if it wasn't for me and the map, if I hadn't come into your life."

"I'm not sorry for that."

Claire couldn't stop the tears now.

"Don't cry."

"I know we haven't known each other long, but I've come . . ." She turned her head and wiped her cheeks. "You're a friend, Vincent, and look what I brought upon you."

"You made me smile, you gave me friendship." He sighed. "I wish I could have met a special woman the way Blake and Nate have."

"Rest," she whispered. She ignored the pain in her ribs when she leaned forward and pressed a hand to his cheek. He looked small and frail in the bed, yet the whiskers beneath her palm proved it wasn't a little boy lying there, no matter how much he looked like one.

"Take care of Nate. The big lubber needs someone to watch over him."

The affection in his fading voice was clear and strong even if the words themselves weren't much above a whisper. Because she cherished Vincent, she didn't lie to him. She simply didn't answer.

Instead she waited until he'd slipped back into sleep, then pressed a kiss to his forehead and left the cabin. Nate's gaze followed her from the hatch to her bed, but she ignored it. She needed to be alone, to grieve alone.

She'd just buried what was left of her father. She knew, as Vincent did, that she was about to lose a friend. There wasn't room in her heart for any more pain, and thinking of Nate would only add more.

Yet despite her best efforts, Vincent's words rode through her mind, even though they were wrong. Nate didn't need anybody. He'd made a life without her, had attained wealth, and though she hated it, had become one of the most notorious pirates. If anybody could manage fine on their own, it was Nate.

Though it was midday, she crawled beneath the lifeboat. The sun was bright behind her closed eyelids, but nothing was bright inside her heart.

It had never been such a relief to see land. The trees of Santo Domingo rose from the ground like the darkest of emeralds. And to Nate's mind, they were even more priceless. They'd made good time. The sun was just now kissing the horizon.

"Hold on," he murmured as he turned the wheel toward port. "Just hold on a little longer."

He shouted orders and his crew snapped to. Sails were trimmed, ropes were coiled. The longboat was readied. Nate took the *Revenge* in as close as he could, cursing under his breath when the ship wouldn't glide fast enough.

"Drop the anchor!" he shouted. He didn't wait for the order to be obeyed. He knew without question it would, as everyone's first thought was of Vincent.

He threw open the hatch, all but flew down the stairs. "We're here."

Blake turned from the bed; his eyes shone.

"He's gone."

Twenty-four

Claire had never felt so superfluous. Nate was carrying Vincent to his house, with Blake walking close at his side. Though no words were spoken, the bond of friendship was strong as steel and didn't leave room for Claire. He hadn't even looked back to see if she was following.

Nate had left some men on board to guard the treasure, and until it was divided—which sounded awful, even in her own thoughts—she had no means of going anywhere. Not that she would until after the burial; she wouldn't leave without paying Vincent the respect he deserved. In the meantime, however, she had no money and nothing to do. A dirty set of clothes, a brush, knife, and pistol wouldn't get her very far.

And so Claire followed behind Nate, figuring maybe there would be something she could do at the house, something that would not only keep her mind busy but make things a little easier for Nate. At the least she could prepare some food for him and Blake, or see to errands that needed to be done. They, too, had enough on their minds.

All thoughts of that, however, vanished like fog in the sun when she saw the house. Her heart stumbled and so did she. It was beautiful. Made of brick with two levels of gleaming windows, it stood proud and tall in a sea of jade green grass. The door, even from as far back as she was standing, was wide gleaming wood with intricate carvings. It was all nestled amid tall stately trees that seemed to surround it lovingly.

It was everything she'd dreamed of as a little girl, and everything she yearned for as a woman. She'd shared that dream once with Nate and now here it was. He'd known, when he'd built it, that it was her dream. Why, when he'd admitted he'd never thought to ever see her again, had he built the home of her heart?

He'd told her she'd like it. Tears of hurt blurred her vision. Oh, she liked it. But he hadn't built the house for her, or for them. He'd built it for himself. He hadn't come looking for her, but now that they'd stumbled upon each other and he'd bedded her, he'd asked her to share it with him. If they hadn't been at the poker game together, he'd have gone on to live here. Without her.

Blake reached the door first and opened it for Nate. Nate went in, stepping sideways to account for Vincent. Neither Blake nor Nate bothered looking back before Blake shut the door.

Claire hung her head. Not only wasn't she needed here, she wasn't wanted. And looking up at the lovely house, then down at her worn, dirty clothing, Claire knew she also didn't belong.

* * *

Nate watched Alicia fly into Blake's arms. There was no escaping the slice of envy that cut through him. Nate hadn't seen Claire in days, not since they'd come ashore. He'd known she'd followed them to the house, but she'd never come inside. And he knew why. He hadn't explained about the house and knew it must have come as a huge shock to her. He'd planned to explain once they came ashore and she came to her senses about their future. But that was before they'd realized how badly Vincent was hurt. After that, there hadn't been room for anything but Vincent.

And though Nate missed Claire, needed her, he simply didn't have the energy to go looking for her. Everything, it seemed, took such effort. Just getting out of bed required giving himself a lecture and forcing his limbs to move when the lecture didn't work.

Even seeing Alicia, a friend he held very dear, couldn't bring a smile to his face. He wondered, as she turned her sorrow-filled blue eyes to him, if he would ever feel like smiling again.

"You look awful," she said before wrapping her arms around him.

She didn't look like a blacksmith today with her blue cotton dress, but the arms that held him had the strength of one. He pressed a kiss to her head, wished for a moment it were Claire in his arms, and held Alicia tightly.

"I'm so sorry," she said and he felt her chin quiver. "I wish I could have said good-bye."

Nate couldn't speak, couldn't find a way to tell her that some of Vincent's last words were of her. Emotion so raw he thought he'd choke from it pressed against his chest. Not able to handle it, Nate stepped away.

"He was thinking of you," Blake managed, through a voice that shook. "He said to say good-bye."

Samantha had come in with Alicia, and while her sister went back into her husband's arms and wept, Samantha took Nate's hand and squeezed it. The woman with the golden eyes, the woman who had originated Sam Steele, looked as heartbroken as he felt.

"I know what it is to lose family. Vincent was part of ours, as are you. If I can do anything to make this easier . . ."

He pulled her into his arms and held her. He'd started out alone, but because of Blake and Vincent, he'd gained family. Blake had married Alicia and by doing so gave him nieces and a nephew as well as Samantha, Luke, Aidan, and Joe. It wasn't a traditional family, but since he'd never had one of those, the one he'd found meant even more to him.

"He wanted to be Steele."

Samantha pulled back. "He did?"

"I didn't know either, not until he told me. He knew I wanted out of it and he wanted a chance to prove something."

"He's asked his brother to do it in his stead."

"What?" Nate turned to Blake. "This is the first I've heard of this."

Blake rubbed his brow. "He asked me to pen a letter, just before . . . well, I wrote the words he asked me to. He has a brother, name of Cale, and I'm to give him this letter."

Nate straightened. "Cale? Did Vincent know where he lives?"

"Last he had heard, Cale lived in Nevis."

Nate drew a sharp breath. Could it be the same Cale that had been at the poker game?

"I'll go there after the burial, see if I can find him. The man could easily refuse—hell, why wouldn't he?—but I promised Vincent I'd give his brother the letter."

Nate didn't hesitate. "I'll go with you."

Samantha shook her head. "But if you've tired of it, Steele can die now."

"That'll be up to Cale. In the meantime, now that you're here, I'll get word to the preacher. We can have the burial this afternoon."

"What about Claire?" Blake asked.

"Who's Claire?" Alicia asked. Despite the seriousness of the occasion, her blue eyes began to twinkle.

Alicia had been trying to find Nate a wife since she'd married Blake. He'd begun to think, on Isla de Hueso, that he'd finally marry the only woman who had ever captured his heart. But since coming back to Santo Domingo, he hadn't seen her. He scraped his hand over his stubbled cheeks; shaving was something else he hadn't bothered doing in days.

"It's a long story. I'm sure you'll see her at the burial. If I can find her in time."

Alicia looked at Samantha. Her sister nodded. She faced Nate, her eyes shining with determination.

"Tell me where you think she is and what she looks like. We'll find her."

Perhaps she was simply getting used to the pain, Claire thought as she poked at the fire. Either way, it wasn't the piercing kind it used to be. She still had to keep her breaths light, but it no longer felt as though someone were taking a red-hot iron to her middle. They'd switched to a club instead.

And after another restless night's sleep, it wasn't only her ribs that throbbed. Her head pounded as well. Which was likely why she hadn't heard the sound of approaching steps until it was almost too late. But hearing them now, and the swish of branches being moved, Claire grabbed her knife with her left hand and her pistol with her right.

She felt like a flaming idiot when two women stepped into her camp, both wearing day dresses, both unarmed. Still, since it was ingrained in her to always be prepared, she kept her weapons in her hands as she lowered her arms to her side.

They were about the same height, but while one had light blond hair and a blue dress, the other had darker hair and wore green. It was the darker-haired one who smiled.

"Claire, I presume?" she said.

Since only a handful of people on the island knew her name, and since she couldn't imagine any other women would come looking for her, Claire threw her pistol onto her bag and put her knife back into her boot. She wiped her hands on her trousers.

"Samantha and Alicia," she sighed. Why was it that when Claire thought her life couldn't get any worse, that she couldn't be more ashamed of herself than she already was, she was proven wrong?

The one in blue came forward, held out her hand. "I'm Alicia, pleased to meet you."

Claire held back. She wasn't going to take her hand, not when her own was as dirty as it was.

"I wish it could be under better circumstances," Claire answered.

"I'm a blacksmith, Claire. Look at my own hands."

Claire did, and felt some of the tension fall away when

she saw a hint of black smears around Alicia's fingernails. Alicia held out her hand again, and this time, Claire took it.

"I'm her sister, Samantha." Samantha angled her head. "I imagine you've heard of me?"

Claire nodded, amazed that this woman, this very pretty woman, had at one time been the fearsome Sam Steele.

"You don't look like a pirate."

Samantha laughed. "I imagine you thought my husband did?"

"Yes, Luke most definitely looks the part."

"And he'll be most pleased to hear you say that." She offered her hand. "Samantha Bradley."

"Claire Gentry."

Suddenly realizing the reason they'd come looking for her, and the very fact that they were on this island, made Claire's stomach clench.

"The burial. It's today?"

Alicia's eyes shone. "It is. Nate and Blake are arranging it. We only arrived a short time ago."

"Thank you for telling me," Claire said. "I'll come once I've . . ." She held her arms aside, looked down, and saw herself through their eyes. Worn, dusty boots that rode to her knee, gray pants that used to be black, and a tan-colored shirt that was worn thin at the elbows. That wasn't to mention the dirt that felt embedded into each fold of her skin, the fact that her hair was cut ragged, or the smell she was sure she wreaked of since it had been days without washing.

Claire looked at Alicia, whose long blond hair was folded into a neat braid, and at Samantha's darker, curled tresses, which flowed loose and clean around her shoulders. There was no judgment in their steady gazes, but

Claire had enough of her own. She looked and felt like an urchin. She'd been alone and miserable and now, not only did she have to face burying a friend, but she had to do it looking and feeling her absolute worst.

It was all too much. Claire felt her face crumple. She'd been battling to hold herself together, but she couldn't do it any longer. She didn't have the strength or the will. The emotions she'd held back burst from the walls she'd pushed them behind and came forth in a flood of tears.

The trees around her blurred into a fog of green. The smell of the fire faded as did the melodic singing of the birds that hid amid the greenery. There was only the emptiness that engulfed her. Her sobs drummed against her ribs and tears slipped into the corner of her mouth as she gasped for breath. She turned away, hands covering her mouth, mortified she'd lost control.

The soft touch that settled onto her shoulder only made her feel worse.

"We loved him, too," Alicia said, her own voice watery.

Claire squeezed her eyes shut. She didn't doubt they knew her tears were about more than Vincent, but thankfully Alicia chose to concentrate on the most obvious reason.

Claire managed a nod and swiped impatiently at her tears. They'd never accomplished anything, she'd learned, yet here she was leaking like a sinking ship. Dammit.

"I'm all right." She wiped her face again and turned.

Alicia kept her hand on Claire. Samantha watched with steady eyes that seemed to miss nothing.

"I think it pays tribute to Vincent to cry. It means he was loved and mattered enough to be wept over."

Claire choked on emotion and had to settle for nodding instead.

Samantha came forward, raised her skirts, and kicked

dirt over the fire. Using Claire's stick, she stirred it, then shoved in more dirt until nothing but a thin finger of gray smoke rose to the tree tops. Then she faced Claire.

"Do you have a gown in your bag?" she asked.

Claire felt her cheeks burn. "I haven't."

"Then we'll buy you one. There's a bathhouse and a barber in town." She came forward and touched the tips of Claire's short hair. "It's such a beautiful color."

"I can't—I don't—" She sighed, then pressed a hand against her sore chest. "I don't have any money, not yet."

"I thought you'd be insulted by the offer," Samantha said.

"Sam has a habit of being very forthright," Alicia agreed with a grin.

Claire shook her head. "How can I be insulted when you're right? I know how I look. And I want to do better by Vincent than to go looking like this. I simply don't have the means to do anything about it."

"Did Nate refuse to help you?" Alicia fisted a hand on her hip. "If he did, I'll—"

"No, no, I didn't ask. He has enough to deal with."

Alicia softened. "As do we all. He'd have helped you. It's in his nature to help."

Claire thought of how he'd offered his cabin when she'd been hurt, how he'd jumped into the pit to help her, how he'd tended to Vincent. Nate would have given her money, had she asked. But she hadn't wanted to. It hurt being near him, and she'd already decided to leave as quickly as possible after the burial. She had plans for her part of the treasure that didn't include Nate or anything on that island.

"I know what it is to be independent, to be used to doing things alone," Samantha offered with a smile of understanding. "But there comes a time when you have to reach out, accept there are people who care about you and want to help you. I hope you'll let us."

"I'm sorry, I'm grateful to you both, truly I am. Especially since you don't know me, but the truth remains that I have no money."

Samantha smiled. "Well, that's no bother. I happen to have more than I need."

Claire's refusal was immediate. "No. I can't accept it."

"Why not?"

Claire bit her lip, thought of the best way to explain without hurting this woman she'd only met, and decided to be as forthright as Samantha had already proven herself to be.

"It's pirate money. I want no part of it."

Alicia's eyes widened and her gaze snapped to her sister. Samantha's gaze had hardened, and in the cold look she shot Claire, Claire saw the pirate she'd once been.

"I've made money legitimately building ships, but yes, prior to that I was a pirate. However, I took no glory in it. I became Steele to avenge my family's murder, nothing more. The ships I took in the interim were treated with as much respect and lack of violence as I could manage."

Claire frowned. "If that's the case, why do you have such a fearsome name? Why does everyone fear Steele?"

"There were many battles that were vicious, too many. Besides, you don't have to be deadly to be feared, you only have to be effective. Most people who came against Steele lost. However, that's the past. The point I wanted to make, Claire, was that when I met Luke, I thought he was no better than the man who murdered my family. Had I not looked past Luke's piracy, I'd have missed the wonderful man he is and all the joy and love he's brought to my life.

"Tell me, are you only an urchin that lives in the forest and forages for food, or are you a woman of substance behind the clothes and the ragged hair?"

Claire felt the sting of Samantha's words as surely as if she'd been slapped. And, she realized, she deserved that and more.

"Hasn't Nate proven to you that he's more than a pirate?" Alicia asked.

Claire nodded, feeling suddenly weighed down. "He has, on more than one occasion."

"Then I don't understand," Alicia said.

"It's a matter of self-respect. Mine." She sighed. "I've tried so hard to maintain my integrity, to come back from the bad decisions I've made in a way I could be proud of. I could have turned to piracy but I wanted people, and that included myself, to look upon Claire Gentry and see a woman worthy of respect." She gestured to her clothes. "As you can see, I've yet to attain my goal."

"Claire," Alicia said, taking her hand. "As a blacksmith, I know what it's like to be regarded with disdain, to not be included or valued for who I am. I'm not a traditional wife and that's fine by me. You don't have to live up to anybody else's values, only your own. In the end, those are the only ones that matter. The fact that you're living as you are, knowing you could have made it easier on yourself by turning pirate, shows me the character you have. You should be proud of yourself."

"It doesn't matter to me how you're dressed or where you live, you already have my respect," Samantha added softly.

Tears once again filled Claire's eyes.

"Thank you both," Claire said as she wiped her eyes. "And to you, Samantha, I apologize."

"Accepted," Samantha answered. "Now, can we take you into town?"

The ceremony was everything Nate thought Vincent would have wanted. It was simple, it was to the point, and it was attended by his family. The crew was gathered round, hats in hand as the afternoon sun spread its glow around those in attendance. Judging from their shiny hair and ruddy faces, they'd taken the time to bathe and shave.

Vincent would have chuckled to see it.

And knowing that pressed on Nate's heart.

Blake had found a woman, the preacher's daughter, to sing. She stepped forward now. Her voice, pure as anything Nate had ever heard, wove around each of them and held them captive. When the words spoke of a being lost, then found, Nate's gaze sought out Claire.

His heart had tumbled when he'd seen her. She wore green to match her eyes and her hair had been cut, the tattered ends smoothed. It was too short to be called fashionable by most standards, but Nate wasn't most men. He thought the way the tips brushed her cheekbones made her look soft and pretty. The dress clung to her waist and the square cut of the bodice offered a hint of the gentle curves beneath it.

She met his gaze across the freshly turned earth, wiped a tear from her cheek. The woman's voice trailed off and the last note of the chorus floated over tear-streaked faces. She stepped back and her father once again came forward. He held his hand over the grave, recited a last prayer.

Nate and Blake knelt down as they'd planned. They reached out, grabbed a handful of the cool dirt, and let it sift over Vincent's grave. Nate's hand remained on the ground long after the last of the dirt had fallen. The earth beneath his hand was cool, and reality was a bitter taste in his mouth.

Vincent would never again tease him mercilessly, would never drag a crate to the helm when it was his turn to man the ship. His friend was lost, and for the life of him, Nate couldn't envision the rest of it without Vincent in it. He buried his face in his hands, clenched his teeth against the grief. *Good-bye, my friend.*

He felt Blake stand, knew he was seeking comfort in his wife. Nate breathed deeply, concentrating on the simple movement rather than the loss. Still, when he opened his eyes and stood, he knew another, equally strong sense of loss.

Claire was nowhere to be seen.

Twenty-five

Claire plodded back to camp, her heart too heavy to care about the thorny fingers that clawed at her skirt. Seeing Nate and Blake at the grave, their eyes wet, had undone Claire. She hadn't been able to endure their pain a moment longer. Not when her own was nearly unbearable. Selfishly, she'd slipped from the assembled group while they'd had their focus elsewhere.

Hours later, after changing back into her trousers and shirt, with her dress carefully folded into her bag, Claire lit a fire out of necessity rather than a need to keep busy. She sat cross-legged on her bed, watched the flames flicker with life. How easily it could all be snuffed out, she thought sadly.

She heard the steps approaching and her belly clutched. Blake stepped into camp. Claire swallowed a hard knot of disappointment.

"Alicia told me where I might find you. We thought you'd come to the house."

"I wanted to give you all the privacy to grieve."

Blake gave her a knowing look. "You were Vincent's friend as well. You didn't have to leave."

She shrugged. "I thought it would be best."

"For who, Claire?"

"For everyone."

"Claire, Nate needed you there today."

"I *was* there."

"No, you weren't. You stood by yourself, you didn't so much as touch Nate's hand, and you ran away right afterward."

"I didn't run."

Blake arched a brow. "Didn't you?"

Claire got up and paced. "You're a family. I didn't belong."

"Only because you didn't want to. Alicia and Samantha both asked for you."

Claire stopped and looked at Blake. "And Nate?"

Blake rubbed his brow. "He missed you."

"But he didn't ask."

Blake sighed. "You of all people know it's complicated. Nate told me what happened between you at the orphanage. He told me he's asked you to marry him. Claire, he's come for you twice now, first at the orphanage and again on his ship. He's not going to do it a third time. I know Nate, and if you want him, you'll have to go to him."

Claire looked away, crossing her arms when she realized her hands were trembling.

"He said to tell you that the treasure will be divided in the morning. Once it is, Nate and I will be going to Nevis, but we shouldn't be long."

"Nevis? Isn't your home Port Royal?"

"I'm not going home yet. We have a last request to grant Vincent."

One Nate hadn't bothered to tell her. Just as she hadn't told him her own plans. Claire shook her head. They may have come together for a while, but she and Nate remained miles apart.

By the time they reached Nevis, Nate wasn't fit company. Three days of thinking about Claire and the treasure had about done him in. He'd given her his share, easily and without question, but she'd refused it. She'd taken only what was hers, given Nate a sad smile, and left. She should have simply shot him. It would have hurt less.

Nate barked orders, ignored the questioning looks of his crew and Blake's amused ones. They could all go to Hell, he thought. Feeling trapped on his ship, something Nate wouldn't have believed to ever be possible, he gladly made port in Nevis.

He had no idea where to look for Cale, or even if it was the same person, but Nate only knew one man by that name and decided to start where he'd last seen him.

The man at the tavern hadn't seen Cale but he did have an idea where the man lived. After vague directions, Blake and Nate headed that way. It was a run-down little house with moss growing on its roof. Nothing about the yard was tended; the grasses grew to the tops of Nate's boots. Before he could stride for the door, a familiar voice came from behind him.

"What do you want?"

Nate turned. Sure enough, it was the same man from the poker game. His icy blue eyes met Nate's then drifted a moment to Blake's.

"Is your family name Hunter?"

"I don't have a family," Cale answered.

Well, damn, Nate thought.

"I think you do," Blake said, taking a step forward. "You have five sisters and a brother. We're here about Vincent."

The flash of recognition came quick to Cale's eyes, and left as fast. Nate turned to Blake and raised a questioning brow.

Blake shrugged. "If we'd asked, he'd have denied it. Now we know he's lying."

An hour later, after a hefty struggle that left all three men panting and breathless, and each with fresh cuts on his face, they finally had Cale's attention.

"You've lost your mind," Cale said. His eyes were pale as the morning fog and certainly no warmer.

"He's asked this of you. Surely a ship is better than this," Blake said as his hand encompassed the dingy one-room cabin.

"I don't want a ship. For the last time, I'm not a pirate."

"You'll have a crew and Vincent's share of the treasure."

Cale's face went red. "I don't want anything to do with that damn treasure! That's why I sold the map to begin with!"

Nate sighed. They weren't getting anywhere with force. He tried again. "Vincent felt inferior. He wanted this to make himself feel like more of a man. We'd never given him the impression he was less of one. Where did he come to believe that?"

The fire went out of Cale. "He had reason to believe that."

Yes, Nate imagined he did. Cale wasn't quite as tall as Nate was, but his shoulders were as wide. It must have been hard to be a dwarf when your brother looked like Cale. Nate couldn't help wondering if Cale hadn't made it worse. Judging by the remorse on his face, he imagined Cale had.

A thought suddenly struck Nate. "He came to see you that night, the night of the poker game?"

Cale was silent, but his large hands had curled into fists.

"Did he tell you that?"

Nate shook his head, regret sitting heavily on his shoulders. He'd felt something was wrong with Vincent that night but he'd been too damn wrapped up in his own problems to take the time for his friend.

"No. All he ever said about you was that you'd left home when he was a young boy." Nate leaned forward, not above using guilt. "I do know that he was upset that night and that when he spoke of being Steele, he got a fire in his eyes I hadn't seen before."

"It meant everything to Vincent to be Steele. Clearly he thought enough of you to ask you to do it in his place. You can't find it in yourself to honor that request?" Blake asked.

Cale looked up and Nate saw what he himself was feeling. Grief, more than he knew what to do with.

"I'll do it," Cale sighed after a long moment. "I'll do it and I'll keep your bloody secrets, but I still don't want his damn share of the treasure."

Bloody family reunion," Cale cursed at the amount of people gathered about the longboat.

He'd met them all, which, as far as he was concerned, wasn't a requirement. All Cale wanted was to get the bloody hell away from them. He was doing this for Vincent—couldn't he just get on with it?

"Boy? You coming or not?"

"Yeah. I'm coming." And Aidan did, with the bag Luke passed him in one hand and a cage containing a red and yellow parrot in the other.

"You've got to be bloody kidding me," Cale roared. "I'm not taking a parrot as well." He jerked his chin at Samantha. "Next you'll have me raise your children for you."

"Don't worry, we won't ask that of you," Samantha replied. Her tone gave Cale's hearty competition.

Luke wrapped an arm around his wife's shoulders and rubbed her arm affectionately. "The bird goes with Aidan," Luke said.

"I can't believe this," Cale said with a shake of his head. "Can we bloody leave now?" he roared.

Samantha turned to Aidan. "I know you're ready to leave us, but we're not quite as ready." She kissed Aidan's cheek. "Carracks will remind you of what's waiting for you at home."

Aidan's smile was gentle, as was his hold when he hugged Samantha. "I don't need a parrot to remind me of that, but I'm glad to have him."

"He's annoying," Luke said, though he poked his fingers through the bars and rubbed the bird's neck. "But he's good company. Just watch what you say. Bloody bird repeats everything."

Squawk. "Bloody bird, bloody bird."

"Christ," Cale cursed as he plunged the oars into the water. "Won't this be fun?"

San Salvador isn't that far," Blake reminded Nate.

Nate took his tankard and cupped it in one large palm. They were continuing the tradition of having a nightly drink—this time in Nate's kitchen—but it wasn't the same. Not without Vincent and not knowing Blake was taking Alicia, Samantha, and Luke and leaving in the morning.

"There's nothing for me in San Salvador. There never

was." Alicia had discovered that Claire had paid for passage to San Salvador and had been very forthcoming giving the information to Nate. He couldn't imagine why Claire would want to go back where the orphanage had been and where so many awful memories awaited her. Would she see her husband? Would he hurt her?

"There's Claire, you big lubber."

Nate choked on his rum. Only Vincent had ever called him that.

"Thought it was appropriate. I'm sure it's what he'd be thinking." Blake smiled, casting his glance upward.

Nate scoffed. "Probably is at that," he agreed and felt a little lighter since Blake had brought Vincent back into the room, if only in words.

"He'd want you to go. *I* want you to go."

"Marriage has made you sentimental," Nate said before taking another drink.

"Maybe. But it's also made me see the value of not wasting time. I lost months with Alicia, months of her first pregnancy that I can't get back. Would you do the same?"

This time Nate did choke. He wiped the rum off his chin with his forearm. "Claire's not expecting."

"Not what I meant, though that was fun. Why won't you go to her?"

He ran a hand over his face. "You don't know Claire. She's independent, she won't lean on me, and she doesn't trust me to come through for her." He shrugged away the pain. "She won't even let me try."

"Then prove her wrong."

"She left, Blake. That tells me everything I need to know."

"Like it did the last time? You thought she gave up on you once, and she didn't. She just ran out of time. You let her walk away, let her keep her secrets to herself. You proved her right, Nate, by doing all those things." Blake leaned forward. "Why don't you try another way this time?"

Nate swallowed the drink along with Blake's words. He knew Blake was right. He had proved her right. But he'd also been hoping she'd come around on her own, that she'd realize what they had and what he felt for her. He'd asked her to share his house, hadn't he?

Yes, he had, but as he closed his eyes, he realized that he'd never explained to her why he'd built the house. He'd never told her he loved her or proposed properly. He'd been as withholding as she'd been.

"Someone has to give in first," Blake said, bursting into his thoughts. "It may as well be you."

When she'd stepped into the abandoned orphanage, Claire had felt like a young girl again. She'd felt the fear, the despair. She'd heard her words echo in her head, "Don't leave, Father. Let me go with you." Her father's response had been, "My sweet girl. I'll be back for you. Trust me."

She had. And he hadn't.

Claire had pushed aside the memory as she'd pushed her fingers through the sticky webs that had filled most doorways. The windows had been broken, likely from the very children who'd been spit out with little thought or care. Dust and misery had lain thick in the air. The walls, a dull and wretched gray, had offered no relief.

Well, Claire thought now as she walked through the entryway, they weren't dull any longer.

She'd helped paint them a cheery yellow, and curtains she'd paid women to sew hung crisply from the newly repaired and gleaming windows. Chairs had been assembled in the parlor and they lined the walls, awaiting the guests she'd invited for the evening. A small platform had been built in the corner to accommodate the musicians that would play lively music.

The new floor beneath her feet was sturdy and polished. Her shoes tapped against it as she made her way to the kitchen. Long tables reflected the sun that streamed into the room. Later, they'd be overflowing with food and drink. The windows were open and the smell of flowers in full bloom drifted in to mix with that of the floor polish and the smell of hope. Because here, finally, was hope.

The cupboards, she knew as she'd personally seen to it, were stocked and ready. The beds upstairs were made with freshly laundered bedding. There were toys waiting on each of them.

She'd pushed hard to have everything completed this quickly, though it nonetheless took months of hard work. Still, it had been worth it. While the repairs were being seen to, she'd found temporary lodging for those children she'd been able to find on the street, or those who had heard there was someone who had the means to help them.

Claire found the women who used to run the orphanage. They'd been doing what they could to help, but there simply wasn't enough time or resources to look after every child that needed help. With Litton withholding his money and threatening to pull his support from the town if anyone spoke against him, there was little help to be found.

Well, Claire thought, her hands on her hips, there was now. She had learned from the gossip that Litton knew about the reopening, but she'd managed to keep her identity from him. Dressing as a man when necessary continued to have its advantages.

She'd found the perfect people to help her run the orphanage and had promised to pay them well. They wouldn't work for an ogre again. Everyone within those walls, Claire promised, would be treated with dignity and respect or they would personally be shown the door.

There wouldn't be any inappropriate touching or crude suggestions. Still, it wasn't all she was after, and she fervently prayed she'd be able to accomplish what she'd planned for so long. Like the treasure she'd dreamed of finding, she'd also dreamed of justice. She'd found the gold; she had to believe that she'd attain her other goal as well.

Even though, she thought with a tug of sadness, she'd failed where Nate was concerned.

She'd had time to think on the voyage to San Salvador, and she'd realized and accepted the mistakes she'd made. She hadn't trusted Nate or anybody. He was right when he'd said she'd been waiting for him to fail her. No man had ever made her a promise and kept it. Yes, Nate had come back, but he hadn't fought for her, hadn't even sought her out to discover why she was marrying another man. He'd simply learned of her engagement and left.

They'd wronged each other, Claire realized. He hadn't trusted in her love enough to realize there had to be a reason she'd marry another man, and she hadn't trusted Nate enough to give him a chance to make amends for that.

She didn't hear anyone coming until a voice spoke from behind her. Claire jumped a little, then turned to face Marie.

"Begging your pardon, miss. I was just saying we are ready for this evening. I've overseen the cooking, and it's going to be ready on time. The flowers will be cut fresh and placed in vases one hour before the guests are due to arrive. The musicians will also be arriving at that time to have everything in order before the guests arrive."

Claire already knew all that as she'd personally seen to it. Trust, she thought again with a sad shake of her head, simply didn't come easily for her. But there was a lot at stake tonight, much more than a ball to raise some money to help keep the orphanage running smoothly. Not that Claire couldn't do it on her own, but there were other wealthy people on the island and it was past time they helped those less fortunate. It was time they paid.

"Thank you, Marie. It all looks wonderful."

Nodding, the woman left and slipped into the kitchen. Claire looked around once more. She pressed a hand to her stomach. Tonight. It all came down to tonight.

Outside, she stopped to look at the sign that hung from a black iron pole. She'd commissioned the local blacksmith to fashion it. Although Alicia could have done the work, it was faster and simpler—the local blacksmith didn't know Nate— to have it made here. It swayed slightly with the breeze.

VINCENT'S HOUSE—WHERE ALL ARE WELCOME

"He'd have loved it."

Claire spun round. Her heart clutched as her eyes latched on to Nate's. He was there. How was it he was there?

"Nate."

He pointed a large hand to the sign. "I'd have helped you with that, had I known."

"I know," she answered, for she'd never doubted that. "It was something I needed to do." She shrugged. "It was the least I could do."

"He didn't blame you. I didn't blame you. None of us did."

She'd realized that on the ship as well. It was easier to assume the worst because then the heart didn't get so deeply involved. But looking at his soft green eyes, seeing his hair play in the breeze, and hearing the deep tone of his voice, she knew it was too late. Her heart was already as involved as it could ever be.

"You didn't have to. I carried enough for everyone."

He angled his head. "And now?"

"I'm working on accepting that some things are simply meant to be."

She saw the change in his eyes immediately. And felt the trip in her heart.

"Would you and I be included in that?"

Her breath caught until she had to remind herself to breathe.

"I'm working my way up to it."

His smile was the most beautiful thing Claire had ever seen. She'd missed it. She'd missed him. Enough to know what needed to be done. Enough to be willing to do it, despite the tremor of fear that rippled along her skin.

"Before we go any further, Nate, there's something I have to do."

He pulled himself back. She saw it in the press of his lips and the flicker of disappointment in his eyes. He scrubbed his hands over his face and dropped them at his sides.

She took one of them between hers and pressed it to her heart.

"I could use your help. Come with me and I'll explain."

Candles flickered from the tables. Soft music drifted through the room. Women in fancy gowns were swept along by their equally attired dance partners. For one night, this one night, there were no children present. Only businessmen. Rich businessmen. One in particular, wearing a dark brown suit, held Claire's interest. Her soon-to-be former husband, Quinn Litton. As the wine and brandy flowed through the room, Claire watched his progress.

She danced with who needed to be danced with in order to extract more money for the orphanage. Her smile was genuine and her laughter soft. As her gown swept the floor in the dance, there was no sign of the Claire who'd lived in the forest, who'd owned nothing. But inside, where her heart impatiently waited for justice, that Claire waited with bated breath.

When Litton excused himself from the man he'd been speaking with, Claire graciously declined another offer to dance and followed him out into the garden.

Like the inside, the outside had been cleaned and tended. Red, yellow, and pink flowers overflowed the pots that had been placed around the yard. Lanterns hung from poles and created a softly lit path designed to lure couples out for a walk. Or in this case, to lure a lone man into taking a stroll while he enjoyed his cigar.

Claire absently smiled at men and women who passed her on their way back inside. She couldn't have said later what they'd looked like. Her attention was all for the bastard she was following. She waited until he stopped and lit his cigar. When the end glowed red and a plume of smoke rose from his mouth, Claire let herself be known.

"I'm glad you came," she said, stepping into the glow of a lantern. "It saves me the trouble of having to go looking for you."

He squinted through the smoke. "Claire? My God, it is you. You look"—his eyes slid over her like a thousand snakes—"delicious."

"And you're vile as you've ever been."

He chuckled. "You're the only one here who thinks so."

"Oh, I think not," Claire said, smiling now. "Everyone in this town hates you."

He chuckled, and inhaled again. "Be that as it may, they'll never say so. I own this town."

"Not anymore."

She had the satisfaction of seeing the cigar in his hand bobble. "I have no idea what you're talking about," he said.

"You will. The merchants in this town will no longer step aside and let you run roughshod on its people. They don't need your money anymore."

He laughed. "Not only do they need it, they already owe it to me. With interest."

"Paid in full, as of today. They aren't dependent on you any longer. I've seen to that."

He threw down his cigar and took a step toward her. "I don't know how you came up with the money to do this"—he gestured to the orphanage—"but I'll see to it the doors close. And this time, they won't reopen. As for the merchants in this town? They would be out of business without me and they know it. They'll never step out against me."

Her smile was fearless. "I've gambled for less. Let's go inside, see where the cards fall."

"You lying—"

His hand came up fast, but Nate was faster. He grabbed Litton from behind, crushed the man's hand in his fist. Quinn yelled, and dropped to his knees when Nate increased the pressure.

"The lady doesn't lie," Nate growled. "And I'll help her bury you any way I can."

Claire beamed when Nate met her gaze and winked.

"What do you want?" Litton whimpered.

Claire bent down so she could look Litton in the eye.

"You closed this orphanage down. I think it only right your money goes into keeping it open."

"What?" His eyes rounded. "I won't! And you can—ah, let go! Let go! You're breaking my hand!"

"Which is such a shame," Nate said.

"Your money for your life. I think that's a fair trade."

Sweat poured down Litton's temples. Spit gathered at the corners of his mouth.

"What'll it be?" she asked.

"I'll do it, I'll do it! How much do you want?"

He whimpered when Claire told him the figure.

"That's robbery!" he yelled.

"That's justice," Claire corrected. She stood upright, turned to go, and knew the sweetest victory when his pathetic voice called her back.

"All right. Dammit. All right. I agree."

"Yes, I thought you might." She signaled to the man who waited on the steps at the back door. "Mr. Anderson, right on time," she said as her attorney joined them. "Quinn, I'd like you to meet Mr. Anderson, my attorney. He has all the papers ready for you to sign."

"Sign?" he whined.

"Yes. I may be a gambler, but some things I want in writing, which includes our divorce.

"Marie is waiting in the office behind the kitchen. She'll witness the transaction. And to ensure you don't run like the coward you are," Claire said, "Nate will escort you inside."

Mr. Anderson went in first, and as Nate pushed Litton along, she heard Nate whisper, "I happen to know Sam Steele personally. If you ever give Claire or the orphanage any more trouble, I'll escort him to your house myself."

Claire threw her head back and laughed. Then, as she waited for Nate to come back outside, she looked at the orphanage, at the people moving behind the windows, and thought to herself, *This is where it all started. It's only right this is where it all ends.*

Nate stepped outside, filling the doorway as surely as he filled her heart. She waited for him to join her in the yard, underneath the stars and the moon, where her heart galloped inside her chest.

"Papers are signed and in Mr. Anderson's hands. The first payment is due on Monday."

Claire breathed deeply, then released a long, slow breath. "Well, that feels good."

Nate swept in and took her in his arms. His kiss was soft, full of promise.

"Not as good as that feels." He grinned.

"No," Claire agreed. "Nothing feels quite as good as that." She breathed him in, then touched her palm to his cheek. "We make a good team. I'm sorry it took me so long to realize that."

He turned his head and kissed her palm. "I love you, Claire. I'm sorry I didn't tell you that back on Isla de Hueso and I'm so damn proud of you. Of what you did here, for yourself, for the children. For Vincent." His eyes shone in the flickering light. "He'd be so touched."

"I'm sorry," Marie said as she came forward. "I didn't mean to interrupt."

"That's all right. Marie, I'd like you to meet—"

"Claire's future husband, if she'll have me."

Claire's hand flew to her chest.

"I mean it. Claire, I love you. I built that house for us. Even when I thought I couldn't have you, I wanted it to remind me of you. Now I want to share it with you."

Marie sniffed. Claire had a hard time containing her heart within her chest.

"I'm sorry it's taken me so long to learn that I don't have to do everything by myself." Her smile was watery. "I can't guarantee that I won't forget every now and then."

"I'll be here to remind you," he said. He pressed a kiss to her forehead then dipped lower and took her mouth. He lingered, his mouth warm and firm against hers. His hands slipped behind her back and drew her tightly against him.

Claire hung on as the kiss turned seductive, as the promises within it sparked her blood. His tongue slid around hers and they both sighed.

"Ahem," Marie said from her side.

Claire smiled, then drew back. She looked at the blushing woman. "I'm sorry, I forgot for a moment you were there."

"Understandable, miss," she replied, and grinned. "I wanted to let you know the food is ready. May we serve it now?"

"Yes, please. And Marie," she called when the woman stepped away. "If I increase your salary, do you think you could manage to run this orphanage without me?"

Marie staggered, then stopped. She studied Claire and Nate for a moment, and when she smiled, it was a knowing smile. "I imagine I could at that. May I ask where it is you're going?"

Claire turned to Nate, her heart so full it was bursting.

"I have a home in Santo Domingo."

Nate took a sharp breath. "But you did this," he said. "You can't walk away from this."

"I'm not walking away. We'll come back, ensure it stays running properly."

"But—"

"Don't you think," she asked, "that other islands could benefit from having a house in Vincent's name?"

"In Santo Domingo?"

Claire shrugged. "I imagine there are children there that need a home as well."

He grinned. "It'll take a lot of money."

"Do you happen to have any to spare, Captain Steele?" she whispered.

His smile wavered. "That's not me. Not anymore."

She kissed him gently. "No, but it was. And I think, from what I learned, you did the name proud."

He spun her in his arms, setting her down lightly. "It no longer bothers you that I was a pirate?"

"That depends."

He frowned. "On what?"

She curled her hands into his hair. "If I wanted to know what it was to be kissed by a pirate, do you think you could oblige me?"

His grin came slow and was full of heat and promise. He brought his mouth down, let it hover over hers.

"Hold on tight, Claire," he growled.

Then he closed his lips over hers and plundered.

Enter the rich world of
historical romance
with Berkley Books . . .

Madeline Hunter

Jennifer Ashley

Joanna Bourne

Lynn Kurland

Jodi Thomas

Anne Gracie

Love is timeless.

berkleyjoveauthors.com

The "masterful"* *New York Times* bestselling author

MADELINE HUNTER

presents the first book in
a magnificent historical romance quartet

*Ravishing
in Red*

Audrianna Kelmsleigh is unattached, independent—and
armed. Her adversary is Lord Sebastian Summerhays. What
they have in common is Audrianna's father, who died in a
scandalous conspiracy—a deserved death, in Sebastian's eyes.
Audrianna vows to clear her father's name, never expecting
to fall in love with the man devoted to destroying it . . .

*Booklist

M579T1009